My Heart is a Mausoleum

adam Šhove

Published by New Generation Publishing in 2013

First Edition

www.newgeneration-publishing.com

New Generation Publishing

This novel would never have been possible without the help from the following people - Erin Mason, Vickie Zodda, Dace Blūma, my mum, Lois Hurst, Dane Haverley and Theresa Spohrer. I'm sure that there is a list of other people that I have forgotten, but please take no offence to the fact that I can't remember every person; it's been a crazy couple of years.

adam

Day 63

And I walked into the building, to say I was livid was an extreme understatement. People passed out drunk on the staircase, the stench of vomit I couldn't locate; there was no denying that it was there.

The apartment that I had to get to was on the 4th floor, I was on the 2nd walking across the next flight of stairs. There was about a 10 metre gap between them. As I came to the next flight of stairs I saw it, stepping over I said to myself, "Why does vomit always look like it has carrots in it?"

Some drunk woman was staggering down the stairs, she tripped over her own feet and fell past me. I repeated the motion between the third and fourth, clocking the apartment at the end of the landing. I walked over stepped past some person with a needle sticking out of their arm. Some prick stood in the door with nothing better to do but try to stop me as I walked in. I looked at him as he said, "venez-vous? C'est un rassemblement privé."[1]

I looked at him, shrugged my shoulders and punched him square in

---

[1] Are you going inside? This is a private gathering.

the throat. As I walked in I said, "Just call me a collector."

As I stepped into the apartment, I looked at the chaos and didn't know where to start in looking for her.

"Erin!" I shouted, moving from room to room. I knew she was in the apartment, finding her was the only issue that I had.

I walked into a room that looked like it should have been a child's bedroom, but had been turned out to make way for something that wasn't quite a brothel or a junkie's safe house. She was in there with Erin and some black guy, I walked up to her.

"Who is this guy?"

I looked at Erin, "We're going." She looked at me,

"Erin is fine; I'll bring her home with me." The black guy looked at me again,

"Somebody tell me who this is." I picked up Erin and we started walking towards the door,

"Why is she going with him?" there was a baseball bat tucked just to the side of the door frame, I said to the Estonian,

"Tell him to stay out of this." She said nothing, he started up again,

"He's not going anywhere." I asked,

"Have you ever picked up your teeth with broken fingers?" He spat on the floor and grinned a Cheshire cat smile. I picked up the baseball bat, cracked it across those gleaming white teeth. Kicked him in both his kneecaps, as his hands hit the floor I slammed the bat on each of them.

"Guess what nigger?" he looked up at me, "I welcome you to the crying game." He was trying to hold back those tears, the same tears that as soon as the room was empty wouldn't be able to stop themselves. I grabbed Erin and we started to leave the apartment. On our way out she said,

"Crying Game, such a fantastic film. Dill really spun me out, nominated for best actor and supporting actor at the Oscars." The Estonian followed us out and down the stairs, leaving the black man to cry by himself. As we walked out the door, I looked back to see that she had sped up to try and catch up with us. As we walked out the front door she screamed,

"Wait!" I stopped turned with Erin holding my left hand, she walked out,

"You didn't need to do that." The heartfelt look in her eyes wasn't going to stick this time. I had fucking told her.

"I really did, she didn't need to see that." There was no point to her even trying to argue the matter, and she knew it. "I'm taking her home, and just for the record; we're talking in the morning." We looked at each other in an idle manner, as I took a fresh grip of Erin's hand she said,

"That guy is a prick, he won't see himself as such a big guy now."

"We're going to walk back, it's not far. May I suggest you leave pretty soon, Like before the police turn up." I turned back to her, before I had chance to add anything she said,

"Tell Erin I am sorry that I took her here, she is a flower like an orchid that needs to be looked after." I said,

"Night." Erin followed suit, "Night." And the Estonian said it as we walked off.

I knew the way back with even knowing what streets we were walking through and across, one of the things that I loved to do was to get myself so lost in a city and just walk the streets in a daze.

"What did she say to you about me?"

"Just that she shouldn't have taken you there."

"She said more than that."

"No she didn't."

"It's hard to tell when you're lying. Who am I to blame you about something like this?"

"The rest of what she said doesn't matter sweetie."

We walked past bakers on their way to the early shift, or the late. Most bakeries in Paris don't have a moment when the kitchens aren't occupied. The prostitutes that work their pitches by the Moulin Rouge looked at us, some stepped aside. One said,

"She looks too young to be working the street." I replied still walking,

"She's not working, she's family and I'm taking her home." I kept my hand firmly on hers as we walked the city street that for all I knew could have faded and changed since the day before. I looked around trying to get my bearing.

"At night this city really is a ghost world." Without missing a beat Erin said,

"2001, Thora Birch. Sublime piece of cinema."

"Do you know every film ever made?" I had to ask.

"Only the ones that were good." She mused, "Did you ever see Battlefield Earth?"

"No, I never did." She looked at the prostitutes with such amazement, like their lives were close to drinking moonshine.

"You **REALLY** don't need to watch that film." I stored that piece of useless information.

We were only a few streets from mine, unexplained reasons why I felt the need to expose the smallest aspects of my own life in my art, poems that nobody was destining to read. My trail of thought was distracted by a dead raven lying by a car; Erin knelt down next to it.

"In the end we all have a wasted life, life we can't go back to or revisit no matter if we're to try and try again." Everything she said seemed to be the musing of some greater idea, Erin's eyes say 10,000 things that I couldn't-no matter how hard I were to contemplate the things that she does.

"C'mon you, we're one street away from being home." She stood back up readjusted her top, brushed whatever was on her jeans off and started walking back towards mine. By the time I was at the street corner she was by the front door, waiting barely near a street lamp; she looked up like a ghost. I got to the front door, unlocked and opened. I had stepped in first but by the time I had made it to the bottom of the stairs; she was half way up the staircase.

"Why didn't you take the flat on the top floor?" she asked, my voice to me sounded pensive,

"I guess if the rapture happens I won't have to look on with envy." I didn't want to give her the real answer, so the best thing to do was lie with something that she could believe.

"Let's just go to bed," I rolled my eyes for no reason as I put the key in the lock I said, "Is there anything that you want to do?" The door swung open, she stepped first and as I pulled the key from the lock and shut the door she was flicking through my vinyl collection.

"Just one song before bed, ok?" I nodded, but she didn't see. She knew that if I didn't want to listen to anything I would have said.

"This is it, this song then we can go to sleep."

"Drop the needle." I said.

"You will remember so much to this, maybe not now but one day a lifetime of things to laugh, cry, remember, muse over, I don't know there is so much that will fill your head." She dropped the needle and I instantly recognised Piggy by Nine Inch Nails. Her stance rocked backwards and forwards as she alternated the foot which took her small and fragile weight. I sat on the floor pulling at my hair, we both stayed in silence with the exception of repeating the line - Nothing can stop me now. - the emotion that ran between us in those 4 minutes and 25 seconds that I'd never be able to explain, like if somebody were to pull a trigger but forgot to cock every shot. We captured lightning in multiple bottles.

When the song finished she lifted the needle and returned the vinyl to its case.

"Time for bed?" I looked up and nodded, as I stood up a dozen strands of my hair fell on the floor. It was too late in the day for me to give a shit. Erin took a glance at the bed, and then her eyes turned to me,

"You sleep on the left side; I'll sleep in the middle. She'll be home some, she'll take the right side." I move over to the bed and sat on the edge, Erin sat next to me. She rested her head on mine,

"Turn out the light, please." I got up, took the 3 steps to the switch and looked back at her as she took my t-shirt off.

"You're not wearing the same underwear as earlier, come to think of it; they're not even yours."

"She said I could wear them so I would look more mature and might have been able to get a guy."

"You don't need to be thinking about that. I can tell you this - guys just want sex, the guys at that party would only want to get their fingers wet."

"What should I do then?" she asked.

"Take the bra off, wear my t-shirt. It looks good on you, what panties have you got on?"

"French knickers," I made some hand gestures before she added, "They're black."

"Great, well if I wake up with morning glory you do nothing because you're still underage." I hit the light and clambered into bed with her, she got really close to me. I spun her round so she had her back to me.

"You're the little spoon," I said, "Now go to sleep."

Day 11

I just finished making the bed, the sun shone in through the window and I wondered if Sacré-Cœur were the same colour as when it was first built? The sun must have taken it toll in the time it had been there. I learnt yesterday that Notre-Dame meant Our Lady, the reverie I was trying to have was interrupted by her shouting from the other room,

"…Think to this?" I didn't hear the start of what she said, so I had no choice but to go to her and see just what she was going on about. I walked into the lounge, which she had transformed into something that could be regarded as a lived in home.

"Looks good." I said as I scanned my eyes around the room. She had pictures from all different periods of both our lives, the first picture we ever had taken together on a frame on the windowsill. Life was simple and carefree back then, sad thing is that you have to keep growing. These days I worry about money, here I am. A stranger, in a strange land. I walked over and picked up our first picture, I looked at her. I looked awful; I had just spent a week traipsing across Europe to get to her.

"It seems like a lifetime ago

doesn't it?" she said, "You never did tell me how you got to Tallinn." I put the picture back down,

"And I never will." I looked at her, "Are you wearing MY chords?"

"No, these are mine. They're more faded than yours, why did you think... are you saying that you have a pair that look like these?" I had left myself wide open for her banter, all I could say was.

"Shit." It didn't realise that she was just as quick witted as me.

"Is there something you want to tell me?" I rolled my eyes to the back of me head, "*Are you suffering from* **Gender Identity Issues?**"

"Christ, I swear you only hear what you want to hear." I had to stretch before adding, "HAD they been mine, YOU would have without a shadow of a doubt told me that they *look so much better on you*." she smiled. I stepped back from the picture to look at us aged 14,

"I don't know who looks prettier, you there or you now."

"Please, I'm 15 lbs heavier now, and besides..." I cut her off, I don't know if she was trying to be modest in herself, frankly I just saw as doing that thing that women do, when if you pay them a complement they say something back as a poignant reminder that your work is good, but not good enough.

"Your eyes are prettier now, than

what they were then." She sneezed; I smiled, as it sounded almost too feminine. She pulled a tissue out of her pocket, clean her nose and hands before throwing the tissue into the bin which was the other side of the room; about 12 feet away.

"5 points." She said,

"How do you get 5 points from that?" I was the confused party, but for some reason she was looking at me like I was speaking Dutch.

"Because, I'm this far away!" How timid and innocent she sounded.

"But in Basketball, you only get 3 points." How quickly the tables had turned in who had the upper hand.

"Why don't you have any pictures of her with you?" I shook my head,

"I didn't want any, I feel that I would rather… recreate this world again." She looked at me with eyes that said 'Why?' I felt so shot down by her silence. While I was gazing at her, something happened. Her eyes - they flickered to green and gold and as quick as I could click my fingers, they were back as dodger blue.

"If I just keep pictures of her lying around all my life, I would just be unbewithable." I started to shake, there was no need for words, but she was making me speak. I thought to myself, I just wanted to shout at her,

'Why aren't you getting it? No I can't forget her, but at the same time I can't let her stick around. The world is moving, each night it feels like we are going to sleep to die and the following morning we are born again. Life won't wait for us. I have thrown so much away. If I spend my time worrying about what I like, and what I hate; it won't matter - the fact of the matter is, life is an…'

"Life is an hourglass glued to the table." She finished my sentence. Had we become that intuitive with each other? That we could without saying anything know where we were in our sentences.

"I don't want the days to fade away from me." She picked up a pillow and threw it at me; I caught it and passed it onto the couch. Something was missing on that couch; I walked back to the bedroom, looked in the cupboard. I couldn't find anything that I thought was suitable. I walked back into the lounge,

"We have to go out," I said as I slipped on a pair of shoes, "The couch is missing something." She looked at it and grew pensive over it,

"I thought that I'd be the one to spot things that I thought would look shoddy? Is that the word I'm thinking of? It must be. Anyway, what were you thinking?" I handed a cardigan to her as she walked to me.

"Plaid, why do you think something

else?" she opened the door and started down the stairs,

"This isn't the bloody 90s; we should get something more…" I locked the door behind me.

"More… retro? Is that what you're thinking? You might if you got dressed up look like Janet Leigh." We started walking down the stairs, after we had passed the halfway point my foot went through one of the steps, she looked at me, she knew if she were to help she'd make it worse. I slipped my other foot out of the shoe,

"Stamp a hole though, and I'll be able to kick the rest of this out." She looked at the thin bit of wood that was designed for the continual usage of supporting the weight of not man, but men.

"Caveat emptor, said the man. And he was right, no wonder we got the place so fucking cheap." She stamped and her foot went straight through, a split second later we heard a thud.

"Was that my…"

"Yep,"

"Think you could retrieve it?" She looked down,

"My foot is also stuck."

"So it seems, but your feet are 4 sizes smaller than mine. Meaning, YOU can slide your foot out and get the shoe while I finish off here." She started walking down; I ripped my foot up, as the fragments of wood went all over the other steps; I hadn't even begun to mention how I looked.

"SHOULD WE LEAVE A NOTE?" she shouted up to me. I walked down to her,

"Godspeed to the person who doesn't see that." We walked out to the morning heat. The Paris streets that a week ago I didn't even know existed, seem to fade into the day before. We eventually found a fabric shop, we stood outside; I had to say it didn't look too appealing to me from the outside.

"I think I'll just wait outside." She looked at me, "I'm not any good at haggling. I really would just end up buying any old shit. No! A job like this I do believe is destining for you."

"You are so *blonde* about such small things **aren't you?**" I helped her along and pushed her inside, I stood outside looking at the world from afar. I got the song Have A Cigar stuck in my head, and I suddenly found myself stood outside singing the lyrics to myself,

"*It's a hell of a start, it could be made into a monster if we all pull together as a team.*" I had a tap on my shoulder, I curiously turned my head to see a woman that I had never seen before in my life,

"As-tu vu mon copain?"[2] the speed at which she spoke was far too much for me to absorb in a second with an accent that I didn't know.

"Désolé, peux tu parler plus lentement s'il te plaît, je…"[3] I suddenly couldn't remember what I needed to say in French. "Look, I'll be honest with you. I can't really understand your accent."

"Écoute! Je veux juste ton aide. Je me suis disputée avec mon copain et il est parti. J'ai essayé de le suivre et je me suis perdue; je t'ai pris pour lui et tu ne m'aides pas avec ton accent américain. Pour l'amour de dieu, vas tu m'écouter s'il te plaît!"[4] I just stood there looking at her, I was unable to say anything to her. I felt bad for saying nothing, the 30 seconds that we were in that awkward silence felt like a lifetime. She broke the silence by saying,

"Bon…"[5] I thought that the woman was going to start up and go on

---

[2] Have you seen my boyfriend?

[3] Sorry, can you please speak more slowly I…

[4] LOOK! I just want your help. I was arguing with my boyfriend, and he walked off. I tried to follow him, I got lost; I thought you were him and you are not helping me by talking AMERICAN! For the love of God will you please listen to me!

[5] Well…

another barrage of screeches and noises that I couldn't define, when she walked out of the shop shouting,

"You fucking pig, you have a sweatshop back there. This is Europe, if I report you, you and your shitty rugs will be deported back to Iran!" he slammed the door on her, "FUCKWIT!!" she then spotted me, **"And *who the* fuck is THIS?"**

"Thank fuck you're back, I have no idea who she is she started saying something to me, but I can't distinguish her accent. Please tell her to leave me alone." She clicked her fingers at her,

"Hey babe, why don't you make like an Asian girl after a night with a black cock and split."

"Je cherche juste mon copain, l'as tu vu?"[6]

She looked around shell-shocked by what she had just been asked,

"Yeah he's just over there." She pointed at her 10 o'clock, the woman turned to look. Our minds had found some kind of juxtaposition, because we just ran off. We must have run for 10 minutes solid, I looked up at a street sign and it said we were in the 16th, on the corner of Rue Baffet and Rue De La Source. As far as I could remember I hadn't been there before, I also don't recall seeing

---

[6] I'm just looking for my boyfriend, have you seen him?

the Arc De Triomphe when running, but there wasn't much that either of us were paying attention to, including the traffic.

I could tell that she was musing something over in her mind about where we were,

"What?" I asked her, she was studying the street names; I had no idea what she was doing.

"It should be this way." She started to continue on down Rue Baffet, I followed her, though I wasn't sure if what she had in mind was of any use to the day. We came to an oddly shaped square.

"And it should be just around there." She curved her arm around to a corner that I couldn't see. "I saw a picture of this back home when I was looking up things in Paris, and to me it is better not to try and find words to say what it makes me think. I don't think that words can really express just how refined and exquisite it really is."

"***Right,***" I said, "Can we at least get around the corner, so I can make a judgement for myself?" she grabbed my hand, it was so obvious that this was the most excited that she had been about seeing anything in a while. I would say she was as excited about seeing me but I wasn't in the greatest of all circumstances, we stood in the middle of a deserted street. I looked at the cars which were parked at all angles, the silence we were in she broke by saying,

"People not inspired by the beauty of this church just haven't had the right food or sex." What a predominately wrong thing to say outside of a catholic church; my mind was saying, but there was no further action from my lips.

"Do you want to have a look inside?" I asked her, she smiled. As we walked towards the church I looked at the brick work and said,

"Do you think we should do our room that colour?" she gave a slight nod as she opened the door, I held it open and watched her step into the darkness. I followed her in; a few candles barely lit the room in erratic places. I sat down as she moved between the shadows that were designed for her to dance between, nobody would have known. A priest walked over to me,

"Quelque chose à confesser?"[7] he questioned as he sat down.

"Non mon père, rien que les Dieux ne savent pas déjà."[8] She came back to me and the priest.

"I can hear all my thoughts like they should be heard in here, you are a lucky man father." I don't know if

---

[7] Anything to confess?

[8] No father, nothing that the Gods don't already know about.

he could speak English but the smile he gave her resonated in my mind that the old man could.

Day 48

She leaned over and turned off the alarm, which in turn woke me up.

"Do you always sleep naked?" I asked.

"Only when I think I will be up and out, before you've woken up." I had a face that looked like she had cluttered up my mind.

"Right," I said, "Do you fancy moving off me? Just…" I lost my trail of thought.

"It is titillating you, and you can't remember what you need to do today."

"Something like that." We both got out of bed; I made it as she got herself ready for the classes that she had that day. She put her French books into her bag, still sodding naked. I thought to myself – 'Do I say something? Do I do something?'

I then watched her as she put on the same pair of black boy shorts that she had leant me 10 days earlier, she readjusted them at the back.

"What?"

"No, they do feel the same. I was going to say they feel different but they are very much the same."

I straighten the sheets before collapsing on them, what was it that I needed?

"I know that I have work tonight from 10 until 5 tomorrow morning. What am I forgetting?" I just yelled at air.

"Help me with my bra strap."

"No, it's not that." She starred something close to machetes never mind daggers at me,

"No, help me with my bra strap. It's an awkward bra and I can never get it done, it always comes undone when I do it myself."

I sat up and helped her with her bra strap, and then it came to me.

"My sister is coming isn't she?" I was fairly sure that I was right.

"Which sister? Your older sister who is worried about everything and had you given her your number she'd be phoning us every other day. Or your younger sisters not able to travel on the Eurostar alone because the security has been upped so much that almost no child can get on it given your escapades 4 years ago."

"I'm fairly sure that has nothing to do with it."

She had to have the final word with,

"I'm sure it had something to do with it."

Yeah, never mind September 11th 2001, the reason why travelling anywhere in this world was so difficult was because I had been able to get across Europe undetected to see her. She looked agitated,

"Right, well I got to go. When you work out what it is that you've forgotten, let me know." We shared a kiss before she went to the front door; I heard it open before she called out,

"One more thing,"

"Being?"

"If you're to do any washing put my stuff in with it."

"Consider it done." She shut the door and I heard nothing after that, either she wasn't wearing shoes or she had found a way to compress the sounds down to nothing. I watched her walk up Rue Des Martyrs; I then headed towards the bathroom. I brushed my teeth and sprayed some deodorant on, whatever it was that I had forgotten I wasn't going to let it bug me too much. I knew that it was going to pray on my mind but, I knew that the more I let it annoy me the less I was going to get done. I walked back into the bedroom, and put on a pair of jeans. I opened the windows in the flat to let some air in; I figured that for the majority of the morning that was the only decent oxygen that could course through my veins. I don't know why but I didn't put any music on, I guess I must have wanted me and my thoughts; not me, my thoughts and The Doors. I did the washing up and I was trying to figure out everything from the past couple of months, things had become a blur, even for me. I remembered hospital lights. I had an arcane of looking at her corpse before coughing up about 40 undigested tablets. There were things that I wasn't sure if they were from dreams or if I had just suppressed them. Kate Bush was stuck in my head. Once I finished the washing up, I walked over and put the Hounds Of Love album on before I proceeded to scan the flat looking for all the clothes that needed to go in the machine, I was so grateful that she wore the same kind of colours as me, otherwise her clothes would be waiting. Part of me felt like a fool for not remembering, I knew right now I couldn't do better with this part of my life even if I were to have tried. I stood holding the clothes, close to tears wanting for this world to just burn away. At that very moment everything could just disintegrate, I knew it was only a matter of time before it all would.

The clothes fell from my hands and it was a few seconds before I realised, and I knelt down to pick them up I said to myself,

"You're still alive man, and that is something." My heart was in total overdrive, it must have been beating about 4 times faster than it should have been.

"You have her; she will take care of you." Why was I talking in an out of body manner? Was that it was I now in a fucking novel and someone was dictating what I was going to say? I regained my composure and put the washing on. As I pressed the start button my mobile started to ring, I quickly ran back to the bedroom and answered it,

"Hello?" I didn't bother to check the number,

"Aha, you're in." I couldn't pinpoint the voice.

"You've phoned my mobile." There was a slight pause where I figured that she had checked her phone to confirm what I had said.

"I knew that, what I was going to say was that my train gets into Gare Du Nord in about 45 minutes…"

"Sorry, I hate to interrupt but I've just woken up. Who is this?"

"It's Erin; did you forget that I was coming?"

"To be fair, I did know that something was happening today."

"You are such a twat," I waited to see if she was going to insult me some more.

"Don't worry; I'll be there to meet you. It's only a 10 minute walk from mine."

"Ok."

"See you shortly."

"Useless."

"What?" She hung up. I returned to sorting the flat out, but got the urge to phone the Estonian.

"You worked it out?"
"Erin is staying."
"YOU worked it out."
I sneezed, "She phoned, I'm picking her up in about 45 minutes."
"Good, well I'm about to go into class right now. So, I will see both of you later."
"We'll have something cooked when you get in."
She hung up and I made sure the flat was more or less tidy. I grabbed my bag and threw my wallet, keys, phone and iPod inside. I figured that I could sort myself out on the walk to the train station. I walked out the flat locked the door before reaching into my bag for my iPod. The headphones went in and as I walked down the stairs I threw on the Wu-Tang Clan, and headed down the stairs. I walked up Rue Des Martyrs as they brought the ruckus. I switched to Boulevard De Rochechouart, and with the road switch I turned to Kanye West and his debut album, forgetting it was the market day and the hustle of people that I had to get through as there was a constant flow of cars and I was unable to cross, until the lights changed, even then it didn't stop moving, French drivers always trying to edge their way forwards. I was able to cross over and get quickly down Rue De Maubeuge, and before I knew it I was inside Gare Du Nord. I

walked through the constant barrage of people to take a look at the arrivals board; I had 8 minutes to spare so I thought it wise to not travel far if the train were to arrive early. I looked around; there was nowhere to sit, so I just had to stand. Waiting to see what platform it was to arrive at. I watched the arrivals board changing, there was something very therapeutic about watching the clippers change, when up it came - platform 8.

I walked over to platform 8 as the train was coming in; I waited at the end as I watched her get off the train and walk down towards me. She was wearing a dress that looked worn, but she wore it and it complimented her waist even if it were to be falling off one shoulder. Her eyes clocked with mine and she gave a rather shy smile, she walked down and I got to see the rest of her. Ripped jeans that made me ignore all the holes except the ones by her knees, a blatantly black bra that was visible under the old dress, she was trying to hold her bags at the same time as not letting her jeans fall down. I walked up to her and we shared a hug, she had to stand on my toes to hug me at my height. I looked down at the white vans that she had on; they were dirty like tennis shoes that had been used on clay.

"Sorry," she giggled, "It's just

really great to see you."

"It's OK," I said, "You still have no tits." She handed me 2 of her bags and undone my belt.

"Spin." She said to the shell-shocked look that I had on my face.

"WHAT?!"

"My jeans are falling down, I need a belt. Spin!"

So I spun round for her, she stole my belt and wore it around the bottom of the zip and it was sported in a very punk way.

We walked outside in silence, once we had made our way outside, she breathed in the Parisian air.

"My first taste of French air."

"I don't know if you know this, but air is more or less the same anywhere you go."

"Bonjour Paris! Je suis jeune et je cherche à expérimenter avec une femme au foyer. Je ne sais pas pourquoi mais le sexe avec un jeune semble attirant maintenant que je suis là!"[9]

I just stood there mouth open, catching both flies and dust.

"What? The fuck! Was that?" she was off, she walked up to a couple of local girls, "excusez-moi," they looked at her, "Tu voudrais baiser ce

---

[9] Hello Paris! I'm young and I want to experiment with a housewife. I don't know why but underage sex seems appealing now I'm here.

soir?"[10] they seemed more shocked, but less offended than I did.

"Sorry I've wanted to say that since I got on the train this morning." Was the response I got when she turned back to me.

"Right? Well people here are quite conservative, so they most likely will take offence to you saying that." She giggled, she pointed down Boulevard De Margneta and said, "Lead the way!"

"That leads to République, we head west chick." I pointed down Rue De Magneta, "This way is the start of our walk back to mine."

I took her hand and we walked towards Maubeuge, the rows of scooters on either side of the street meant that any cars looking to park would be on quite a walk back to Dunkerque. The confusing nature of a simple task like crossing a road in France, I held her hand by a zebra crossing; as the cars went past she asked,

"Why are we not crossing?"

"Because in France, they have the genius idea that cars are more important than people so, unless we are in the road the car doesn't need to stop for us."

"What a fucking stupid idea," she said; I looked down the street,

"On 3," I said as a silver Renault

---

[10] Do you want to fuck this evening?

pulled up towards us, "1, 2," it pulled away and before the next car which I think was a Ford of some description was able to get to us I shouted, "3." We ran across the road and were able to stop just next to an old couple that looked at us and said,

"Vous les jeunes et votre mode de vie a 100 a l'heure, vous n'atteindrez pas nos âges."[11]

"We are sorry sir, traffic is awful today. You must have seen it." His eyes looked glazed almost like he was trying to work out my accent, but had never heard anything like it. We crossed the road when the lights turned red and made our way down Maubeuge. We were on the right side of the street; the few bistros and small shops that we passed were never going to live up to what Erin was expecting to see in Paris, I looked at her as we walked down towards the next zebra crossing. The pensive look in her eyes was going to bring me down if I were to see it anymore.

"Erin," she looked over to me, "You'll have to get used to this. It is not all cute boutiques and good looking women riding around wearing berets, for the most part it is immigrants and shitty shops."

The rest of the walk home was

---

[11] You kids and your live fast lifestyles, you won't get to our age

pretty quiet and uneventful; Rue Condorcet played out and looked like any other street, the few cars that went down there were clearly driving too fast, so I walked on the curb. When we made it onto Rue Des Martyrs Erin then asked,

"Is she in?" I shook my head and at the same time I pointed up.

"She has class at the moment, you will meet her tonight. That is where we live, we'll drop you're stuff off and then we have to get some things for dinner."

"Can I cook?" was all Erin said, I was taken by surprise a little which caused me to forget where in my bag I had left my keys.

"Please yes, she rarely ever cooks. It would be nice to not have to cook for one night."

I unlocked the door and as we stepped in she said, "I only know a couple of recipes, can we make spekulatius?" I had no idea what it was so I guess I needed to find out.

"Which is?"

"They are these really cute biscuits, that people normally make around Christmas time but where,"

I cut her off, "I thought that you meant a meal, we can make them. But we have to eat something proper. What were you going to say before I rudely interrupted you?"

"I was going to say where I work we make them all year round. We do them in all different shapes."

"You work as a baker?"

"No I work as a Kassiererin,[12] I take the money."

"A cashier, aha."

"Is that how you say it? Cashier, I will remember that." I was stood a few steps in front of her, "Are you not going to keep going?" she asked.

"You can go ahead." I replied, only for her to shake her head, "Bad luck to cross on the stairs." So I had to carry on up. When we got to the front door she reached into my bag and pulled out the key chain and insisted on opening the door.

I let her walk inside first, we put the bags down and she was off walking through the rooms.

"Where will I be sleeping?" I didn't have a clue where she'd be sleeping, so I told her straight.

"As you can remember, I forgot that you were coming. So will you be OK in sharing a bed with her?"

"Where will you sleep?" She then asked.

"I can take the couch." I felt pensive, and it showed; I didn't know why.

"Don't be silly, is there any reason we can't have 3 in the bed."

"There is a quite serious reason why, you're 15. I don't know what the sentence is over here, and I have no

[12] Cashier

intention of finding out."

"We'll sort something out. What else do we have to do before bed?"

"Get some food." She kept moving from room to room, until I eventually heard, "Here it is."

"Here what is?"

"The bathroom."

She was only in there for a minute or 90 seconds, before I knew it she was back with me.

"What will we eat tonight? Don't you go out to eat often?" I shook my head,

"The only people who can afford to go out and eat every night are tourists, and before you say anything - no tourists will be staying in my flat."

"So what are we eating? I didn't hear that in and amongst your rant there."

"Coq au vin." She seemed to approve, she picked up her bag, check to see if all that she needed was inside. Nodding to herself she walked into the kitchen and started to go through the fridge,

"I already know what we need, chicken, mustard and cream."

"You forgot mushrooms." I thought that we had some. In fact, I was so sure of it I had to go and check myself.

"Remember that when we are at the shop. Oh and potatoes, we need to have them with something."

We left the flat again, as I locked the door Erin asked,

"How have you been?" she was a few steps ahead of me, I turned to face her - I gave a half-hearted smile, but it was something.

"We take it one day at a time, if I have a bad day it is a bad day. The next day I will try and make a better period of time. Like to try and shine through shadows, but it is a long and slow way until I'm really able to be by myself."

We walked down the stairs and she got the street door, as we stepped out she then asked,

"Have you tried to get back on it while you've been in Paris?"

"No, I just… I don't know, here I don't want to impress anyone I'm here with her, I know like half a dozen people here and to them I'm just a scared guy."

She didn't say anything; I know that it was easier for her to say nothing than be seeking tears. We walked into the supermarket she picked up a basket, followed quickly by a French stick.

"Put it back." I said.

"Why?"

"Because, we use the bakery across the road from mine. I work there, so it's free. Makes more sense."

She put the French stick back, very unwillingly.

"You work in a bakery; you should

know that it's hard to compete with supermarkets."

"That is a fair point."

We walked around the store collecting the things that we needed, I couldn't remember where in the store the mustard was; and as a typical male instead of asking I decided it would be much easier to search every shelf of the store hunting for the fucking thing. We split up to find it all the easier, I was looking through the crisps to see if it had been misplaced, when I heard from afar.

"Found it." She walked back around to me; I was stood half way down the aisle when out of nowhere she threw the jar to me. I was lucky to just about catch it; I placed it in the basket and walked back to her.

"Don't throw things, if you break something in a store here. You pay for it."

"Still, you caught it." Was all she said. We went and paid, as we walked out of the supermarket she asked,

"I don't understand why you still drink, I thought you told me you moved out here to get and stay healthy."

"I did." We return back down Rue Des Martyrs, she then said.

"But still you are drinking."

"Drinking wasn't the problem that I had, I can't drink a lot so it never really effects me." She mused over what I said, as we walked back to mine in pretty much total silence.

We walked in and just got straight on with cooking dinner, I did the bulk of the work, Erin was in charge of the potatoes and mange tout.

"Can I ask you something?" she said, I looked up to her.

"When you're strung out, what is it like?" I didn't want to answer the question, but knew if I were to avoid it then she would just keep on asking.

"I would have to say I can't really remember, so take it from me not being able to remember that it can't have been that great a place." She was silent. "You're not thinking of trying are you?"

"No, mum told me not to ask you about it. But I guess that curiosity got the better of me."

"It's ok, I realise now that I was such a fool for thinking I was important to the world, now I realise just how the world is important to me. Guess it does show what a fool a person can be."

"You're not a fool."

"Everyone is a fool to some degree; it's just a matter of how much you really let it be seen by the people who are around you."

She sat down on the floor, I sat down with her. I heard the door go, I thought about standing up as she walked in.

"Which room are you in?" she asked to the void.

"We're in the kitchen."

She walked through to join us, when looking at us sat on the floor she then joined us.

"So, you are Erin." She said, Erin smiled to which she repeated the action.

"He talks a lot about you." She then added.

"He talks about you almost all the time, he says that you're the reason he is still alive."

"We need each other, but at the moment - he is the priority." I stayed quiet during their chat before the Estonian asked,

"So what have you cooked?"

"Coq au Vin, we were just waiting for you." She stood up and dished up the food, handing each of us a plate.

"Do you ever cook?" she shook her head whilst eating, waiting to finish her mouthful before saying,

"No I'm very much the one who washes up." Erin smiled; she knew that her first night in the city was best spent inside.

"Can we watch a film tonight?" she asked, I looked at the Estonian and we both nodded our heads before we returned to our food.

Day 55

We walked into Père Lachaise Cemetery, Erin had her hair brushed to one side; I had never seen anyone with hair like that before. Wearing that strapless dress, I knew it was only really being held up by the piano belt which she had stolen from me that morning.

"Where is Oscar Wilde's grave?" she asked, there were jitters in her voice; and it was a voice that I had not heard anyone else be so excited about seeing a person's grave.

"It's in the 89th, and we're in the 1st. so we have to walk to the other side of the graveyard." As we started to walk up Erin noticed a map, examining it; proving to herself that it was nothing more than a straight line we were walking in. satisfied with what she had seen, she had vindication that I did know where we were walking. I don't think that either of us were really paying attention to the graves that we were walking past, as we walked up steps and around graves. Erin went to step over a grave, I grabbed her hand and made her walk around; she gave me a disgruntled look as my eyes cast their way back to her.

"A graveyard has its own life, I see the graves as people's houses, and you shouldn't walk across them." I knew she wanted to give an answer back to me, but she wasn't going to get anywhere with it. Even the dead need their peace.

"What do you think happens when you die?" Erin would often muse about things to do with her surroundings, but this was awkward like when my science teacher got arrested in class for having child porn on his laptop. As we sat in the classroom, looking at each other, with the assumption that it had become a free period.

"I don't know, it's all grey to me. I always thought that you'd float around for a few hours and get to see anyone you cared about." We stood between the graves, she retighten my belt around her waist, the way she was dressing was like a younger and quirkier version of Amélie. We started walking again,

"So who would you see?" she asked, I thought about it for a minute. When we came to a footpath I waited facing her as she stepped out onto the footpath.

"I'd make sure that she were ok, and you kept your heart strong. Mum and my sisters go without saying, I guess the only other person is the journalist."

"You have moved on to her very quickly." I knew she was going to say something along those lines,

"Nothing is happening, you really

do have the wrong end of things."

"Yeah, but she is seriously beautiful."

"I'm never going to deny that, and I expect I will end up in bed with her at some point. But, she does know how I feel about life and the world in this present moment of time." A group of people walked past us, we were silent looking at them as they fell to an obtrusive volume. We watched them go past, as they started to hunt for their next target through the fields of graves Erin started again,

"Can I sleep with her?"

"What?!"

"Well you're not interested, why can't I try?"

"You're 15!"

"There's a goalkeeper in football, that didn't stop Aílton from scoring 28 goals last season." I had to bite my tongue, her wit was getting better, had the Estonian been giving lessons? I wasn't to know.

"It's not a case of I'm not interested in her, I'm just waiting for the time when I feel ready. It could be in the morning, or a years' time; I really don't know much more than that never is a long time." We carried on walking through the lots, after a couple more footpaths we came out at section 87. Erin started to walk in the wrong direction, I didn't have the strength to walk after her;

almost as if talking about the journalist had not only mentally, but physically drained me.

"This way," There was almost a sigh to how I said it, but I felt heart soft and head-gone. As she walked back towards me, her head touched mine, I wasn't sure if it were affection. She started to walk down a small foot path, I dragged her between some graves explaining,

"We're on the wrong side. We'll walk in a straight line and be right beside it." The smile that she wore looked like she wanted to forgive me, but didn't know what she wanted to forgive me for.

There was a throng of people gathered around the stone, people left flowers and cigarettes. A few people had left notes saying things like 'Thank you for the literature.' Along with many of his famous quotes. Erin reached into her bag, and after rooting around for something like 30 seconds she pulled out a tube of lipstick. As she was applying the lipstick I looked at the people around the grave. There was a couple holding hands, he was trying to comfort her; she was acting like he had just died. I thought to myself 'How can you have nostalgia for a time you didn't know?' The sun was going to start burning giant cigarette holes in the sky, the heat it was emanating was close to torture. I could see the sweat on me, I didn't even want to see the sweat on others. Shame I could.

"He was such a modest man." I heard the woman say to her partner, I couldn't believe what she said.

"Seriously, you actually think that?" Erin walked over to the grave and laid a kiss with blue lipstick,

"Yes." She snapped, ah the audacity of some people's stupidity.

"He was so vain, the man died penniless and had this as his grave?" She just stared at me, I felt compelled to quote him,

"We are all in the gutter, but some of us are looking at the stars."

"What a shit attempt at a metaphor." I started to laugh at her,

"Well he's the man who wrote those words down." She snubbed my words, and walked off. There was a tap on the shoulder I turned to see a new couple with a camera in hand.

"Can you take a picture of us?"

"Certainly." They handed me the camera and went and stood either side of the grave. Just after I took 2 pictures the girl said,

"You were right; he was a very vain man."

"It doesn't matter how much great you do, if you can't stay human there was no point in doing what it was you were trying to do before." I handed the camera back, the boyfriend asked us,

"Do you know where the grave of Modigliani is?" I looked at Erin, it sounded more like something that she would know.

"Who was he?"

"He was a painter, he was friends with Picasso." We looked at each other; it was then than I noticed the blue lipstick she was wearing.

"Why blue?"

"People will see it, and think that it's different. I don't care what people think, so long as it's about me." She could say things that sounded so much like me, but from the way it's presented she would make me look like the person caught up with copying. We returned our attention to the couple,

"It's in the 96th, this much we do know." We started to walk over towards the 96th lot,

"Is it your first time in Paris?" Erin asked, the woman smiled, her boyfriend said,

"It is, it's also our first holiday together. We're from Bari, we study in Milan. She studies, I paint." She whispered something into his ear, he then reached into his pocket and pulled out their camera. As he scrolled through the photographs, I asked the Italian woman,

"So what do you study?"

"Business communications, I have one year left." She replied with, to which Erin and I said in unison,

"Isn't that just talking?" we instantly realised that the reply was quite rude, but we did find it humorous.

We came to lot 96, a barrage of caskets that most likely had its contents fermenting. As we walked amongst the sarcophagi, I started to feel the morbid atmosphere that was around us. It seemed to take longer to find the grave than it did for us to walk here. I eventually found this tiny grave, with a few dried out pastels on top; the painter pulled out a used brush and placed it on the grave; I didn't know what to make of it so I turned away. I am relearning to be in this world, for someone to feel that they have a connection with somebody that died so long ago is just mad; but these days my brain does feel fried.

"You don't like graveyards?" he asked me, I started to walk backwards to face him,

"I think about a lot in graveyards, I fear I will end up in a place like this."

"You're afraid of when you will die?" the woman asked, I shook my head.

"No, I'm afraid that people will want me to be remembered. I don't want to be stuck in the ground, I'll die with my name."

"Which is?" I smiled and gave no reply, my name wasn't very important they would see me today, and today only.

"Come on," I deflected the conversation, "Let's show you all Jim Morrison's grave." We started to follow the curve of the footpath around towards the entrance, I knew how far we had to walk and more or less where the tiny monument to the last real poet was.

"Which section are we looking for?" I took a left when I saw the tree,

"Here, section 6." We walked through, there was a group stood around his grave. I didn't look at the grave, it's not something that I have a great passion for; even if it does belong to an icon. As the other people left and the 4 of us moved closer to the grave, Erin started to tap her feet on the floor; my eyes were on the tree next to the grave. The graffiti gave it a slight human pulse. All of a sudden Erin started singing to herself,

"You know the day destroys the night, night divides the day. Tried to run, tried to hide. Break on through to the other side; break on through to the other side. Break on through to the other side, yeah." I was expecting someone to join her in singing, I'm glad she was happy to fly that flag solo. The Italians looked at her confused by the act she was in, and her in a trancelike state unaware of the action she was committing along with the number of people who were looking at her.

When she was done with her rendition, I took her hand and we walked out to let the next lot in. we walked back onto the footpath, as we continued away from the way in which we had come; from the Italians said something to each other before asking us,

"Do you know where the nearest Metro is? We are going to go into the main part of the city and have lunch." I pointed, we continued to walk to the gates.

"Just on the corner, I can't remember its name; but you can't miss the signs." We shook hands and they gave us their email address, I looked at Erin as they left.

"Do you want to see Victor Hugo's grave?" she shook her head,

"How do you see death?" she asked me. I had never really given it much thought, so I tried to answer as honestly as I could.

"It's cold, I guess." We sat on a bench outside; the wall didn't look to enticing for people who had family there let alone tourists. "I don't know, to me it's more nothing than it is something." She looked at me, "When we die, that is game over. The soul is said to be just fragments of past people, I sometimes wonder what mundane people of the past were like. Things like that really do keep me up for days." Then silence.

Day 1

Everyone else had already left me, I'd never remember if what was on my mind was important or even remotely relevant, to anything.

From looking at the sun I figured that it was time to go, I felt so fucking awful. I was walking out of the cemetery; the graveyard seemed a little less bleak than I thought it would be. I walked down a path, and looked to my right, there was a grave for a Stanley Vom-Berg, he died April 13th 1993, his wife was buried with him, but I can't remember her name. I carried on walking until I came to the main gates on Bear Road, I looked across the road at the crematorium, and both made me feel quite nauseous.

I started to walk down Bear Road; I didn't hear a sound that was being made by the cars as they drove past me, they would speed away unaware of my pain. I came to the corner by Bevendean Road I crossed the road and continued to walk down Bear Road, when from out of nowhere I got a tap on the shoulder; I turned my head to look at someone who did but didn't look familiar to me.

"Alright mate," I just looked straight through him, "How have you been?" his girlfriend joined him, she was slightly more honest.

"You look awful." I looked up and down at her, sure I looked bad, but she was looking like she had just rolled out of a bed made of sandpaper.

"Maybe, but the diet you're on, is making your pussy look like it's eaten cheesecake."

They both didn't know how to react, they stood still, with that I turned my head back and carried on my walk.

I carried on walking down the road, when a bald black woman with her left arm in a cast was walking up; she looked at me and gave a half-hearted smile, I couldn't bring myself to show an emotion, so I just carried on walking. The further down I walked the less I thought like myself. There was an old mattress on the pavement; a homeless person was sat on it.

"Spare some change?" he asked, as I walked by I mused to him,

"I wish my problems. Were as easy to resolve, as yours." Yet another person left speechless by me, I don't know why I felt that everyone else needed to endure my pain.

I carried on walking down the road, I saw the Sainsbury's store from afar. I got to the bottom of the road and walked out in front of the 49 bus. East Moulsecoomb was like paradise when you compare it to the world that I was in, a shithole like that was a worthwhile place. The bus driver really did go for it at letting me know that he wasn't happy that I had walked out in front of him, but when he saw the look in my eyes that I just didn't care he did nothing. Almost like, I had ripped the earth out from underneath his feet. I made it to the other side of the road, and as I walked around to cross the road again I stepped on a snail. I heard the crush through the white noise that was filling my ears; I looked down only to say,

"You lost all inhibitions, I guess everyone will adore you."

I walked around to the next traffic island, when the lights changed to red I crossed over only to have to wait on the traffic island, each second that I was there felt like a lifetime; I was certain that I could feel myself aging. There was a man also standing on the traffic island with his daughter, she was holding his hand. she looked up at me as I looked around before down at her, she smiled - I tried to smile back to her but only the sadness inside me came out; almost like it was the end of the world. She pulled on her father's hand, as she did the lights turned red and I started to cross the road. I was still able to hear her ask him,

"Dad, why did he look so sad?"

I never heard what he said back to her I was heading straight up Hollingdean Road. There were a couple of cars parked on the pavement, an old woman was walking in the gap that was the pavement between the cars and houses, I had no desire to wait for anyone, so I walked up on the road. There was nothing really to think about, my brain couldn't even try and concentrate, I looked up the billboard it had something that would be dated within a fortnight. The road forks round so I carried on walking up towards Hollingdean Lane, the sun blinded my eyes for a brief second, but it felt like too long. A cloud hid the sun, I took that moment to look at the sky, and the aeroplane paths added an extra heartbeat to the world. My mind was so confused. Again there was a cast of the sunlight, thought this time it was blocked out by the tower blocks. Tower blocks, what a sad sight, they look so grey even when the sun is showing off its best features.

I made it up the hill so the sun was now behind me, there was no pavement and the road was so unkempt, it was too late to cry. If I could stop as me and start being someone else midway through their existence I would quite gladly take it, at this moment in time. This one was so overrated. I came out on Ditchling Road I walked across the entrance to the BP petrol station causing a car to crash into the Toyota that was about to roll into the pumps. I walked down to a wine store called

Rose when I crossed the road to head down Ditchling Rise.

The sign at the top of the road was pointing down to London Road train station, though I couldn't remember how far down it was to it or even if it were off on a side road. I must have only taken 10 steps when I read a sign for a missing cat, I think it was a lemony colour, though it could have been blue. I don't know, it was only a quick glance. The steps I was taking, seemed more like miles than anything. I walked a little further down, before I crossed over the road to slow down an already quite slow pace along Vere Street; I had no point of reference as to how long it had taken me to get this far. I guess it didn't matter. I stood on the corner of Vere Street and Clyde Road. I don't, know why I couldn't move. I needed to sleep, it wouldn't resolve anything but I knew I wouldn't have to think about breathing while I was asleep.

I plucked up the courage to carry on with my walk; I walked past 8 or 9 houses before I saw a woman stood in the doorway of her house; she was watering her plants that she had hanging either side of the doorframe, as I got closer I noticed that she was pregnant. As I walked along side where she was I said to her, "Congratulations."

She looked but before she had

chance to say anything to the compliment that I had just given I had already walked on by.

There was a smell of burnt lavender; I couldn't tell where it was coming from. I found it to be quite over powering, to the point that it was gagging. I kept on walking, the road veered left and I followed suit. There's an old second hand shop on the corner adjacent to the Duke Of York's Cinema, the owner of the second hand shop was sat in a rocking chair out the front of the store, smoking a very finely rolled cigarette. The way it was rolled looked like something that you would see in a soviet prison environment. I glanced at the things that he had outside of the shop as I made my progression, the only thing that stuck out in my mind was the mannequin; the thing had nipples and no head, I couldn't think if I had ever seen a mannequin like that before. It didn't really matter, I was nothing more than a commuter at that moment with one thing on my mind. I looked at the posters outside, but my mind just couldn't make any words out. I remember taking her there to watch City Of God, she wanted to watch it and I just became so interested in the world of foreign films. It took me a few minutes to cross the road but once I had made it across I walked pass the bank that was on the corner, I think it was NatWest. I crossed over again, so I was on the side of the road that I lived, before I started the final walk.

New England Road, I just walked up the hill what felt an extreme amount steeper than what it actually is. The footsteps that I was taking felt so torturous, I couldn't even think of a reason to put one foot in front of the other. Everything was gone. I came to the underpass; there was a huge amount of broken glass sprawled across the floor. It could have been a bed for a less fortunate homeless person than the one I had met earlier. I stepped around it and carried on, I think it must have taken me something like 8 minutes to walk from there to the Shakespeare's Head pub.

I could see from the window that there were a few people in there, not too crowded - and I could take solace in the barmaid who was only a few years older than myself. I walked in, a couple of people looked over but quickly returned to their discussion. I walked over to the barmaid, who took a quick glance at me before reaching for the Grey Goose and pouring me a shot,

"Rough day?" she asked.

"You have no idea of the pain I've had today." I knocked back the shot.

"If you don't mind me asking, do

you care to share with me?"

I pointed at the glass with my index and middle fingers slightly apart; she added another shot to the glass.

"Thank you," I whispered before knocking that back, "I just buried my girlfriend." I took a deep breath before exhaling, "And now, now I'm nothing." She moved the bottle to one side before wiping the tear that had started to form in my right eye.

"Babe, I am so sorry. I hope that you don't think it's your fault."

I shrugged my shoulders; I didn't know what to think. I looked at her, she was going to reflect a hint of sadness on others as she had a tear trickling down the side of her face, and I knew that her mascara would run.

"How old are you?"

"18." I said.

"You shouldn't know hurt at your age." Was what she started with, "You should be out enjoying life."

"I know. Can I have one more for the road, please?"

She poured me the last shot, she made it a double.

"How much do I…"

She shook her head, "Your money isn't needed here today babe, these are on me." I toasted to her, before raising my glass to the ceiling. She poured herself a glass and joined me in raising her glass.

"I'll be with her again, someday. But please wipe the tear away, it looks like it could form in the shape of a square."

We both knocked back our shots, I put the glass on the bar looked at her and said, "Thank you." She smiled and closed our conversation with,

"Take care."

I walked out of the pub and carried on up the road, after a few houses I came to mine. I let myself in and walked to my room, I have no idea if anyone were already in, I just crawled on my bed and just went to sleep.

Day 2

I woke up, I looked at the clock, it said 4:35am. Had I really slept for 10 hours? I got up and walked to the bathroom. I washed my face and wondered to myself why I was awake, before realising that I HAD been asleep for 10 hours. I looked at myself in the mirror, I was wasting away. I figured that as I was up, I might as well try and get my body clock back to normal by staying up until that evening. I had a shower before I brushed my teeth; I was shaking all over, it was a massive heat wave, and I'm cold, my body looked grey. I'm here shaking all over like a meth addict, nothing eating my pain. I decided that I needed to go for a walk; I went back into my bedroom and got myself dressed. My jeans were basically falling off me, I hadn't had anything to eat in around 4 or 5 days; it fucking showed. I took my shoes off and walked to the kitchen in my socks and picked up 3 apples before opening the cupboards, there was a granola bar so I took that. I went back into my room and finished getting dressed. I had on a fading Hard Rock Cafe t-shirt from Puerto Vallarta, some jeans with holes taking their place in the cliché that is the knees, as well as holding my old vans. I looked just like you imagined. I picked up my shoes, put the bits to eat except one apple, in my bag and walked to the front door. I kept as quiet as I could; I let myself out and slipped into my shoes. With no agenda as to where I was going to walk to I just started off walking down the road, I made it to the underpass when I couldn't breathe, hyperventilating, I screamed.

"ARRRRRRRRRRRRRGGGGGGGGGHHHHHHHHH!!!!!" I looked around before I shouted,

"I WISH I FELT SOMETHING!!!!!!!"

I could still hear the first yell bouncing off the walls; if anyone were sleeping in there, I would have put a cease to that.

I kept on walking with no real agenda; the sun was starting to come up so it was pretty much 5am. I couldn't see the sun coming up, I don't remember the last time I saw a sunrise; feels like a lifetime ago. I looked around to get my bearings, only to find myself walking back towards the graveyard. I figured that as I had started I might as well carry on; I will never know why I wanted to see it again. It wasn't going to make me happy. I had before I knew it made my way to the bottom of Bear Road. I looked back at Lewis Road, there was nothing really in the way of traffic. I saw the entrance to the crematorium, looked to my left and there was the entrance to the graveyard.

I walked in, I think that the silence was more haunting than the fact that I couldn't see if there was anybody around. I walked amongst the epitaphs, looking at the fading names. Nothing stuck in my mind; I thought that I heard voices coming from near where her grave was. I walked up to see what was going on, there was a man in a digger setting the place for a new grave. I walked up to where he was working, waiting for him to take a break. Eventually he got out of his digger,

"Excuse me," I said, he turned to face me.

"Yeah,"

"Did you," I found myself stuttering. "Did you dig my girlfriends grave?"

"Look man, I don't want a fight. There's nothing to you." I threw up on the ground. "And now there's even less of you."

I wiped the vomit off my mouth, he handed me a bottle of water, to which I took a swig and then spat it on the earth beneath my feet.

"Thank you," I wiped my lips to dry them, "I don't want to fight anyone; I just feel like I need to know."

"Which grave?" He asked. I walked over to it and he followed a few steps behind, I point when I reached it.

"This 1."

He looked at her name, recalling his work from the day before. He eventually did nod his head.

"I remember now, I did this grave. I found it sad that somebody so young would die."

"You dug, my girlfriends' grave."

"I dug, your girlfriends' grave."

I knelt down, I knew that I was going to cry, I just didn't want him to see me do so.

"Look mate, this is my job. I don't mean to offend anyone by doing this, I'm not the cause of anything."

"You put her 6 feet below." I said, before I wiped the tears away from my eyes.

"Don't worry about me seeing you cry." He said,

"Men don't cry," I mused, "And I am a man. Even if you think I'm not."

"I think you are a man, if you cry that makes you no less a man."

"What?"

"Crying isn't for girls, crying shows that you really do feel pain, that you understand what a dog feels when it's bitten by a flea."

He put out his hand, "Would she want to see you like this?"

"No." I shook his hand.

"It's going to rain today, I think. I have to get this finished and get the sheets in so the ground doesn't slide away."

I looked at the sky, it did look like rain.

"I'm sorry that I dug your girlfriends' grave, it's just a job to me. The sorrow will be lifted in time, until then you need to ride this out man."

He walked back to his digger, I turned around and left the graveyard.

I walked back down Bear Road, I forgot everything that I knew; when walking down the road I noticed, the homeless person who spoke to me the day before; today I think our problems were about the same. When I made it to the bottom of the road, there was still nobody about but I was able to see the sun; at least that was something. There were a couple of buses that went along Lewis Road other than that all I saw in the way of cars was a Royal Mail van. I walked along Lewis Road, there were 2 couples walking home together, I didn't hear a word that they said, it was all reverb and background noise. All that I had I could hear was the conversation I had with the gravedigger. All the off streets blended into 1, and what I would normally be able to name without thinking about; had become a grand overture of a struggle. I had thrown away everything - orange had turned to blue, which in turn had become oh so grey. The walk along Lewis Road was a contemplative one to say the least, I looked up Elm Grove unable to remember who I knew that lived up there. Was it a friend of my mother's? Had I picked up my little sister from her friend's house there? I couldn't remember.

By the time that I had made it down to the Grand Parade it must have been an hour that had past, I was walking so slow. I looked at the business houses that were disguised as £350,000 houses. The Brighton Pavilion, would I miss looking at that? Old Steine was the busiest part of the walk, the school children and suits all heading to their consumer destinations. Me, I was caught with a lost designation.

When I reached the bottom of Old Steine and had crossed over to Grand Junction Road, down a flight of steps onto the beach. All the cafes and restaurants were closed, I wasn't interested in that. I walked across the pebbles and stones to the edge of the beach, I didn't notice that an old school friend of mine was right next to me.

"I heard man, I'm really sorry." I looked over at him,

"Thanks for caring mate."

The seagulls moved away from me as I took off my shoes and socks, and I walked towards the water.

"What are you doing? You can't swim."

I stared straight out into the

open,

"Where does the beach become the water?"

"What?"

"WHERE DOES THE BEACH BECOME THE WATER?"

A fisherman up on the pier shouted out to me,

"Do you mind? You're scaring away the fish!"

I looked up, only to shout out to him, "Fuck off!"

"You're not really going to go in are you?"

I shook my head, "I'm hydrophobic. You'll never catch me ever going into water."

"What about a…"

"Deep water." Fucking stupid question he was going to ask.

"Do you want to go get a drink?" he asked, I looked quite mortified.

"It's too early for that; why in God's name would you suggest such a thing?"

"I thought depressed drank their problems away, isn't that what you do?"

I really couldn't believe just how blasé he was to my predicament.

"I'm not depressed. Besides, even if I were why would I drink? To try and tell you what was worse the pain or the hangover."

"Ummm, yeah."

I put my socks and shoes back on, I turned and walked back up the beach.

"When will I see you again?" He shouted out to me, I turned continued to walk up the beach just backwards.

"When you know the answer to the question I asked the fish."

He just looked at me so blankly; I couldn't be bothered to explain it to him, so I walked off. I walked up the next set of stairs and along King's Road, I walked towards the basically non-existent west pier. I wish I had my camera on me, it looked so picturesque with the sunrise. I stopped in my tracks, there was no chance I was going to spend the morning let alone the day with anyone. I changed direction and started to walk back the way I came, I was going to walk away from the city today.

I walked along the Marine Drive, my intention was simple I was going to go to the windmill by Rottingdean and waste my day there. The cars past me by, it was only when a car blaring out some loud bass music drove past that I remembered that I had left my iPod in my bag from a few days ago. I stopped where I was, spun my bag around, grabbed the iPod - in went the headphones, the bag got zipped back up and I was back on foot. I don't remember what I put on, it was something from the 90's, I am certain it had a big beat and was slightly dated. The Chemical Brothers Out Of Control, it was. I really did take my time with the footsteps that I was taking, I'm certain that anyone would have walked faster than me. It took me close to 90 minutes to make my way from the pier to the Beacon Mill near Rottingdean. When I got there, I saw a few people walking their dogs and a bus with school children getting off, I subsequently recalled days when I had to come out here with my art class to draw the windmill.

As the last of the students got off the bus I saw my old art teacher, she saw me and after giving her students instructions of how to draw the windmill came over to see me.

"Good morning Miss." I said, she looked at me before asking,

"Have you slept since?" I was tilling my head slightly before saying,

"I slept for 10 hours last night, other than that I've not really." We started to walk around the structure as she asked,

"Do you have any plans today?" I shook my head and looked towards the sea,

"No, I was just going to reflect about everything. I don't really know what is happening with me at the moment."

"I'm feeling for you right now, when I heard I just…"

"Can you not, please. I'm just trying to feel something close to normal, it's hard and at the moment

I'm just taking each moment as they come." We took a few steps before she then said,

"I only ask what you were doing today because I care." I looked at her with my left eye,

"I know, I just." I gave up on my sentence.

"Do you have any plans tonight?" she quizzed me.

"What did you have in mind?" she was just about to pitch her reply when a student came up to her, I turned and faced the other way. The sun looked so much more intuitive than what I do. When the student left, I turned back to face her.

"I was going to say you could come around for dinner."

"OK, but are you expecting me to cook? Everyone always wants me to cook."

"We can cook together." I looked at her so inquisitively.

"This isn't like Oedipus complex is it? No, it wouldn't be that would it? It would be like some reverse Oedipus complex, besides aren't I far too young for you?"

She laughed at me.

"I'm not like that. Besides, I've just become divorced so it would be nice to have someone to spend the night with who doesn't want sex for 3 hours after eating."

I looked a bit shocked by what she said, I had to ask.

"Is that enough grounds for divorce?" she shook her head while pulling a pear out of her handbag.

"No, but sleeping with another woman is."

"Now I feel like I'm the one who needs to say I'm sorry."

"It's ok, my place is quite unorganised. But you'll find the photographs that I have scattered around the place to be quite interesting." I decided that I would go, so upon nodding my head she asked.

"Do you drink…" she got interrupted by a student asking her to check their work; I was only half paying attention so all I caught was, "Draw it from that angle, don't make your work easy for yourself. Really challenge yourself to do something that you feel like you can't do, it doesn't matter if you fail; we all fail at things."

I was nodding my head to myself as her student walked off to the angle that she said, she faced me, "What?"

"We do all fail at things, right now I'm just failing with myself. What were you going to ask me?"

"Sorry, I was going to ask do you drink beer?"

"No, I'm not able to stomach the taste, I'll bring some vodka for you to try." She looked wary of what I said,

"Are you sure that's wise?"

"I don't drink my problems away, besides I don't drink a lot because of my size."

"Makes sense, I don't think that I've ever seen you smaller than what you are now."

I felt quite pensive, but I tried to not let it show.

"I'll let you return to your class, I'll meet you at the gates to the school when you finish with the bits to cook with."

"That's fine, I'll see you then." I let her return to the students that she had in her current class, I felt slightly nostalgic but I didn't want to show it. I said goodbye and headed back along the seafront to the city.

I felt a little bit more secure in myself from when I woke up, I felt a bit more connected towards myself from the fragile entity screaming in an underpass.

I was walking along and I caught a glimpse of the scar on my left forearm, I got that in a fight over her. There was nothing to be done today, I had already finished college, I was on leave from work. There was nothing to be done today, so it was home for me to walk.

I made it into Kemp Town, noticed that Sainsbury's was there and decided that would be the place where I'd get my shopping before I head back across to Rottingdean to meet my old art teacher. I kept my arms crossed as I walked home, the remnants of my heart were staying with me. By the time I had made my way back home it was close to midday, I wasn't expecting anyone to be inside so I let myself in. I stepped inside and the first thing that I got was my mum shouting out to me,

"That you?"

"Who else would it be?" was my reply, before I then added, "Why are you home?"

"Trying to catch your sister ditching school. You were gone pretty early this morning, what time did you leave?"

"4:35 please don't ask me where I went or what I did, I'm just in and then out; I have to go get some food because I'm cooking for someone tonight."

"OK. But who are you cooking for tonight?" before I had chance to even compose an answer she then asked, "Don't you think that you should be spending some time at home?"

"I'm going to be having dinner with my old art teacher." My mother finally stepped into my room, she gave me the oddest look. "What?" I replied with.

"You're going to have dinner with your old art teacher? Don't you think that is a little inappropriate?"

"I left school 2 years ago, she's like 10 years older than you, and besides isn't it better to be with someone who won't judge me than those who will all whisper when I'm out of the room." The silence she created I found quite annoying, there was nothing left to do but leave.

I picked up my wallet, I had about £25 more or less inside.

"I need to go to Sainsbury's, so can you please…" she didn't move. "Mum, I need to go." She just stood there, so I slipped past.

"You're tearing us all apart."

"No I'm not; I am just taking everything as it comes right now. When I feel ready to make some more long term plans I will, but until that day you lot will have to be patient with me."

She turned her head away in disgust, her attempts to make me feel guilty weren't going to work. I walked to the front door, she still hadn't given a reply.

"I'll be back tonight." I heard her throw something right before the screaming that was, "Why don't you fall down dead with her!" I had had enough, I stormed back into the house. When I came into sight she launched a Glass at me, which shattered as I caught it.

"You'd like that WOULDN'T YOU? A house with just women! You wouldn't know what to do with yourself if I FUCKING LEFT! Be careful what your wishes are, some get ignored and OTHERS GET CASHED!!!" I walked with the glass in my hand out of the house. When I got outside I threw the glass across the street. I didn't even bother to look to see if there were a car there, I just stormed around the corner and back towards the train station.

I kept moving, I don't think that I stopped until I made it to Western Road, I decided to change where I was going to pick the food up from; no idea as to why but I did. I walked into Waitrose, picked up a basket and started to walk around. The first aisle that I went to was the alcohol. I needed a bottle of brandy to cook with, but given how irate I was I feeling it would have been just as easy to have downed the bottle. I walked around the rest of the supermarket picking up bits as and when I needed them. When I came to the meat counter I noticed that there was nobody else waiting so I stepped up,

"How can I help?" the woman asked me,

"Can I have…" I paused because she gave me the most peculiar look; I looked around before asking, "What's wrong?"

"Your hand is bleeding quite badly sir." I looked down, the glass had clearly cut through on quite a deep scale.

"So it is," I said, "I'll deal with that in due course. Right, where was

I? Can I please have 8 ounces of Sirloin."

"Sir,"

"Yes."

"Your hand is bleeding quite badly, you need to get that looked at."

"Very well, but can I still have the 8 ounces of Sirloin that I asked you for?"

"Not right now."

"Why not?" I asked,

"Because your hand is bleeding."

"Well that isn't going to prevent you from cutting a steak is it?"

"Sorry?" this guy was clearly the definition of a dingbat, should I ever use it as an insult.

"Cut the steak, and then we shall get my hand sorted." He quickly cut the steak; then only put half on the scales subsequently only charging me a fraction of the price; because he was in such a rush to get things done.

"Can you just wait there?" He asked, I replied with.

"OK." He walked off. I waited for about 30 seconds before realising I had all my shopping in the basket. I walked to the checkout going straight up to the first one that I saw, the girl working on the checkout was in my Math class at high school.

"I thought it was you." She said. She handed each of the items to me as she scanned them; she tried to make conversation by saying,

"I saw what happened in the paper, how are you doing?" I didn't answer, I read the total on the screen and handed her £15 in notes.

"You know I'm here for you if you want to talk."

"Why lie?" I asked, she had nothing to answer back with. "You want to know how bad my life is so you can tell your friends and thus feel better about your lives. Even though you have no vindication of who you are so you attach yourselves to others art to express how much of an individual you are. I don't buy phoney people, go look for my name in the obituaries next week." I didn't even wait for the 47 pence change, I zipped up my bag and was out of the store with a blood stained receipt. I walked around to the Boots store on the corner of Queens Road, I walked straight in and just went up to the first woman I saw working there and said,

"Excuse me," she looked over to me and smiled. "I need something to contain this." I lifted up my hand to turn her face from passive to mortified, "Can you help me please?"

"My God, what happened?" she quizzed.

"My mother threw a glass at me, not too sure if she meant to but she did. So, can you please help me?"

"Yes, of course." She said, "Please follow me and I'll get you everything." We walked across the store to the antiseptic wipes, she asked, "If you don't want to answer that is fine, but why did your mother throw a glass at you?"

"It's ok, we were fighting about me, she thinks I'm tearing the family apart and killing myself in the process."

"Are you?" she asked, I shrugged my shoulders.

"I'm not sure, I just miss my girlfriend."

"Well why don't you go get her back then?" She must have seen the tear swelling up in my eye right before I said,

"I buried her yesterday." The poor girl looked shocked; this was a day of work she would never forget. A quiet day at work and then BOOM - she is helping me with a nasty cut and learning about a complete strangers' life. She composed herself extremely well before she told me,

"Of all the people you meet in life, you realise who is important. So when your song is sung, you are reunited to share your songs with each other."

"Is that what death is like?" I asked, she picked up 2 antiseptic pads and started to walk towards the bandages.

"I have no idea; to me I guess it is. But anyone who tells you that your idea is wrong, is nothing more than a fool." We got to the bandages, she mused over which ones before deciding. We then moved on to the pads that collect the excess blood, I didn't know what they were called; and I didn't feel too compelled to ask. Once we had found them she said, "We're done."

"Are there any tills where you can ring the bits through for me?" I asked. She looked around, before starting to walk to the perfumes. I followed, as we were walking over she asked, "Are you one of those men who has a boots card?"

"I get a lot of pictures developed, so it helps because every now and again I can get a load for free."

"D'you want to know something."

"Go for it." We arrived at the till.

"A lot of middle aged men have them, they say it's their wives but, it has their names on them."

"Strange." I said. She sent the items through; I paid her before saying, "Well thank you very much for your help."

"Are you not going to put it on?"

"I'll do it later, besides I'm right handed so it would be quite difficult."

"Let me help you." Before taking the antiseptic pad out, "This will sting." She said literally a moment before putting the pad on.

"FUCK ME SIDEWAYS!!" A couple of

old women looked at me and before they even had chance to say a word I snapped, "SHUT, UP. I'm in no fit state to argue, but if you say a single word I will bring the motherfucking ruckus!" they went back to their Lilly of the Valley and Egyptian Musk.

"Rant over?" she asked, I nodded my head. "Right let's get you fixed up for wherever it is you'll be going after here."

"I'm going to cook dinner for my old art teacher; she wanted to check up on me."

"Thoughtful of her,"

"I'm trying to work out right now who is genuine and who is just acting like a barnacle. Frankly, you're the most genuine person I've met these past few days."

"I was going to ask you if you wanted to meet up for a coffee during the week and I can check on how that is coming along."

"That would be nice; I'll come in and see you."

She smiled, "My name is…"

"I already have it memorised."

"Well take care, and I hope to see you soon enough."

I smiled before I walked out of the shop. I walked down to the bottom of the hill where I waited for the number 2 bus; it wasn't long I waited, no more than 2 or 3 minutes. I got on, showed my pass and walked to the back of the bus where there were a few seats left. A mother and her daughter who must have been about 6 years old were sat opposite me, the pensive look in my eyes turned to one of optimism. She was so innocent, she didn't know of the problems that I had; I doubt she was even aware of the problems that riddled her mother. It suddenly occurred to me that I had a bar of white chocolate in the side pocket of my bag, I broke off a few pieces had one for myself and gave one to the little girl. She said really quietly,"Thank you."

"You're quite welcome." I said back to her.

I put my headphones back in my ears and put something on, I think it was My Lovely Man by Red Hot Chili Peppers.

We came to Ovingdean, and I felt a tap on my leg. I looked down to see the little girl waving to me, I waved back to her before saying, "Take care." She got off the bus and gave me one last wave with her mother also waving. I couldn't help but wave back.

When the bus got to Rottingdean, I got off by the High School, crossed the road and walked down to the building. My old art teacher was already waiting by her car, she noticed my hand and as I got closer she asked,

"What happened?"

"Accident at home." She looked satisfied with the answer that I gave, "How are you?" I asked.

"Looking forward to your cooking, and how are you?"

"My heart is a mausoleum." We got into her Audi and she drove us to her place.

Day 24

I had only gone out to buy a bottle of wine to replace the one that we drank a few nights before. I found myself at Parc De Monceau, I sat there watching the hours tick away from me. The people constantly jogging around the park, the kids playing football deciding who would be Zidane, Gallas and Thuram. While the others bicker, nobody wanted to be the English players. Though frankly the French lost to an underrated Greek side that won me £330 so I wasn't too bothered by the English playing crappy unattractive football, my heart was with the outsiders. The kids who played football in this park today, would be wearing PSG shirts in 8/10 years' time. I was watching a mother with her twins, they must have been about 5 years old. She was showing them how to feed the pigeons, the boy was more interested in eating the stale baguette. As the girl was trying to throw the bread so she could watch the birds from afar, she hadn't realised that an underarm throw would go further and she could watch everything from a safe distance. I contemplated going over and showing her, I decided against it. It was more amusing to watch her. My phone went off, I looked to see who it was and answered.

"Yeah,"

"I got a surprise for you." She said, I thought to myself, *Right,* before saying.

"Is it Cate Blanchett?"

"What? No, I wouldn't know how to get a hold of her. It's nothing like that." I watched the joggers run past me for a third or fourth time.

"Then what is it?"

"You just have to come home, I can't tell you; it's something that you have to see." I sighed, it was probably nothing, a spider she wanted to kill; a wasp in the flat. I stood up, and walked towards the entrance to the gate.

"Right, I'm on my way. I'll be like 15 minutes or so."

"15 minutes? I know that walk only takes you about 5/6 minutes, 8 minutes at a top." I walked out of the gates and enjoyed the décor of the building across the road, Villiers is such a peaceful area if I had bad days I would go for a walk there to clear my head. I couldn't be bothered with walking through the main streets, enduring the claustrophobic nature that those Paris street corners had for comfort. It would also help in justifying my lateness. I walked down Malesherbes, I wasn't really paying attention to the world around me. A guy in his early 20's ran past me, another 2 guys ran past me chasing him, they were as Hench as fuck.

"Somebody should have just paid the money when they asked." I said to myself while I was putting my headphones on and turning on my iPod, a little Portishead to take me around to Rue De Madrid. I looked more at the architecture of the area than I did paying attention to what was happening around me. A car with black out windows was the next thing to go past me at some speed, I looked around to see if anything else was following,

"Shit is going down for that unfortunate fucker." The dulcet tones of what rung clear in my ears, as I came to Place De L'Europe I knew that the architecture that I love in the 8th, the architecture that I associate with Paris would soon come to an end. The ghetto that is the 9th had such horrible buildings, there was no care to my home district. I stood and enjoyed the buildings, the stone colour, and the way that the penthouse apartments are a black, while the rest of the building is a taupe to greyish colour. I had to stand on the street corner for a minute, to look at each of the buildings, wishing I had the money to live in this part of the city, sadly it wasn't to be. I carried on towards Rue D'Amsterdam, unsure of which way was the quickest or for that matter easiest route back to ours. I walked up to Place De Clichy, the strangers walked past me, and I paid some attention to their faces, nobody would ever lock eyes, but I did try to subtly study each of their faces. A group of children were playing some game in the streets, that I never played when I was their age. I couldn't work out the objective of the game, guess it is something I would never know. I turned off on to Rue De Douai, there was a couple a little older than me on bikes waiting to pull out and head towards Boulevard De Clichy, tourists so clearly in love. He would look at her inside Gare Du Nord, and declare his love for her; she would say that their love was pure and original. He would think that she was being honest with him, yet me a stranger passing by on my way home to see what surprise I had waiting for me; I could tell that she didn't love him as much as he loved her. I watched them leave, and I thought he is just like that guy I went to school with, he'll go from one heartache to another.

I caught a glimpse of my reflection in the window of a car, I could barely recognise myself. It made me feel like I hadn't slept, and I subsequently lost concentration for a moment, which caused me to bump into a stranger.

"Sorry," I said, I tried to keep walking forwards. A hand that felt coarse, but too small to be a man's hand grabbed me, I turned to see a prostitute aging more than her years. She smelt of caustic soda and corrosion, looking 76, but claiming to be 34. Jessica Tandy looked young in Driving Miss Daisy, compared to her.

"Looking for a good time?" I just wanted to go back to the flat, so I could see just what the surprise is that she had for me.

"In English." I said in a tone that made it very obvious that I wasn't interested.

"Looking for a good time?"

"I think not, I'm going home to an 18 year old Estonian girl. Who, lets' face it, is younger, better looking, and doesn't have her clitoris hanging down by her ankles."

"I can do things that she never could."

"I think the only thing you can do what she can't is have your vagina in a different postcode to your fingertips. Now I'm in a rush." I returned to continue walking home.

"You'll regret saying that!" she shouted out at me. I wasn't even aware of how long I had been walking for at that point in time, I knew she was going to be mad that I was late. I kept going forwards.

I came to an intersection where the road split into 7 directions; it reminded me of being where I live in Brighton. The top of the road had 7 directions of traffic. I had never walked down the road before, so I was a little confused as to the direction that I was to take. I looked up to see what street I was on,

"Rue De Douai." I said to myself, I decided to walk around and pick what seemed like the best road to take. Mansart was the first street I came to, heading south but back the way I came. I looked at Rue Fontaine, and contemplated the idea that the street was named after the French footballer of the 1958 world cup scoring a record 13 goals, the man holds such a fantastic status, yet in my mind all he has been given to remember him by is this street, this tiny almost unknown street. I decided that it must be the only reason why the street would be named as such. It also looked to be leading me quite out of my way. I looked up at the next street sign, Douai. I carried on with the street I was already on. I thought about the prostitute, her skin looked like the after effects of an atom bomb, there was little chance that she would be paying her pimp tonight unless she were to get a call out from a lonely old man in a state of bereft, looking for comfort from the realisation that he would also die alone.

I waited on the corner of Pigalle, as a car with a couple who had just got married drove past me. The bride looked out at me, smiled and waved. I smiled at her, leaning down so she could see that I gave my regards. I wondered how long they had been together, was it a shotgun wedding or had she planned this day for weeks to pass away adolescent being 18 pounds overweight. Today, today she looked a million dollars, that virgin white dress wouldn't ever be worn again; but that wasn't for time to dictate to her. The cars all went past, it wasn't for me to obstruct them from reaching the wedding reception. 300€ spent on a cake, a drunk aunt staggering between ushers telling them to fuck her while her husband is passed out from taking a bottle of brandy in less than an hour. A day I would share with them by giving the bride an unexpected smile. I crossed the road looked up at the street sign and said to myself,

"Victor Masse, now I know where I am." I walked the short distance to the next junction, Rue Frochot a road that I had never seen a car drive up, and today was no exception. There was 2-tone playing from a 3rd storey apartment, it sounded very early 80's. I put the iPod back into my bag, as I continued my way round to Rue Des Martyrs. The 80 feet or so I was from the front door, was paved in insignificance. I looked at a car parked just before the building, filled with some unfortunate soul's possessions. I didn't notice at first the person asleep in the driver's seat, the drool going from his mouth to form an ever growing wet patch just below his collar. I did notice the 3 parking tickets his car had acquired, each with its own place on the dashboard.

I unlocked the door, looked up and down the streets and slipped in unnoticed by anyone. I walked up the stairs, nobody had sorted out the step which we had destroyed, I would have never been surprised if one day I was to walk down and somebody had left flowers by it, maybe some lilies or a begonia. I've never had to know what people leave by graves.

The door was slightly ajar, I went in, she had some Estonian folk music playing that I had never heard before. I walked into the kitchen, she was cooking?

"What are you doing?" I asked,

"AAAAAAAAAAAAAARRRRRRRRRRGH!!!!" she screamed as she turned to face me, "Jesus, you scared the living shit out of me! Are you a cat burglar on the side?"

"No, that's a fucking ridiculous thing to say. What is all this?" I looked around the room, she had cooked dinner, via some means got a bottle of Viru Valge, laid the table set for 2, shot glasses and everything. "Why have you done this?"

"You always cook, I figured it was my turn to return the favour. So we're eating spinach and red pepper risotto. Don't worry, we'll finish the wine later in the week."

"So how did you get the Viru Valge?"

"Friend passing through, on her way to Barcelona. She owed me a favour." Her eyes segregated to the colours of her flag, our flag as she looked at me. "You never really ask me for anything, I just wanted to surprise you and say thank you."

She smiled, I held her close, ran my fingers through her hair.

Day 35

"So yeah, that's what I've done today." I said through the door, I heard no sound. I knocked on the door, "Are you going to be long?" I opened the door to her in the bath shaving her legs.

"Yes," she said,

"I really need a shit." I said to her, she looked at the toilet,

"If it smells, you'll be buying the first 3 drinks." I looked at the can, petrified; knowing that I was in a kangaroo court. If she says it smells bad and I don't - she wins; if I think it smells bad - it smells bad and she wins.

"I've seen it all before, not unless something has drastically changed." I sat down, I was watching her shave. I began to wonder why it takes so long for her to get ready in the morning, then I realised - she isn't me. I brush my teeth and don a hat of some description to hide my bedhead, other days I just embrace the bedhead that I woke up with. We were sat in our respective seats waiting for the other to make a move, eventually she asked,

"So where are we going tonight?" I shrugged my shoulders,

"I have no idea, we can just move from one bar to another. Like…" she

cut my trail of thought dead,
"Like a dandelion's seeds." I smiled as I handed her the towel as she got out,
"Yeah, like that." I said. She was such an enticing figure in just her underwear, she had put some lipstick on very faintly whilst she was in the bath; her and the colour blue went together like nothing I had ever pictured in my mind.
"The person you marry will never wank." She gave me a sullen look,
"Gross, but I will take your compliment." She replied with a smile, I stood up and flushed. As I washed my hands she out of the corner of my eye was putting on a dress. I had never seen the dress before, her national colours, but it was so subtle. She faced me, I studied her every inch as she asked; "How do I look?"
"Beautiful enough to make both Venus and Aphrodite jealous, and there will be nothing that the other Gods can do about it." She shook out her hair,
"My blonde Parisian nights." She walked out of the bathroom; I in a second locked the door, sat down and did what had to be done.
I return to the rest of the flat, she was in the kitchen. I stood in the door way, she was leaning against the sink.
"Why don't you send a text to that

journalist, she if she wants to join us?" I shook my head as she handed me a glass of wine,

"She is too old to be going out drinking with us, I wouldn't be surprised if she were married. She is a very attractive woman."

"So how old is she? Or, how old does she look? Rather." I couldn't even mull it in my head.

"I really haven't got a clue, she looks about 23. It's when you hear her talk about things, she speaks like she is in her mid-30's. I don't know how old Julie Delpy is, and I think she looks stunning."

"French women are hard to age, us eastern European girls we look young…" it was finally my turn to cut her off,

"Until you reach about 40, then you all fall off the map." We each finished our glasses and as I handed her my glass she commented saying,

"The next 22 years for you will be alright then, won't they?"

"You and I will stay together until we're ghosts, and when the earth beneath our feet is no longer here; we'll still be together." She put the glasses in the sink and came back over, as she leaned into me she asked,

"Is there anyone else other than me that you really care for?" I kissed the back of her head, I wasn't sure if the question was rhetorical or she was looking for reassurance; but I felt in my heart that what I had said before should have been enough. I went into the bedroom, as I finished to get changed she called out to me,

"Where are we going tonight?" I really had no idea,

"Not sure, we can go to a few bars. See what becomes of that." She didn't reply, so I was assuming that it sounded like a plan.

"One more warm up drink?" she said from the door, I gave a nod and she brought me another glass of wine. I still couldn't believe that she looked so enchanting, and we were not going home with anyone else. We left the flat and went bar-hopping, each bar we tried different vodkas. There were a dozen small possibly illegal Russian bars selling vodkas that we couldn't dream of tasting so cheap.

We went into this one bar, it just looked like someone's house; there were a few Albanian sat at the bar with their tiny shot glasses. Nursing their drinks, knowing the second they finished their drinks they would have to leave. She asked the barman for us,

"Parlez-vous anglais?" The barman gave a nod, which meant that we were able to get a drink on our grounds,

"What *vodkas* do you have?" he pointed at a series of bottles, some of which we had already had that night.

"No, no. Do you have any homemade?" he walked down to the end of the bar and we followed,

"There is only one man I tell you to go see for homemade vodka," His Russian accent was thick and some of his words got lost in his beard, "He has tiny bar on Rue D'Uzès. It is highly illegal, so in and out." We looked at each other,

"Who do we ask for?" she asked, he pulled out 2 shot glasses and poured vodka into both.

"This is Snow Queen, from Kazakhstan. You ask for the man from Tomsk, he make the purest vodka you will ever try." We took the shots down in 1, put a 5€ note on the bar; he picked it up and gave a nod. As we walked out I asked her,

"How far is it to the bar he told us?" she got her sense of direction and told me,

"It's about an 8 minute walk to this bar, I wonder how we'll know when we're there?" her musings were always something to really watch.

"Where are we right now?" she looked up and pointed, Boulevard Des Italiens, we're just inside the 9th. As we walked up towards Montmartre, we saw a couple leaving their apartment for a night out, they noticed us – to which we smiled. There was no doubt in our eyes that she had been cheating on him, she was dressed up to the nines, we were never to know if she was eyeing up me or the Estonian. As we got closer I reached into my pocket pulled out a condom and handed it to him as we passed.

"Rag the life out of her on us." He winked and we carried on in our different directions. We made it to Montmartre, as we were walking along she asked,

"What did you hand him?"

"Condom, should have bumped with him; Would have been better." She smiled and we carried on. We eventually made our way to Rue D'Uzès, pacing up and down the street multiple times; looking for an illegal bar that may or may not exist.

"Did the man in the last bar give us a number or some sort of sign for us to look for?" I asked, she gave no sign of knowing. We stood facing each other, I was looking in the east march, while her eyes gazed west. I watched a man walk out of a building and spark up a cigarette, the packet of cigarettes was nothing I had ever seen in Europe.

"Is that the place?" walking towards it, it became quite apparent that it was the place. The large Russian flag was our biggest indication; the man flicked his cigarette butt into the road and walked back inside. We crept in with him, if this was an illegal bar, then it would have been matching the bars of the prohibition times in the United States. We walked up to the bar, a man wearing a string vest covered in prison tattoos came up to serve us,

"Parlez-vous anglais?" he gave a nod, "We're looking for the man from Tomsk."

"I will get him." And with that he walked off, we stood waiting she leaned her head on my shoulder when a huge man, sporting a cathedral tattoo on his left arm came walking towards us.

"Yes," he said, we looked at one another and I knew that I was going to be on vocal duties,

"Are you *The Man from Tomsk*?" he smiled, you couldn't see it behind that beard that would have made wolverine jealous, but you knew it was there.

"I am man from Tomsk."

"We were told to come to you to try homemade vodka." He gave a nod and pulled out a bottle of Evian mineral water,

"Before I pour 10€ for shot, each. Ok." I put a 20 note on the bar, the seedy smell of cigarettes and bad gambling decisions came wafting towards us from all directions. He poured the drinks into 2 shot glasses, before giving us a motion with his hand to try before saying, "Na zdrowie."

"Na zdrowie." We said back before sending the moonshine to the backs of our throats. It hit, it burnt at first, but then there was this unwordable sensation. A hint of vanilla, most certainly made of grain and a purer cleansing on my tongue than anything I had ever tried in my life.

"You like it?" he said,

"If that vodka was a woman, it would be Cate Blanchett. I would gaze into her eyes every morning."

"I am happy you like it."

"How did you create such a unique flavour?"

"It was 1967 I would have been little older than you. Brezhnev was in power, and price of vodka was expensive. People in Tomsk, very poor. I created many recipes…" a man about 4 feet away from us with his girlfriend who looked strangely familiar to us.

"Drink!" he shouted,

"Shut it! You're killing his story!" I shouted at him, he remained quiet. "Sorry about that," I whispered, "Please continue."

"I created the recipe and had it with friends, it grew and I was distilling more vodka. People came from many parts of Siberia to try. Police shut me down many times, then I have to go to prison for what do they say these day?"

"Racketeering?" she asked, he gave

a nod.

"16 years I was in prison, nobody get my recipe." The man who was 4 feet away from us, now was next to us; he slammed a 50 note on the bar.

"I want a drink." She turned and slapped him.

"Shut up, just shut up." He lifted his fist, I stood up and pushed him back.

"Lay a finger on her and I'll severe your head from your body." Then it occurred to me where we knew the girl from.

"You've been round our flat?" I said pointing at her, "Is this the guy you were fighting with in the street?"

"Yes." She tried to hide behind a smile.

"I'll tell you what, you and me have an arm wrestle and whoever wins spends the rest of the night with your girl." I won't lie, he was 3 times the size of me; able to crush my hand like it were twiglets.

"Seems too easy to me." He said arrogantly,

"Fine, we'll have a Polish arm wrestling match." He was flexing his muscles, trying to show off to anyone who was watching.

"So how do we do this?" I put his arm into position,

"You have to pull my arms up and I have to bring yours down." I turned to the man from Tomsk, put a 20€ note on the bar, he poured 2 more shots; we downed them in 1. I then said to her, "When I give the word, grab her and run." The man from Tomsk, held our knuckles.

"Fight!" he shouted, I immediately started to pull down his arm, he started to get the upper hand but my footing was stronger. I almost had him, he was red in the face; which you could combined with the etching of rage on his face, to see one extremely fucked off moron. I looked at her, shouted,

"Now!" She grabbed the other girl and started to run, I let go watched him bang his own lights out.

As I made it outside, they were waiting;

"Where shall we head to now?" I asked, she smiled and we interlocked our fingers. We then looked at the new girl, who said,

"I know a bar, a little bohemian, but the drinks are fairly cheap."

Day 51

I woke up something like 35 minutes before Erin, the Estonian had already left for class. I started to make Erin breakfast, I hope that she was enjoying sleeping in my bed with her, the couch was comfortable enough but the constant noise was enough to make a saint fucking swear. When she came into the kitchen, eyes pretty much kept shut from the sleep; her hair was a mess, but nobody could rock bedhead quite like Erin.

"G'morning," Her Werder Bremen shirt was barely staying on her, I looked at her as she scratched the back of her head. The top rose up and all I could see was her legs, "Why do you have that shirt?" I asked.

"They are a great team, better than who you support. Bremen won the Bundesliga."

"And I'm sure next season you will have a different shirt, I should get you a spurs shirt show off my team to your friends." She leaned past me and picked up a rasher of bacon burning her finger tips in the process but eating it nonetheless. As she was licking her fingers, trying to get some feeling back into her fingertip she said,

"I don't like mushrooms, so no mushrooms." I looked shocked as she sat down, I then noticed that the only other thing that she was wearing was her underwear.

"Well I don't like mushrooms, so even if you did want mushroom; you wouldn't be getting any."

"Can I get some French toast?" I looked at her,

"I'm not making you French toast for you to then say that you're in a food coma and we can't go out and see the city."

"Answer for everything." She muttered under her breath as I handed her the plate.

"If you have it today you won't want it tomorrow, pace yourself; otherwise, you'll be slowly clawing your way to hating this place." She took her time when eating, the city wasn't going to vanish; she knew that and nobody would lose sleep over it.

By the time that she was finishing up she was more awake, still rocking the bedhead but I think that she looks better with it.

"Do you want a shower?" I asked, her mouth was full and I hadn't noticed. She shook her head,

"I never shower in the morning, I'm normally running late for school that I don't have time. So force of habit, I'll have one tonight." She finished her plate and took both of ours to the sink,

"Are you going to be OK with getting changed in the same room?" I asked,

"Are you?" she said sarcastically back,

"The law says I shouldn't but we've known each other for time, and we're like family so I'm cool with it if you are." She tucked her chair in and started to walk to the bedroom, I sat there for a minute finished my glass of water and followed her.

By the time I had made it to the bedroom she was putting on a pair of jeans, I got changed in a matter of 90 seconds or so; when I turned back to face her she was still trying to pull the jeans up.

"***Still?!?!***" Nobody should spend this long putting on a sodding pair of jeans, as she was on the bed trying to hope that gravity would pull them down.

"Come here." I walked around to the other side of the bed, picked her up and grabbed her jeans, "This might hurt." I put my thumbs in the back of the jeans, pulled her close and yanked them up first time.

"Fuck a prophet, if you ever do this again I'll cut your shitting dick off."

"Then buy some jeans that fit." She picked up her bag and like a renegade to their comrades; we were subsequently ready to leave.

"What do you stand for?" she asked me once we had made our way down and onto the street, we started to walk down Rue Des Martyrs, towards Place De L'Opera.

"Ummm, I look at things and I know what is worth my time, something's you need to just walk on by." She held my hand,

"So what is worth standing for? Mum said if you don't stand for something then people fall for anything."

"Your mum is very right. But it's better to keep your cards close to your chest than to shout what you have." She looked at a small church at the bottom of the street, she made a cross.

"The Gods need respect as you don't want to be caught out when you die." I pulled 2 coins of my pocket, holding them up in front of her I said,

"I will always be able to pay the boatman, how can anything be more important than that?" she took the coins from me, examined them and gave them back.

"They are just coins. Why would the boatman want these coins?" as I put the coins back into my wallet and returned my attention back to Erin I said,

"Because even when you're dead, people still expect to be paid. Sad fact, but that's how we all survive."

"So you're not too worried if the Gods are to cast you out?" we had by this time walked our way down to Opera.

"If I get cast out, then I know that the time here was interesting enough for the entities to acknowledge that I'm here. And better still that I was able to offend someone." She started to giggle, I pulled her in and hugged her. If I had a rewind button I would have done it every time, like a guitarist obsessed with a loop pedal. The past of everything was starting to ring through, I could see it all; the whole area allowing time to go back. Before me and Erin, what was now suddenly became 1901, the cinemas had all reverted back to matinée theatres. The actors would be at the side door smoking, in costume just lacking the make-up. Handing each other their cigarettes so they could sign playbills, in their heads thinking of lines to adlib for lines they dislike or can't remember. We looked at each other in our period clothes, we didn't fit in. I was waiting for her to click her fingers or clap her hands, and we'd be back in our present.

Eventually we did return to the 21st century, we started walking between the streets and in the 2nd district, I wasn't going to tell Erin about the Russians that are there; I wasn't dragging a drunken wench back to the flat. I looked at the clock on my phone, it was later in the day than what I had thought it was.

"Come on," I took her hand and we started to walk towards Bonne Nouvelle,

"So where are we going?" she asked, I merely pointed ahead. As we walked at no real pace, but somehow faster than the people that surrounded us. "So will you at least tell me what your politics are?" I smiled,

"I didn't say this because I don't want your mother to have a moan at me, but I'm a socialist. I was really influenced by Ché Guevara, he was just a man… but, he was able to stand up to a nation and create the change that was needed." She was so enthralled by what I said, I could see her franticly searching the library when she got back to Germany looking for any books, films, newspaper articles that she could find on Ché. The whole time thinking to herself - is he the political icon for me? Time would give the answers to both her and me. If she felt after a while that they were the wrong answers, time could heal her thoughts, by which time she would have moved out of the punk image and found her voice to the world, along with a decent pair of heels to walk in. Erin was going to be an iconoclastic person, it was an obvious thing to whoever met her, all she just needed to find out what it was she really stood for.

This is a world where you need to

know what you are, and what you're not.

We kept walking along, I could see the statue that showed we were at République a few minutes before her.

"This looks familiar," When Erin mused over things there was such emotion in her eyes and lips, I could only compare it to a mother who had lost her husband, or children reading Sylvia Plath poems without a care as to her tears or where they choose to commute.

"We just need to walk around the corner." I told her, I reached into my bag and after a minute of reaching around I was able to find what I was looking for.

"Here," I handed her some flat stones, those electric eyes of hers lit up.

"Is this where…"

"Yep," she started taking more than she could hold, Erin scanned her surrounding,

"So where is it?" I took her hand and we walked around to the cannel, I went to walk up the steps looking round to see that she was balancing on the wooden beam that separates the water.

"*What are you doing?!*" she really didn't have a care in the world,

"I've wanted to do this ever since I saw the film," she started to skim the stone, she was in all fairness quite good at it; but still.

"DON'T even think about telling your mother, if she finds out about this she will string me up by my bollocks!" she skimmed one and we watched it hit the water 12 times, "Come back, we still have to go to…"

"Das ist ein langweiler."[13] I rolled my eyes and shook my head, for a moment I thought I could see the back of my head.

"That's just mean, and I can't even phone her up; as she doesn't speak German." She started walking back across, jokingly acting like she was going to fall, unaware that I can't swim. I held out my hand as she took it I said,

"Had you fallen in, I wouldn't have saved you?"

"Oh, thank you. It's wonderful to know you think that highly of me."

"I can't swim."

"You what?" I closed my eyes, took her hand and started walking towards "You live by the sea, how can't you swim?" I was about to start speaking when she said, "I live inland, you're by the sea. How can I swim but you can't?"

"I never learnt, my mum can't swim, nor can my sisters." She started to walk slightly quicker than me, I ducked into a coffee shop, I didn't bother to look at the name of the café; come whatever may of this place

---

[13] You are such a square

I thought to myself. We each had a legumes soup, I left a 10€ note and Erin left the tip. As we walked out I looked up Café Restaurant Sésame, Erin was looking at some exiting through a large set of doors to the right of the café,

"Why did you not get an apartment here?" I took her hand and we started to walk up the street,

"The apartments here are seriously expensive, and I wouldn't want to live here. People pretend to have money, to be happy. Everyone can see they are not."

"There are parts of Köln that are like that, I'd rather avoid those places." We carried on walking up Quai De Valmy, the people around us had no idea of the age difference between me and her; then again she looked older and I looked like I was fresh out of a hospital. Teenagers went racing past us on their bikes, tennis rackets on their backs.

"We'll have to get some people to join us and play a game of baseball while you're here." Her eyes lit up, I rarely saw real colour in them; even when they did shine.

"For a moment I thought you were going to suggest a game of football, and I was going to say I could never see her playing football. You'd have to get your weight up either way." She had her point, also if the Estonian and the journalist were to join us that would make 4; who else could I ask? Well, for now it wasn't important. We stood and looked at a wall of graffiti, Erin became lost inside the street art moving from one section to another while I took a few photographs. After she had scanned the whole wall studying every individual work of art she was ready to move on. As we walked a young family with 2 boys that couldn't have been any older than 5 or 6 had just left a shop each holding ice creams, the kids would run forward a few steps wait for the parents to catch up, and then run on ahead. To me the action was like being in Derby, hoping to see a lighthouse at night, if only just a little fog. We crossed the bridge and started to walk first along Richerant, and then Bichat, Erin looked around a little confused.

"Which district are we in?" I looked up at the street sign and pointed,

"The 10th, that's what the numbers mean." As I finished my sentence I started to hear music, just a trumpet as we looked around we saw on the 4th floor a black man leaning out of his window playing,

"Play something that will make me want to dance!" Erin shouted up at him, he started to play Right Off by Miles Davis. She started dancing, it left me with very little option but to dance with her. As the people in the restaurant opposite stopped stuffing their faces with paté on Melba toast, and started watching us. I have no idea how long we were dancing for, or even how I hadn't fallen over my feet as I'm a terrible dancer. When he stopped we looked up and before we had chance to say anything he said,

"Anytime." As we continued up Bichat, and the swine returned to their paté, salads and uneventful lives. The pavement had a series of steps or a slanted piece of asphalt.

"Which do we take?" my words fell on death ears as Erin dragged me up the steps, an elderly couple were sat on the steps on the other side of the street each smoking a cigarette. The elderly lady offered us 1, Erin shook her head and I ignored the offer so they didn't get confused. I looked back and saw a series of joggers.

As we walked up Quai De Jemmapes a few taxis went past, but nobody was walking around. We walked past a basketball court that had a 4-on-4 game going on, there was no means of an outsider knowing who was on what team; they knew that was the main thing. We crossed the bridge and started walking back on ourselves, there was 2 tower blocks facing each other with a statue of someone I wasn't aware of. As I started to walk between the tower blocks Erin asked,

"So where does this lead to?" I

told her straight,

"I don't know, but if it's not interesting we'll just head back." The unreal amount of rubbish that was lying around, and just making the place look worse than what it already looked. We came out the other side, I looked at the road, it looked slightly familiar though I couldn't determine where I recognised the street from.

"Are we at Gare Du Nord?" Erin asked, I shook my head; not noticing the train tracks I said,

"We have to go past Gare De L'Est first… wait, are we at Gare De L'Est?" We must have been, I couldn't see us being anywhere else. The closer we got the more obvious it was becoming, we had walked around almost full circle. We walked inside, cutting out the pointless walk around to the steps that she remembered so well from Amiéle. A train had recently arrived, I didn't bother to look to see where it had come in from. As we came out the other side there was a group of men smoking, as we got closer they started to pay more attention to Erin. When we got close enough for us to be able to hear them an overweight man with 2 days of stubble and a cigarette burn on his t-shirt that was a size too small for him.

"Jolie fille, laisse moi rentrer dans cette chatte, je vais te montrer ce que c'est qu'un vrai mec."[14] I heard word for word what he said, my fingers were starting to make a fist, and my mind had no say in the matter. I was trying to stay as passive as I could, but it wasn't going to work.

"What did he say?" Erin asked,

"You don't want to know." She nervously started to laugh, I took me eye off her for a second as I punched the dirty old fucker in his collar bone. He went down like a sack of shit, the other men stopped laughing and stepped back in unison before going to help him up.

"Apologise, or end up on the floor again." He lit up a new cigarette and took a drag, holding the smoke in his mouth before blowing it into my face. I punched him in the same spot, he went down but just about kept his balance.

"Go fuck yourself." I told him, he took another drag. Holding the smoke in his mouth he turned and faced Erin, blowing the smoke into her face this time. She had her index and middle finger from her left hand over her closed lips. She closed her eyes as the smoke made its way past her face, opening them once it had past. Standing very calmly she separated her fingers and spat in his face. The other men just stood there, unsure of

---

[14] Pretty girl let me enter that pussy, I will show you what a real man feels like.

what to do towards the escapades that myself and Erin had created. We walked off before he had wiped away the phlegm from his face.

We walked out of the station and Erin looked at the steps that she had watched Amélie Poulain run up time and time again. There was a melancholy feel emanating off her,

"What is it?" I asked, her eyes didn't look away from the steps.

"I can look past the homeless people, they need a place to sleep just like everyone else. But these steps have been ruined by the graffiti." I got the feeling that the chase of running after a stranger with a folder full of passport photos was losing its appeal exceedingly quickly to her.

"Come on, let's show you something that you might have not seen in a movie." An optimistic gambit I will admit, but there was always a chance of something along those lines happening.

"You're forgetting I was the one that told you about The Exterminating Angel."

"I am still questioning if you have seen every movie ever made." She took the first steps up the witless graffiti doused staircase, a homeless person who had clearly been asking people for cigarettes could clearly see that both Erin and myself didn't smoke and just ignored us as we walked past.

"I'm still wondering that same question, have you seen Twisted?" I had never even heard of the film, let alone seen it.

"No, when did it come out?"

"Not too long ago, you don't need to see Twisted." I guess that was that. By the time we had walked up the steps and could look to our left and see Gare Du Nord, we were walking forwards; she wanted to head left, I had to drag her to the right. When we came to the cross roads, I dragged her towards Fayette. As we walked across the bridge a scooter almost hit us, I gave him the finger and we continued to walk along Fayette. A group of English students walked past us, the group wasn't as large as what I thought it was. A homeless woman was sat in the doorway of a building with her child, Erin reached into her pocket and gave her some loose change. I wasn't too happy with her for doing so, but I couldn't tell her, it wasn't my place to say.

"It doesn't solve a problem by giving her your change," I couldn't help myself; I had been able to bite my tongue for a good couple of minutes; but no more.

"It makes her feel a little less alone." It was a fair point, but it still isn't an act that should be undertaken.

"In The Atlas Mountains the

children there pester tourists for sweets and pens, but you shouldn't give them anything because they don't learn anything. They see tourists and instantly beg, ruining their time to enjoy the world." We came to a cross roads, Erin looked around.

"Where now?" I pointed up Saint Martin, she looked past the finger and saw the scooter that nearly run us over.

"There is the twat that nearly hit us, can I say something?" I shook my head, she saw him waiting by a door to an apartment. Erin stood and watched him walk in when a guy answered the door, she went over to his bike and just kicked it over.

"You're a *fucking liability.*" It seemed that Erin was a series of incidents over the course of a day strung together by me telling the Estonian about them. She'd hit the roof while the ceiling was the target.

"Shouldn't have tried to run us over." She said on her return to me, before she followed it up with. "It's all shits and giggles isn't it?" I tried to get us to walk up Saint Martin as quickly as we could.

The metro train went past, we looked at the collection of cardboard. A pile stood there underneath the tracks, all flatten down.

"Why is it there?" The innocence in

the way Erin asked about them, it would have been enough to make the most cauliflower eared boxer cry.

"The local shops around here leave them for the homeless, I, I guess it helps them sleep during the summer months." I was trying to hold back the tears, the bigger man in me wanted to just let go.

"And in the winter?" the anxiety in her voice was almost too much to handle.

"I've not made it to a winter here." The emotions in her were running higher than a derby football match on the final game of the season, 3 points to play for and positions at stake. Tensions run high as goals are scored, cards are given and players really start to show that they will wear their hearts on their sleeves. As the players clash with one another and the locking of heads continue, some people get lost in the moment and everyone forgets the realisation that it's nothing more than a 90 minute match. But the beautiful game touches the heart, for Erin the game would be Werder Bremen against Hamburger SV. I knew, she knew and all of time knew that really it was meant to be, 1. F.C Köln against Bayern Leverkusen. I never wanted to talk about the derby between Tottenham and Arsenal, they were more often than not black days falling over White Hart Lane.

I took her hand and we walked to the other side of the road, before we walked up to look at the building I told her,

"Before we look at the building, I want you to remember that no building should make you remember that you have a human pulse. Except, Sacré-Cœur." She glanced towards me, seeing the tear in my eye; she asked,

"Has life made you cry or will you give some lame excuse?"

"No, it was…" I had to pause if only for a second, "It was the sound of your voice." After a moment she stood up, I felt drained but still I had to show her.

Day 3

I woke up, I don't recall having fallen asleep at my old teachers house. I walked to a door opened it up and found her half way through getting dressed,

"Sorry," I said before shutting the door. She replied with,

"It's ok. You can come back in." I reopened the door to see her readjusting her skirt,

"I was looking for the bathroom, I got a headache. What happened last night?" she was looking in her wardrobe for a blouse to wear, she picked out a blue blouse - I shook my head.

"No, No. You shouldn't wear blue today." She stood there holding the blouse in her hand; I walked over to her wardrobe.

"Today you would look better wearing Taupe rather than blue, it's more informative and it suits your complexion better with the way the sun is today." She smiled, I then asked, "Where is the bathroom? And do you have any paracetamol?" she put on the blouse that I picked out for her and lead me to the bathroom.

"Did you sleep well?" she asked,

"I don't recall falling asleep, so it couldn't have been too bad. Did you?"

"After you left the bed it was ok." I looked quite shocked,

"Did we?"

"I've not been fucked like that since I was your age." I started to hyperventilate. I couldn't believe that I had fucked my old teacher, what was wrong with me?

She opened the bathroom door, pointing as she said things,

"Toothpaste, mouthwash, the paracetamols are in the cupboard." I smiled as she shut the door. I washed my face, and opened the draw to discover about 18 boxes of paracetamols. I looked at them and put 4 boxes in my pockets, 2 down my boxers and decided that I would collect the rest before I left. I brushed my teeth with my right index finger. A temporary solution. I opened the door slightly and said,

"How long until you need to go?"

"About 5 minutes." Was her reply. I slipped out and collected my bag, made my way back to the bathroom and filled my bag with the remaining boxes. Before making my way to the kitchen where she was undetected. She looked at me,

"Ready?" I nodded, she picked up her bag and we headed out the door.

"Where do you want me to drop you?"

"Anywhere in town would be great, but…" she stopped walking and looked at me, "Did we really have sex?" she smiled,

"No, but you did start off sleeping in my bed. I think that I was an unfamiliar woman to you in bed, which scared you a little and caused you to leave."

We walked out of her place and up to her car, she used the keys on the central locking as we walked up I opened her door before walking around and letting myself in.

"Thank you," she said as I sat down, she started the car and we were off. I wasn't really paying attention as she drove through the streets towards before I knew what was what, we were outside my house and the car was parked,

"You'll have to come around again." She said to me, I smiled before unstrapping my seatbelt to share a hug. I got out of the car and walked across the road to the front door. The woman in the flat below was cleaning something away, she lived with her ex, something that I found a little strange but they were both happy enough. She was just about to go back inside when I stopped her,

"Rachael," I don't think she was fully aware of everything that was going on.

"Morning, whose car was that you just out of?"

"My old art teachers I fell asleep at her house, but that's not important."

"What were you going to ask me, I

need to feed Lootie."

"Do you have a spare bottle of wine?"

"Older women, wine in the morning. I'm sure you're trying to live and die like the poet Bukowski." She wasn't a million miles away from the truth,

"Somewhere close to being right, I'll take any scraps that you have."

"I have about half a bottle of red wine, are you going to go and write some songs?" I shook my head,

"Not this early." She indicated that she was only going to be a minute. She walked in her house and came back out a minute later with a half drunk bottle of red.

"It's not the nicest wine you will ever drink."

"So long as it does the trick." She handed me the bottle, I started to walk up the steps,

"You'll have to take the long walk downstairs in the next few days and let me know everything that has been happening."

"I will." I said, right before I walked indoors.

I walked to the kitchen, everyone had already gone out. I opened the cupboard where the glasses are, I got one out and put it on the side. Opening up my bag and pulled out the paracetamols, opening up packets I got to the pills one by one, by one, by one, by one. I have a handful take them like they were fruit pastilles, pouring out a glass of wine and trying the swallow. I don't remember how many of the boxes that I had fully consumed but the wine was gone. I felt weak, I felt drowsy as fuck! I needed to be sick. I ran through the house crashing into walls as I franticly made my way to the bathroom. I threw up down the toilet, I couldn't see myself being sick a second time; still I was. I was eventually able to walk away from the can, I went to the phone, it wasn't on the receiver and that was bloody typical. I paged it and traced the noise to my mums room. Typing in my doctor's number and getting nothing but an engaged tone, I launched the phone at the wall and paced the floor before I decided that it would be easier for me to walk across to Kemp Town and see a doctor. I walked back into the kitchen only to re-put on my shoes, I grabbed my bag, pulled my iPod out and set out again. I walked around to the train station; Queen's Road was full of old people walking slowly up and down the street. My frustration towards being at a virtual standstill caused me to just walk straight down the centre of the street looking directly at the buses and taxis that were heading towards me with eyes that said I really didn't care what the results were. I cut through Boots, the hordes of people waiting to cross the road would only hold me up, how I was feeling 2 days ago was seriously fucking awful, and today was somewhere very close.

I came out on North Street, I hadn't missed the traffic by much, but nonetheless I had missed it. I walked as quickly down the street as I could, I didn't know what the effects were to taking 18 packets of paracetamols - but I knew I couldn't be good. I saw the back of the pavilion, and I went across Old Steine, I looked at the traffic, John Street and the traffic that I faced. I made a run for it just before they left, making it across the road but the left light of a Golf clipped my heel as I spun to try and avoid it. My heel didn't hurt a tremendous amount, and if it did then it would have been amongst the least of my worries.

John street was a nightmare for me to walk along at that exact moment in time, there I was having taken enough to kill an average family, and there I was massively underweight walking past the police station, two police officers were walking towards me,

"Morning," One of them said to me, I nodded. They then said,

"Have a good day." My reply was simple but I said,

"I'll try." I made my walking a little quicker before they had chance to stop me and say anything. The sun was really emanating on the world, and I was feeling it. My mouth was dry and I felt like I had taken a sabbatical from my normal life and invested in some time spent in the Sahara. The road intertwined with Edward Street, and before I knew it I was walking past American Express. The business men sat outside having a cigarette, talking of their problems with the fiscal year and how they couldn't support their wives, 2nd homes and yachts. Come to think of it, they could have been smoking cigars the capitalist pigs. Wheels turning, I was waiting at the end of a road.

Looking at the bingo hall, wondering why the train was outside the wretched building. I'm sure if I were to wait long enough I'd watch a series of buses stop by it, which would be followed by a series of old people getting off and slowly walking their way inside. The short distances of the pavements broke up my journey as my body became riddled with pain, I'd rather that I had just walked without stopping all the way there. My feet were hurting like I couldn't comprehend, it was just unbearable; but I had to keep myself going. When I saw Brighton College School I knew that I was almost there. I felt worse than a toilet after 4 day drinking bender with the only sustenance coming from kebabs and curries. There were some students who were walking towards me; one of them bumped into me, I almost lost my balance.

"You mind?" he asked me, he looked like his parents had the perfect marriage - sending him here so they could actually fuck.

"Not really, my problems are bigger than yours. Besides, when the silver spoon is taken out of your mouth you will be nothing more than a dyslexic crayon." They looked at one another confused by my insult, trying to find something to say back. There was never going to be a reply.

"Nothing? Now, fuck off." I carried on walking I could see the hospital, I stopped by the post box on the corner of Walpole Road, an old lady was slowly walking towards the post box. She handed me the letter and I put it in for her.

"I could have done it myself." She said to me.

"Then in future may I suggest that you don't look like you need the help of others." I'm not sure if she could tell I had no means of caring at that exact moment of time. I walked the short distance that I had remaining. When I walked up the ramp into the reception went up to the first nurse I saw and said,

"I fucked up."

Everything beyond that faded out and just became white noise.

Day 4

A doctor walked into the room, I had only been awake for a few minutes,

"You gave me a huge scare, what were you trying to prove in taking 14 packets of paracetamols?"

"I don't know." I could hear myself breathing, but he didn't seem to be able to hear so.

"Everything has a limit, and you almost took enough to kill you. So for today, you're sedated with methadone."

"That'll be interesting; I used to be on mescaline. So come what may doctor."

"Well the police want to talk to you, but I'm not letting anyone in to see you. You will have to at some point face them."

"Is there any way out of talking to them?" I asked, he looked up from his papers.

"A suicide attempt is considered to be attempted murder, so I'm sorry to tell you but unless you can get out of this hospital undetected then you will be arrested." And for the first time since I was 14 years old I was petrified.

I didn't know how to get out of the room without being seen, let alone out of the building. I wasn't going to let anyone take me alive. I sat up very slightly,

"Can you please do me 2 favours?" he put his papers to one side.

"People always ask me for daft things when they are in a state like this, so be sure to try your worse. I've heard everything."

"Can you get me the Björk album Homogenic?"

"That's no problem, what is the other thing that you want?"

"I need you to phone someone for me, I'll write the number down, but you have to tell her what has happened and she will help me get out of this?"

"Is it a lawyer or a family member?"

"It's complicated, but she will be over as soon as she knows." The doctor nodded his head, he was a little confused by then number of digits.

"Is this the right number?" I nodded my head to which he said, "Right, well I'll get straight on that for you. But for now, I want you to get some rest."

I led back down and was gone to the world. The last thing I heard him say was,

"Who is this John Doe?" as he went out of the room.

My eyes were flickering when I realised that Alarm Call was playing in my ear, I turned and sat up.

"You got it for me." The doctor smiled,

"I told you that I would."

"And the..."

"I phoned her, she will be here tomorrow morning."

"Thank you."

"But tell me," He said, "How did you get those scars?"

I had to think about what he meant when he said, "The one on your wrist is quite obvious, but tell me how many people have seen the scar by your collarbone?"

"Not many people." He seemed convinced by the words I had said,

"So how did you get it?"

"Can I tell you tomorrow, I'll feel better once I've seen her." The doctor smiled,

"So long as you do. The police are still going to want to question you, and from what I gather from eavesdropping they will charge you with attempted murder."

"Even though it's my own?"

"Nobody has the power to take a life in this country, anyone who does..." I cut him off,

"Will be tried in a court of law by corrupt bureaucrats."

"That is one way of putting it, the other problem is we're on the 14th floor."

"So, I won't, be climbing out of the window?" he shook his head, "If I can figure out a way out, would you help me as best as you can."

"You will never just walk out the front door." He said, "Now I want you to get some sleep, I fear that your mind could very well go into overdrive and you won't rest at all, and subsequently won't convalesce."

Day 5

There was a spate of conversations all going on at once in my room. I looked out the window it was dawn. I turned to look towards the door; I saw the doctor was there with her and another female figure.

"Am I interrupting something?" I asked,

"I'm trying to ask these 2 how they got past all the security doors, but they are…"

"It's O.K," I said, "They have their means and ways, and you'll never get a word out of her."

"Shall I leave you alone with them?" he asked,

"That would be great, thank you."

"Well I still want that answer from you today." He walked out of the room leaving me alone with her, I still wasn't able to work out who the other person was. I sat up, I was able to sit up properly which was an improvement on the day before.

"How did you get in?" I asked her,

"You should know better than to question how I can do things." She did have a point, "But why did I get a phone call saying that you had tried to top yourself?"

"Don't ask I've had a seriously awful fortnight. Besides, right now I have a bigger problem."

"What's the bigger problem?" asked the other person. I recognised her accent; I looked at her and asked,

"Is it?" she smiled. I turned to her, "You should have said, I feared it was my mother." She laughed, I was feeling like joining her.

"Anyway, my bigger problem is the second I'm well enough to leave the hospital; or this room at least, the police will arrest me for attempted murder."

"How come I've never seen or heard about your other scar?" she asked me,

"What?"

"Well the doctor has seen it, and you've known him for like 2 days. Sa reisisid üle terve kontinendi vaid minu pärast ja ma ei ole kunagi midagi sellist näinud."[15]

"This early? Really? I can barely think and you're arguing with me in Estonian about something that until 5 minutes ago you didn't even know existed." I waited for her to give some kind of answer before I said, "Anyway, enough of your childish cries, how am I going to get out of this room without being arrested?"

The room was silent as they let what I said sink in and I was holding my breath, hoping that one of them would give a good answer. The Latvian looked like she was going to say

[15] You travelled across a continent for me and I've never seen it.

something before she just gave a sigh.

"I was going to say we can put you in a body bag and say you've died, but it's been done before."

"That's the problem that I'm seeing, any idea that comes to my mind, someone has done it before in a movie that I have watched." I looked at the Latvian, hoping that as the eldest in the room she would put the best suggestions.

"You must have something," I said to the Latvian, she shook her head. "Who knows that you're in the building?" I asked, the looked at each other and simultaneously said,

"Nobody." Before she said, "You should know that I can get passed everything undetected." She did make a fitting point. "Why? How strong are you feeling?" she then asked.

"Not brilliant, why do you ask?" She looked at the floor,

"Better start doing push-ups, you're going to need to get some strength if it is your intention to just walk out the front door." For a girl who had just flown the continent, she was seriously on the ball. I got out of the bed, and stared at the floor, I felt a long way up even though I had hit the bottom. I looked at the Latvian only to say,

"My nihilism keeps me just about alive."

"Your what?"

"Nihilisms, tas ir, kad jūs redzat kaut ko sliktu kādā situācijā un jums ir vienalga."[16]

"Tiesiskuma un kārtības noraidīšana."[17] The Latvian said,

"Nekārtības kārtība."[18] I had to stop them from whatever they were talking about, and at the same time ask,

"Since when do you speak Latvian?" Her eyes revolved towards me,

"I can do many things that you don't know about. I'm also very good at picking up languages, so after a few weeks in a city I know the basics of what I'm saying. Therefore able to speak Latvian."

"So you were just explaining the word nihilism?"

"Pretty much." It seemed reasonable enough to me. "Now stop sitting there moping about nothing and start doing some push ups."

"And when the doctor returns…"

"You say something witty; you'll know what to say when the time comes." I stood up, slowly went down to the floor and started doing press ups. I didn't count, I just went for it. I had no agenda, though it was not a new feeling in the past 10 days

---

[16] Nihilism, it's when you see the bad in a situation and you just don't care.

[17] A rejection of law and order.

[18] Order from disorder.

or so. Her and the Latvian gave me a look before she walked to the window, the Latvian said to the room,

"This room is making me feel quite claustrophobic. I'm going to go get a coffee in town, have a think about how I can get you out of this mess." She was standing with her back to the window, the Latvian said to her,

"Neviens no jums neiet projām un, ja durvis tiks atvērtas no ārpuses, nerādieties acīs."[19] The Latvian gazed her eyes down on me still doing press ups, she crouched down and looked at me,

"I'll do what I can to get you out of this. But for now, just get some strength in your system and be prepared to go in an instant."

She slipped out the door and closed it behind her, I didn't even hear it close. I returned to the calisthenics that I was doing. It was just me and her in the room, she opened the window and lent out,

"You should see the view from up here, sunset would be magical I think." I shook my head, I love her to bits but sometimes she is too ditzy for this world to ignore. We carried on in silence for a few more minutes before she asked,

"Why did you shake your head?" I

---

[19] Neither of you leave, and if the door is to be opened from the outside just stay out of sight.

stopped what I was doing, spun round and sat on the floor,

"Because you wouldn't be able to watch the sunset from that window." I pointed west, she couldn't get the hint.

"The sun rises in the east,"

"WOW, you are some kind of genius, no wonder you're stuck in…" I cut her off and shot he down by saying,

"That window faces east, so miss nameless female genius given that there are none that any fucker can remember a female genius. But if the sun rises in the east and that window faces east, then the sun must set in the west and the west must be…" I walked over to the wall, "Right beyond this fucking wall. Knock it down and everything else in the way and you can enjoy a sunset from this room." She was wishing she hadn't tried to speak in a condescending manner towards me at that very moment.

"But whatever, you're the smarter one out of us."

She shook her head and smiled in the fact that she knew she had been defeated.

"Can I help you with your…"

"Calisthenics, and I'd like that, there isn't anything else around here I can work with for lifting."

She looked around the room, I will never be too sure as to what she was looking for.

"Won't I be too much for you to lift?" she asked.

"No, I'll use you on my legs muscles."

"But I'm fat." I just had to shake my head,

"No, you're not. I'm quite unhealthily underweight, and that is making you think that you are fat. It's not you, it really is me that has fucked up."

We spent the next few hours in silence, she helped me work on the muscles, we worked until they ached and I couldn't get anything else done. The doctor came back into the room,

"Funny," he said in looking around the room, "there were 2 guests in this room this morning, nobody has seen anyone leave and as I stand here now there is only 1. Where did she go?"

"Ta ütles, et ta läheb võtab ühe kohvi ja mõtleb elu üle ning asjadest, mida ta pole filmides varem juba näinud."[20]

The doctor just looked at her in an annoyed way replied,

"Did you understand what she said?" I sat up on the bed,

"I don't speak much Estonian, I

---

[20] She said she was going to get a coffee and to have a think about life and about things that she hadn't seen in the movies.

hear words here and there she said something about coffee and thinking, beyond that I didn't really hear much." He was nodding his head. I think he thought that I knew more than I was letting on,

"So tell me of the scars that you have?"

"The one on my forearm I got the same time as the one on my…" My mind had gone blank and I just pointed at the other,

"The Clavicle, the collar bone if you'd rather." The doctor said.

"That's the one," I said as I pointed at him, "I got them when I was, 15. I got them, in…"

"Go on," said the doctor, "Nobody will judge you."

I contemplated giving a smile to what he said, but I just carried on with the dialect.

"I was in New York, with my then girlfriend; I was walking back to her aunts after I had been on a walk around a few streets to clear my head and think about things; I do it a lot. But a guy stopped me and asked me who my girlfriend was, I told him and went to walk on by; he told me that I was wrong. I tried to brush him off but he wasn't having any of my words, it quickly escalated to an argument, what in turn became a fight he pulled a knife on me. I in turn used an illegal judo move, he cracked his head on the concrete, and I ran off. I neither know, nor care what happened to him."

"You know I have to tell the police what you just said, don't you?" my heart stopped, jaw dropped and in that instant I thought to myself 'I am truly fucked!'

"Please tell me that you are joking." He shook his head, eyes closed.

"Well what about doctor patient confidentiality?"

"With me, that means very little when you are talking about a person's life." I stood up and started to pace the floor, all I had in my head was 25 to life - I'll be 43 if I were to be released from prison, if I were to make it that long.

"You cozen bastard! Your tongue tastes caviar, while your head is up someone's asshole! If I EVER see you again, I'll make sure that I push you in front of a bus!" he started to slowly step backwards. He opened the door and before he had chance to say any more words of bile I simply shouted,

"CUNT!!" at him, before slamming the door in his face.

Day 6

I woke up. I didn't recall falling asleep, but I there I was in the chair; she was on one side on the bed. The room was starting to get to me; there was a knock at the door. I went over to her and shook her,

"Someone is knocking on the door, move over to the chair." She was barely awake, and here I am telling her to move.

"Wh-what?" I'm pointing at the chair; she slowly gets up and shifts over.

I opened the door, a Pilipino nurse was standing in the door,

"Can I come in?" she asked. I nodded and opened the door for her to come in, closing it very swiftly behind her. She looked at her pointed before asking,

"Who is she?" She stood up, walked towards the window and said,

"Nobody important, so don't concern yourself with ghosts." The nurse looked confused and turned to me.

"So how are you feeling?"

"Better." I said.

"You threw quite a tantrum at the doctor yesterday."

"Well there are 3 sides to every story." She looked more baffled than what I said with the first statement.

"Well, there's his, mine and the

truth." The acknowledgement that she gave was that she agreed. The Estonian was looking out of the window, her gaze was something the world needed to see.

"I think you're all ok, do you need anything?" I took a minute to think about if I actually needed anything.

"Is there any chance you could get me some chocolate?" she thought about it for a second before saying,

"I'll see what I can do for you." She headed towards the door,

"Oh, I almost forgot." She said, "You'll be asked to move from this room in 3 days' time." She shut the door behind herself. My jaw dropped, I was truly fucked. She came over and hugged me from behind.

"You're keeping this one very calm; I was expecting you to punch a wall or something."

"I don't know what to say or do, hamartia? It's not exactly the word I'd use to describe this situation, but it's pretty fucking close." I hanged my head in shame, "Guess we might be fighting our way out of here. Nothing to do but carry on with getting myself fit and some calisthenics." She helped me and for the next few hours we were really getting somewhere with them.

All of a sudden the door opened, in stepped a woman wearing a white coat and a clipboard.

"Can I help you?" I asked as she

closed the door. Her eyes just focused on the clipboard; after a minute or so, she put the clipboard down and lifted her head up,

"Time to leave the building, Elvis." The Latvian, of course. Don't get me wrong, if anything were to ever happen the Estonian would be in the back of the police car with me thinking up a better way of doing it, but the Latvian would have thought up the initial idea.

"And I must ask, are we just going to walk out the front door?"

"More or less, we won't be wearing what we're wearing now. But this is like a bullet proof idea." She reached into her doctors' jacket and pulled out a set of scrubs. She gave them to her, she changed into them. I sat there wondering; I had to ask,

"What is my part in this?" the Latvian just pointed at the bed,

"You stay in there and say nothing." I got on the bed, they put the sheet over my lap and kicked the bed off the brakes,

"Almost forgot," the Latvian said, "Sign this." She handed a letter in front of me.

"Well what is it?"

"Your release form." The clever shrew, there was no taming her. I read through the form, signed and dated where I needed to; gave her the form back which she in turn put back on her clipboard, and we went out of the room.

The police were standing around, like the National Guard with Maggie's Pa. One of the police officers looked at the other; before snapping,

"Where are you taking him t-?" she cut him off, saying,

"When I know what room I'm going to move him to I'll be sure to let you know." He went to say something else when she shot him down again, "My orders are the top, and that means in here God would answer to me." He stood up straight, and let us through. We went towards the lift, she pressed the button and we waited for the lift to come.

"Quite an impressive English accent you can pull off." I whispered,

"Years of watching British comedies." I had to hand it to her, I was fearing that she was going to slip into a bad accent and expose us. We were in the lift, I got out of the bed. All of a sudden the lift stopped, the doors opened and the Latvian started to walk out of the lift.

"Why are we getting off here? We've only gone 2 floors. What is the point of that?"

"If we go the full distance then we will create suspicion. From here to the door we'll be walking." It was a good point, we left the bed jamming open the lift.

We walked down the stairs in

silence; it felt like we were moving between the sparse shadows at that hour of the day. We passed a doctor on the stairs, myself and the Estonian walked on ahead as the Latvian asked him,

"Excuse me," he smiled at her, "I've just started working here and I have a patient release form. Can you tell me where I have to take it." Her accent wasn't going away any time soon.

"I've not been here long myself," he had a west coast American accent, "Everyone looked at me strangely when I kept asking where an A.M.A until I explained that A.M.A meant Against Medical Advice."

"Sounds better if you ask me." It didn't take an existentialist to see that he wanted to ask her something, but he clearly didn't want to fail.

"I can take it for you, if you want." The Latvian smiled,

"That is kind of you." He did it, he asked her.

"Maybe, you would like to get a drink together some time." You could see the lump in her throat within an instant; he shook his head and instantly said,

"Sorry I didn't mean it like that,"

"No, it's just I," she said, "I have this thing where I don't date people from work." His face had gone red.

"No, not like that. It was silly of

me; please just forget I said anything." She handed him the form,

"I just got to go do something, so can I meet you back here in an hour and we can talk about it properly." He started heading up the stairs, when he shouted down,

"I might be a few minutes late but I will be here." She walked down to us and we carried on. We made it down to the ground floor. The Latvian took off the coat and handed it to a girl at the reception as we went in front,

"I'm just heading out for a coffee with a friend, I'll be back in about 30 minutes, would you mind watching this for me? I just hate to wear it out."

"Oh, sure. Just look for me and I'll have it for you." We sat down as she walked past us, we got up and followed. We walked through the automatic doors, down the ramp and were then on the street. I was out, and now I had no idea as to what I was going to do.

"I'm going to be heading back home tomorrow," said the Latvian, "I fear that there could be a bounty on my head for helping a fugitive escape." We started to walk slowly towards the city,

"I've got a lease for an apartment in Paris for a couple of months, would you like to join me out there? So that all this is to be forgotten?" I smiled.

Day 26

The metro wasn't as crowded as usual for lunch time, I guess the tourists were trying to be French and by stuffing their faces full of paté thinking that they were French. I had my note pad on my lap, I was scribbling something down. A couple of people were standing, I guess they were waiting for their stop. I could hear a couple arguing, they weren't speaking French and I couldn't understand the dialect. The wife was getting more irate over her husband ignoring her, she kept repeating the same line over and over again. A woman who was sat next to them, her brunette hair slightly starting to lose its colour held up with the exception of a few strands in a rather suiting way. She looked to be in her early 20s, but I wouldn't have been surprised if she was much older. Her light blue top was slightly too see through for her complexion, and it was very easy to tell that she wasn't wearing a bra. The man looked at his wife, she was just in a constant ramble to him; I wouldn't have been surprised if he was contemplating divorce or suicide. She said something that touched a nerve because he went to hit her, the woman sat opposite them put her hand up and stopped him.

"Tu ne pas frapper personne, c'est le 21ème siècle. Gros porc."[21] There was something really sensual about her accent, it could just be me but, French women have something about the way they talk that if I was a woman would make me wet to the quim. She got up and walked over sitting opposite me,

"Je déteste les hommes qui pensent que c'est ok de frapper les femmes. Ils me rendent malade!"[22]

"I'm really sorry," I said, "My French isn't that good." She gave a half-hearted smile,

"What are you writing?" she asked, I turned the sheet to face her. She started reading; she then flicked through the pages, intrigued by what she was finding. Like a child making a scrap book of the things that she wished she could have, then waking up on their birthday to see that all the things that made up the pages were wrapped up.

"You are a poet?" I didn't to disappoint her and say that I was a chef, that has just moved here and didn't have a job, so I simply agreed with her.

"Yes, I'm trying to get a new

---

[21] You hit nobody, this is the 21st century. Pig.

[22] I hate men who think it is OK to hit women. They make me sick!

collection done before I show it to people." She was nodding her head, flicking between the pages.

"I can help you with that." Part of me wanted to shout out 'Bluff!' but I felt that I could at least get her to prove it. Nothing worse than being guilty before any evidence has been shown, and I don't want to run a Kangaroo Court. I looked at her cautiously, I didn't want to hand over a new part of my life. The train came into Louvre Rivoli, I looked at the name on the wall from the window.

"Do you have any plans today?" she asked me, I shook my head before I even thought about it.

"No, I've not got myself a job just yet. So **this** takes up a lot of my time." Her eyes glistened in the darkness. "What were you going to suggest?" The artificial light brought out the shades in her complexion.

"Such green eyes you have, I have only ever seen one person with an eye that green."

"An eye?" she looked confused.

"She had one green eye and one gold, she was the world. Now, now I am learning to be…" she looked at me, through the words that I allowed to echo between us. I could have walked out to an ice age and not been too bothered. She understood what was really being said from my words.

"Would you like to join me for a

coffee? You can tell me about what you're writing."

"That sounds nice." I said in front of a broken smile, "I'm new to the city, so I wouldn't be able to say where we could go."

"It's ok, I have lived in Paris since I was 8." She said, "I have to collect a parcel in the Bastille, then I can take you to a café." I watched the people get on and off at Châtelet, when I asked her,

"Will it take you long to collect your parcel?" the train started moving again when she said,

"Oh no, I have to knock on a door and they will hand it to me. They know I am coming." The train came into Hôtel De Ville, and the woman who was sat next to the journalist got up, guess it was her stop. She looked at both of us, only to give a failed attempt at directing a scoff at both of us. Is it really such a crime to speak to a stranger? The woman who scoffed at us doesn't even realise that her own existence is a crime. I put my feet on the seat that was next to her, she looked down as the train rolled down towards St-Paul. When the train got to the Bastille she stood up and said,

"This is us," I stood up next to her as we waited on the doors to open; my head was shaking like a schizoid. My heart was beating faster and faster, it was like a kick drum playing a 6/4 time signature. There were only a few other people that got off the train with us, we mingled in with everyone else as we walked out onto the street. She was silent until we walked up to the street when she said,

"We have to stop off at Passage De La Main D'or, because I have to collect a book from a friend of a friend."

"What is the book about?" I asked as we crossed the road, her eyes were firmly fixed on crossing the road. We remained still for a moment as a Renault drove past us, she gripped my hand so tight, if someone were to look at my hand you'd think I had just had an arm wrestle with the incredible Hulk. We made it to Roquette, she finally let go of my hand. I looked down to survey the damage.

"Well, no bones appear to be broken." She looked at my hand, her nails had left imprints across the palm of my hand.

"You should not act like a, hypochondriac. Or… you will be what you are not." We turned onto Rue De Lappe, and as we walked along the asphalt I pointed out to her,

"You have not said what the book is about."

"Oh sorry, it is for my nephew. He is very much interested in football from the 1970's. He is a fan of Paris

Saint-Germain, so he has become interested in the football that was around when they formed." As we came onto Charonne I said,

"It was a great time for world football."

"Really?"

"Of course, you had Pelé and Yashin ending their careers. You had Zico, Beckenbaur, Gerd Müller coming through." We came to the next junction in the road, when we stopped I had to say it. "And of course, the player that I regard as the player of the decade - Johan Cruyff." She put her hand out, I was a little reluctant to take it, given the abuse it suffered the first time. We crossed Ledru Rollin, her hand was slightly looser, though it was still a very firm grip she had.

"It is just on the right after we walk down a short distance. The post modern look of the buildings in a way reminded me of buildings that I had seen in Los Angeles years before. Architecture is made, not repeated. Paris was a place that I would live that could never become outdated. I walked on the side of the road, cars parked both sides of the road, with cars prowling up and down waiting for somebody to leave. She dragged me down what I gathered to be Passage De La Main D'or, to the business man who was walking towards me, I am sorry I wasn't a passing emotion, she dragged me away.

We came to a large collection of apartments, I had not been to this part of the city before.

"Let me just phone her," she said as she pulled out her mobile, "Bonjour c'est moi. Je suis un peu occupé, pouvez-vous jeter par la fenêtre." She turned to me, "I am most sorry."[23]

"It's ok, I understand enough French to know what you're saying." She started laughing, "OK, OK. Merci." She hung up, put her phone back into her pocket, and looked up. "She says it is a large book and if it hits us, she is not to blame." A head popped out of the 4th floor window, she look pretty; though her hair was quite unkempt. I thought to myself that all her clothes would be folded neatly into squares.

"Prêt?" I looked up and shouted,

"Come on, throw it down." She dropped it, I moved to my left slightly and caught it.

"Un fantastique arrêt, tu devrais remplacer Barthez."[24]

"Merci." I said.

"au revoir."

"au revoir." We shouted up to her.

---

[23] Hello, it's me. I'm a little busy, is there any chance you can drop it from the window.

[24] A fantastic save, you should replace Barthez.

We then quickly walked around to the café which she still had yet to have told me the name of, the only thing I could remember is that it was on Rue Jean Macé.

We walked in, I found a table in the corner for us to sit.

"What do you want to drink?" she asked, my mind went blank; what did I want to drink?

"I don't know, what were you going to have?"

"I was going to ask you if you wanted to share a bottle of wine with me." My mind snapped in and thought, 'why ask? Surely it would make more sense to just come out and ask.'

"Sounds a little clichéd, but it is better than scolding my throat with a hot chocolate." I sat down, and a moment later she was with me.

"So,"

"So?"

"Can I see the poems?" I reached into my bag and pulled out the notepad, I handed them over to her.

"It is like nothing I have ever read before. You have nods towards Bukowski and Sylvia Plath, but nothing sticks as a true influence. What are the flower references in context to?"

"The flowers are my way to remind myself about someone. Influences…" I paused, I wanted to impress her, say a French writer. "I really like Camus, Emily Dickinson, Dickens, the

Brontë sisters and of course Bukowski and Plath." She put them down, as the waiter poured 2 glasses of white wine.

"It's a medium, I don't like dry wine."

"How can a liquid be dry?"

"I'm not a sommelier, so I could never say. Are you looking for much exposure?" I took a bit of the wine, it didn't taste too bad. Guess it was true, the French do know their wine.

"I am not too sure, I don't want to be in anyone's eye, but I won't ignore the big fish if they come knocking." She knocked back her glass, filled up her glass and asked,

"They will be critical of what they read, ***VERY CRITICAL***."

"I don't give a fraction of a fuck what people think about anything I do, I'm finding it hard to provide evidence that I exist - let alone anyone else." She looked rather stunned by what I said, she downed her second glass of wine before asking,

"Do you want some before I finish the bottle." I looked out the window at the teenage girl who was getting on her bike, her short skirt exposing her cellulite resembled the genetic make-up for flowers that I would never hold. The little she was wearing underneath was for the world to see; but it seemed like it was only me who did care to look. She rode off and I brought my attention back to the room.

"You can polish off the bottle, I'm more a connoisseur of vodka." She looked at the poems again,

"Where do you think up the titles?" she turned around to the waiter and said, "Grey Goose."

"The title is just something that lives at the top of a page. Would you rather give me a proper interview than just ask me questions which you'll forgot that you asked come the morning."

"Shall we make it in 4 days' time? At Shakespeare and co." I gave an agreeing nod, as the waiter put the Grey Goose in front of me. She raised her glass, and I joined her.

"To atmosphere of blank doors." She said right before we knocked back our drinks.

Day 30

She gave me the address to a bookstore near Notre-Dame called Shakespeare & company, I got off the metro at Saint Michel, the number of tourists was close to being unbearable. I had to push my way through the Asians all holding cameras with ridiculously long lenses, why they feel the need to carry them at all times is beyond me. I made my way through the streets as quickly as I could, though it still took me the better part of 8 minutes to get there. The journalist was waiting outside when I got there, arms crossed; it was blantantly obvious that she had just looked at the clock on her phone.

"Traffic," I said to her as I approached.

"You're here now, that's what is important." Was all she said as a reply, I looked around before asking,

"Where are we going to do this interview?" with her head she motioned towards the bookstore, I nodded before stating,

"So it feels easier on you?"

"No, easier for you." I walked in first as she pulled out a notepad, once she had stepped into the store I stopped, facing her I asked,

"Are we going to do this in English

or French?" her soft spoken reply was,

"What would you rather do it in?"

"English, if it's OK with you?"

"That is fine." I started walked around the shop, looking at all the different categories of books,

"So how are we going to do this?"

"As we walk around the shop, I will ask you the questions that I have set for today." I was looking at the biography section, there wasn't anything that I regarded as worth reading.

"Do you mind if I'm to take a few photographs of you for my article."

"Do you need to?" I asked, I was hoping that she could read between the lines and see I don't like having my picture taken.

"I've been told that I have to." Was her reply.

"Then I guess you can, so long as they are natural pictures, I *can't stand* people who feel the need to have big photo shoots. Just photograph me reading The Bell Jar on the stairs, or at home brushing my teeth. I'm not an extraordinary person, so I don't wish to be shown as one." I looked over at her, "Can I photograph you?"

"excusez-moi?" her eyes retracted then grew.

"It doesn't matter, are you going to ask your first question?"

"Oui, do you find it awkward when

people try to put an influence to your work given your method?" I wasn't expecting that as her opening gambit for our Q&A, I put back the book, which I was about to start moaning about. I didn't even get to look at the title, I needed less to be distracted by than what I would normally let distract me. I decided to not even think about an answer, in the same way a flower doesn't take too much care as to where it wishes to grow.

"I think it's not really too important, I mean how many people have whatever it was that they were influenced by all the time in their head? Regardless of if they are doing a painting, composition, a poem or a novel. You know what I mean, don't you?" she nodded as she jotted the last of my words.

"What does influence you?"

"The sick things that I've seen." She didn't write anything down,

"Can I reword the question?" I nodded, "What artists are you influenced by?" I had to applaud the quickness that her mind was working at, for her to reconstruct a question.

"I guess Dali, the sad thing about Dali was by far a better writer than anything else he did." I couldn't tell if her short hand was in English or French, then again it was no concern of mine. I wasn't going to let it play on my mind.

"Would you say your recent suicide attempt has shaped the way that you write?" I was waiting for the real questions, waiting but I knew that I'd be shitting myself when they were thrown my way.

"Well if I hadn't done that, I most likely wouldn't be writing. I am sure I wouldn't be in Paris, and I know for a fact that I wouldn't have met you."

"So why did you start?" she asked as we walked up the stairs,

"It's easier on my hands than punching a brick wall." She had the sense of looking shocked by the statement; not sure what the next question she had planned to ask next, when she gave the 6-year-old question of,

"Why?" I picked up a copy of Wuthering heights, looked at it and said,

"Cath wouldn't understand why he loved her so much." I then brought my attention back to her, "My anger outweighs my guilt, to such an extent that I'm to either self-destruct or create something that might just keep me sane to some extent." She didn't know what to add to the conversation, once she finished her shorthand I said to her, "Sorry for giving you my burdens, it's not fair on you to be subjected to that." Before I closes with, "My personal hell."

She saw it as the perfect moment to change the subject, without having to add anything to what I said.

"Can you sit down for me, I think it will make a good picture to take of you."

"Is there any reason you said now?" I asked, she pointed at my hand.

"Because you're holding Wuthering Heights." Tapping the book with her camera lens, "It would be very fitting to show your love of the Brontë sisters, by showing you reading Emily's masterpiece." I looked at the book, I flickered through the pages, I was able to recall lines but nothing too solid.

"I've not read this since I was 16."

"Read it, no; just look what is the word triste? Non, pensive?"

"Pensive? Oh pensive. I'm sure I can do that." Just as I was about to sit on the floor, an American couple walked past me; causing me to have to stand back up so they could go past. I made my way back down to the floor, the journalist pulled her camera out of her bag.

"It's a nice camera that you have." I said to her,

"Do you have 1?"

"Next time we're out I will show you my camera." She smiled as she started taking the photographs, she looked up only to say,

"Can you look a little bit more

sad?"

"I love the way your voice sounds when you talk French."

"You look so beautiful when you're pensive." I didn't really know how to take what she said, the sunlight changed slightly and in an instant I had a dark shade across the right side of my face.

"What's your next question?" I asked.

"Do you find that not putting the title in the poems helps create a different feel to the poems?" I slanted my head, musing my answer,

"Not really, the title to me is just something that takes up space at the top of the page."

"So is there any reason for the titles?"

"Not really, you could just regard them as inside jokes." She smiled,

"So is anyone else on the inside?" I chucked to myself,

"No, no it's just me." She gave a half smile before looking down at her notepad,

"Are there any subliminal messages within your works? Anything that people should look at when they read your pieces?"

"Meie vahel ei ole saladusi, sest sa näed läbi minu silmade."[25]

---

[25] There are no secrets, because you can see through my eyes.

"Et là je ne te comprends pas."[26] I don't know why but I started laughing really violently.

"I don't think that my French is good enough for me to say that." I said,

"But your Estonian is?" she asked.

"Haha, it's getting there." I said, "There are no secrets, because you can see through my eyes."

"That's quite a beautiful statement. Where did you pluck that from?" with a blank stare I said,

"I don't know." She looked sad over the fact that she couldn't put down an origin to the phrase, I tried to satisfy her need for words. "It might have been, something that I had seen written down; or the way that I read something."

"I will google it when I get home." I stood back up and put Wuthering Heights back on the shelf, the journalist was putting her camera away,

"I just have 2 more questions for you today," she smiled, "Is that ok?"

"It's fine," I said, "What have you got?"

"Did you, did you move to Paris to be more surrounded by the art museums and the vibes of the city with how it is constantly changing?" I took a minute to let the question sink in, the idea was to make it look like I

[26] And now I don't understand you.

had taken my time to compose an answer.

"I moved here because I felt like I needed a fresh start, after all that had happened back in Brighton. It's nice to be here, nobody knows me and people just leave me alone. My mind is always racing around with thoughts." She was nodding as she was going.

"And my last question, do you feel healthier now you're living here in Paris?"

"Fuck, I do feel healthier; but it's hard. The thing that I am enjoying the most is that I don't feel tired all the time." She finished writing down what she needed, after she put her notepad back in her bag she walked towards a room we hadn't yet ventured into.

"As a child, I used to sit in this room, wishing I could read the books." I looked around the room, it was full from the floor to the ceiling with stacks of books. All different sizes, for all different ages. I saw a few books that I had read through-out my life,

"Are there no books in French?" I asked her, she turned faced me, her figure was blocking out the sunlight coming in the window.

"No, and that's why I loved this shop as a child. It was all mystical and very other-worldly to me back then." I picked up a book and handed it to her, I didn't even look to see the title or the author.

"Can you read something to me?" I asked her, she put the book on the top of another pile.

"I was going to ask if you would read me your poetry… over a drink?" I knew I had some of the poems in my bag, the heat of the city was being too harsh to me.

"Can we go to a coffee shop and not end up drinking wine? I don't like to drink very often." As she took a step closer to me I could smell her perfume, it was light and youthful; surely it was meant for a woman who was as young as she looks. The vanilla that I could smell on her was much the same as the Viru Valge that I had in the apartment.

"That's ok," Was whispered from her lips, "Too much wine on a day like today can make a woman anybody's, and I need you to look after me." Her flirtatious nature was very appealing, but she really didn't know the wealth of my problems.

"I trust you to try and not lead me astray." She took me by the hand and we made our way through the people and out of the shop.

We were standing outside, she eventually let go of my hand,

"It's not far," she pointed at the corner of Notre-Dame, "It's just over there." I was trusting her judgement, though I was sure she was going to lure me into something sexual. Her hair was looking radiant even if she had it up and it was looking like a 1960's factory worker. She interlocked arms with me and we walked along Montebello, there was a bridge on the other side of the road which we eventually made our way to. I looked up at Notre-Dame the whole time we were walking past it, the journalist was something special in the way that women look, but that cathedral was something close to perfection.

"What," she said, trying to take my attention away from it.

"You're beautiful, but ***THIS*** is an architect's zenith." She reached up and kissed me on the cheek,

"You flatter, but want nothing. Why?" We carried on walking,

"I'm just a man, the truth of me is something that I'm trying to work out. For now I want nothing, but someday I'll want it all, because I'll feel it all." We walked across another bridge, she pointed,

"Just there, we'll sit out front and read to each other." We walked up, she gave an indication that we wanted to have a drink and the waiter pulled an order pad out of his apron. As she asked for a coffee and a hot chocolate I grabbed some of the pages and got my composure to read to her.

Day 44

Her text said to meet her at Gare De L'Est, it seemed like an odd place to meet her, but I was going to play by her rules. As I walked into the station, every wall seemed to have posters with question marks, someone had been busy. I was slightly cautious of what she had planned given the fiasco the day before, I followed the posters. They led me on a wild goose chase that eventually came to a photo booth, in looking down at the dainty shoes inside; I instantly recognised them as being hers. I pulled back the curtain to reveal her dressed as Zorro,

"Cute." I spurted through laughing, "Is it Amélie? Or are you going to tell me that you want to become a vigilante?"

"You saw the film?" she asked,

"I did, it's one of my favourite films of all time. How did you get your hair so short? You didn't cut it did you?" she took the mask off, and the locks revealed themselves to any souls looking to find solace with us.

"When you've been a journalist as long as I have, you get to meet some good hairdressers. I phoned one up and she helped me out." As she stepped out of the booth, we shared a hug followed by a kiss on each cheek.

It's important to exchange cultures she said, though my brain was wondering what she had planned.

"So do you have anywhere that we're going to do this interview?" she reached into her bag and pulled out a pen and pad, and put me into the photo booth, "Here?" she gave no indication that we were going elsewhere, "Right, but if someone else needs the booth we will have to move." She smiled,

"Do you have any method to how you write?" I was starting to feel a little claustrophobic; the question could have been the opening to an impending doom. I stood up and walked out passed her; she spun to face me,

"Not really, if a line comes to me I'll get it down. Some days I can get pages written, but if it's not going to happen I won't try and work it. There's no point, you admit defeat for that moment; later it might happen." As she was jotting down what I said, I asked her,

"You spend your days writing, have you never been tempted to write like a novel or short stories yourself."

"I'll come back to that later," she commented, "Would your life change much if you became famous?" I didn't really know what the question meant, so I tried to answer it as best I could,

"I'd like to think I'd stay the same, you know… work at the bakery, still spend time with the Estonian and Erin, and most of all that I wouldn't ever forget about her. Why are we stuck inside? Today is a gift that the Gods gave us to spend outside."

"You are religious?" she asked,

"No, it's a phrase. Come on, I'm sure we can walk you ask and we can stop as the answers get fired your way." She locked arms with me, and we left the train station, the suns' rays seemed to resemble different constellations leaving me to rely on her to be my guide. She took me down Avenue De Verdun, I looked up and down the street; both were dead ends.

"This way the sun won't blind us, and we can get some pictures taken. I want to photograph you in a more, honest way." It seemed like a legit reason for her antics,

"No trying anything, it will make me feel sad that you'd go against a simple request." She smiled,

"Are there any things you read these days that you wish you had written?"

"Yeah, there is so much." Her interruption was quite needed to the question,

"Not dead writers, things that are about here and now. We all have books that we wish we had written."

"What do you wish you had written?" I asked, I became intrigued,

"The Outsider by Camus." It was

such an important book to modern literature, and the beauty was nobody had adapted it.

"Good choice, I'd say the only modern book I like is House of Leaves. Things like Fight Club, I found to be better films than books." I let her keep up with me, "And if you read it it's very childlike in the approach."

"Ok, my last question for today is - If you were to ask the readers to do one thing for you, what would it be?"

"Well I'm starting to have enough of the world, I don't know what that means… I think the last few months I've noticed how mindless, pointless and just how heartless people are; not everyone but it's a case of either me or them burst into immolating flames." She wrote down what I said word for word, "I'm not sure if that's the right thing to say, but it's what I needed to get out of my head." She looked up,

"It's ok, I'm not going to put it. People can be like…"

"Barnacles." I knew she was never going to get the word herself.

"I was going to say pretentious pricks." Her accent sounded so funny when she said those words.

"You can always put it like that." I looked around, I guessed that she was just going to photograph me here.

"What are you calling the article?"

"The Shape of Poetry to Come. They wanted you to dress up like a more suave writer, I told them it wouldn't suit you. These pictures are my vindication." I handed her my bag and let her do her worst, I wasn't really thinking about the camera being there.

"You are easier to photograph today, has someone told you to do anything different?"

"I don't like to be this side of the camera, so I am trying to think to myself that the camera isn't here."

"But I am?" she asked,

"I enjoy your company," she put the camera down from her eye to smile, "When you're not trying to get me into your bed." She instantly snapped me, blinding me with the flash; I was waiting for the slap to come. It made me surprised when it didn't.

"One day you will move back to England, and after a while; you will suddenly realise that we should have been together." I walked over to her, took her hand and we started to walk back towards the train station,

"Now it's a little bit claustrophobic in there, so you're going to buy me a drink."

"I knew that you would come round, I know…"

"Not alcohol, we won't be going to bed today. *That*, I do promise you." I was starting to think that she was older than what I thought, wanting a younger man. But why me? I was nothing special, I'm just a guy who is learning to be. I have her to help me, and the journalist makes my levels of normal mundane existence seem that more interesting to the rest of time.

We walked up to the train station, a hoard of people were walking out so I simply assumed that a couple of trains had just arrived. That, or a lot of people had gone to say goodbye. Stranger things had happened.

"Why do you always want us to drink together?" I asked, she clenched my arm tighter and whispered into my ear,

"I ask, because I want you to loosen up when you are with me." We walked into a coffee shop, I went to ask her but she got there first,

"What do you want?"

"Just water please, I'm not really wanting a hot drink on a day that is as hot as today. I'll just be in need of a drink constantly for the rest of the day." She went over and placed the order while I sat down and looked out at the street, the bumbling tourists wearing their 'I love Paris' t-shirts, expecting the inhabitants to be wondering round wearing berets, garlic round the neck and seducing the women from all over the world. And we're not. It was at this point that I did regret sitting outside,

"BONJOUR, PARLEZ-VOUS ANGLAIS?" I had to roll my eyes at them, Americans were quite wasted anywhere in Europe outside of England. I hold no qualm with Americans, I have don't like to be spoken to like I'm 7.

"You know, if you speak to people in a patronising manner; they will be rude to you." They became so excited, I could see the journalist out the corner of my eye.

"Oh my God, you're British, from your accent you're from BirmingHAM." I feared that the questions couldn't be any more stupid,

"No, I'm from Brighton. And I hate to be rude but, I'm actually with someone right now. So could you please leave us alone?" I have American friends, but these people wouldn't leave me alone. All I wanted to do was have a drink with the journalist, and if by some stroke of luck on her part; she did get me back to hers - I wouldn't mind watching her get undressed.

"Can we get a picture? And do you know my friend Terry? He lives in Leicester."

"Yeah I know Terry," they reached into their bag for the camera, "He's a prick. NOW, please leave me alone." They walked off, as they went I heard them say,

"The British really are nothing more than the 51st state."

"I'M ESTONIAN, YOU WANKERS!" I shouted back to them, they carried on walking. Hopefully in the wrong direction.

"What was that about?" the journalist asked,

"Don't ask."

"But I just did."

"Then Americans being Americans, when they come to Europe. Loud, rude and just what I hate to be around."

"They always think because I'm French that I want to be with them. How they are the greatest country in the world, and they can never guess my age."

"I don't know your age."

"Really?" She was genuinely shocked by that,

"You've never told me, so I always assumed that you were about 22/24."

"I'm 29." She didn't look it, I knew of people who people who were 29 and didn't look as good as her.

"I'm 11 years younger than you, why do you want to be with me so much."

"You are a good looking guy, you remind me of a young Ché Guevara. Have you never been with a woman as old as me?" I shook my head, it felt like she was teasing me.

"I've only been with one woman, and she was… she was," I wiped a tear from my eye, I looked at it and saw the outline of her hourglass. There wasn't anything there for me, I had no option but to wipe it away.

"I'm sorry, I didn't know. I just thought that you were somebody who is not going to be tied down." She looked down at her coffee, stirring it in a lackadaisical manner. I lifted her head up to face me,

"You didn't know, and what has happened to me over the last few months is my own fault. It isn't fair to take the blame for your words or their action, on another earth my mind wouldn't care more than a fraction." There was a tear in the shape of a square, I wasn't going to let her see it. As I wiped it away she went to lean in to give me a hug, I turned and faced her; as our eyelashes touched I said,

"The next time you get that sinking feeling, you'll understand my pain." I looked at all the emotions caught up in her eyes. Her mother finding out about her father's mistress, as a student walking home after not meeting a guy on a night out with the girls, her being 12 and the boy she loved lusting after her best friend. I see it all, I feel it all. She kissed me, as she brought her head back she said,

"You didn't resist, why?"

"You know, I really don't know. I feel free, and I now know that you understand where I am; I thought I was alone, now I feel like I can put things to rest." She picked up her coffee, and I thought to myself - the only thing that I know as a certainty, is that I’ll never know what coffee tastes like.

Day 58

The journalist had phoned to say that she was going to take the 3 of us out for lunch, Erin saw it as the perfect opportunity to dress to the nines for her.

"What are you hoping to achieve from this?" I asked Erin, the Estonian was none the wiser to the fact that Erin was very much hoping to bag herself a woman almost twice her age.

"Guess I will know if women are worth taking to bed or not."

"We don't even know where she is taking us, we can't have you dressed like Nicole Kidman in Moulin Rouge." I swear she has seen every film ever made, she would have been more inclined to be dressed like Charlize Theron in 2 Days In The Valley.

"I don't have a red dress." Taking a bite out of an apple I shook my head, she was rolling her hand waiting for me to start talking again; unable to because my mouth was full. As I finished up, Erin put Tiny Dancer on.

"I was more thinking corset, suspenders and just the general look of being able to arouse me and not her."

"Do you feel better in yourself? You seem to be moving forward?" I moved and sat on the bed as she looked at her clothes spread out across the room.

"Why change the subject?"

"You do it all the time, you seem to me to be much like the person I met all that time ago." I picked up a fading t-shirt, I knew that in a couple of washes it would start to acquire holes. I didn't see the problem with it, I did however know that Erin's mum would see that very problem. Her little soul has the heart of a wolf.

"I now know that I will never see her again, I'm not going to sit around and stop living. A man who only exists is not worth talking about, a man not worth talking about isn't real to the world." She took the t-shirt out of my hand, looking at it she said,

"You and I are the only people I know, who don't seem to be caught in a view from a place where time is flat." I liked that,

So into my phone it went. 'A View From A Place Where Time Is Flat.' I'm still to this day not fully aware what it means. I watched her as she changed from one set of clothes to the next, the 3 of us had become so comfortable in our own skins that Erin could change in front of me and I wouldn't be phased by it. The Estonian walked in the bedroom, looking at the clothes flung everywhere she asked,

"Who are you hoping to take to bed?" I didn't even let her open her mouth when I said,

"The journalist." I smiled because I knew how quickly the Estonian was going to start laughing, and then it came…

"Hahahahhahahahahahahaha, you really think she will be interested?" Erin to her credit, stood her ground as she took the top that she was wearing off and the skirt. Standing with the Estonian and myself either side of her, looking at her, Erin's husky dulcet tones said.

"I might be young, but you tell me what is wrong with my body?" The Estonian stood there looking at her, I knew from the view I had that it would be hard to find a fault line.

"You're just too young for her. I'll tell you what, if you ask her in front of us and she says yes to going on a date with you; I'll pay for it." Erin stood contemplating the wager which was put in front of her, on one side of the coin she could stand the chance to take a beautiful French woman out for dinner with the possibility of ending up in her bed if she were to play her cards right. She could however ask and get told no with myself and the Estonian watching, as we sit there in an awkward silence while the waitress brings us a bottle of wine before asking Erin to present proof of her age. I did hope for Erin's sake that she didn't go through with it, given just how stubborn she is I knew that she would.

The Estonian walked to her wardrobe and pulled out a khaki green dress that I had bought her the year before for her birthday, handing it to her she went through the clothes that were lying on the bed; pulling a faded pair of jeans that needed to be washed, but with the right look could be given the benefit of the doubt. Handing them to her she said,

"This is how we'll start, put them on and I'll be able to see what we need to add or takeaway for you to have your desired effect." Erin put the jeans on, looking at the dress in such a way that she thought she would never fill it out; given her framework was almost as fragile as mine.

"You think this will work?" I got off the bed, walked round to look at her, she looked the part; though something was missing.

"You got 20 minutes before she gets here." The journalist was too stylish a woman for me to have, but for some reason she wanted me in my situation as a vulnerable entity. In that moment I pondered in my mind that if I were to end up in bed with the journalist would it give a sensation as euphoric as living inside lightning. Was my fate really mine? I knew that I'd die I wasn't really bothered if someone were to stop me in the street and tell me the exact day I was going to die. But would it change my fate? Would I not find myself in cities I was destining to visit? In bed with women for a night, to promise I would write them sonnets, that nobody will ever read. What if?

I'm not dead yet, so this shouldn't be something to concern me too much. Would I end up in bed with the journalist, would I visit Stockholm, end up marrying the Estonian. Walk Erin down the aisle on her wedding day, ever have a niece and nephew to care for? I guess these are things that could start a bucket list.

I brought my mind back to the room, as I looked at each of them; they seemed to be caught up in a debate about something. I walked out of the room, leaving them to continue their mothers meeting. As I walked into the bathroom, I locked the door behind me; a moment of peace while I sat down to do what needed to be done. All thoughts suddenly became eradicated from my mind, I found peace whilst taking a shit. Once I had finished and sorted myself out, I returned from the bedroom to find Erin pretty much ready.

"Think she has what it takes?" The Estonian asked me, I looked at Erin, for a moment I had forgotten that she was German; and there I was looking at her dressed to the nines, thinking to myself that she was from the Ukraine. I was certain that inside that head of hers she was practicing lines to say to the journalist, I would never know what she was going to be using as an opening gambit. I did hope for her sake that she could work with improvising what needed to be said. The time was getting closer, and she was quite punctual.

"Shall we meet her outside? Today is a day given to us by the Gods and we are going to stay stuck inside until she gets here." After looking at both of them, we all came to the conclusion without any words being said that it was a worthwhile thing to do. We each collected the things that we would need, and as we left Erin locked the door behind us before passing the key to me. We walked down the stairs as Erin started to sing Feelin' Blue. As I opened the front door the journalist was walking down the street in a thin black and blue stripped jumper that came to half way down her thighs and I very much doubt she had too much on beneath that.

Day 19

I was sat on the couch; I watch the colours form off the vase. I wondered what flowers would look best in the room, some Crysthanamum, perhaps an Orchid? I contemplated going to a florist to buy some yellow French Marigold. She walked into the room, she was holding a faded shoulder bag,

"I have to go and meet my lectures, what are you going to do today?" I kept my eyes on the vase, trying to remember from school about the spectrum of light and how the light hitting it truly worked. I couldn't remember so I wasn't going to eradicate my own time over it.

"I'm not sure, I think I might get a little writing done. Though, I have no idea what I'll write though." She picked up a pen and threw it to me,

"The words will come, but don't lock yourself away today, do get out and feel the sun on you." I picked the pen up, as I heard her open the front door I shouted out to her,

"Give me a title to get me started." I heard her footsteps walking back to me.

"7 Story Russian Doll." She said from the doorframe, the size of her was like an ant wearing a person's shoe; that doorframe didn't have her or me in mind.

She walked out of the flat and I muttered the title to myself a few times,

"It's only a title." I said, I wrote it at the top of the page. Words started to form in my head, I couldn't work out the order so I was just scribbling at random throughout the page; I didn't even look at what I was doing. I don't know why but I knew the page was done. I had 10,000 more lines roaming around inside my head, I wrote them all down across 20 sheets of paper. Every time I felt I had it all out of me, new thoughts came into my head. I didn't know if this was a passing whim, or the shape of poetry to come. I wasn't to know, I did think to myself that it was good to be getting the weight of years of my chest, the pot inside me was starting to boil over, and my problems were not things that I wanted to keep with me for too long.

The sun glared across the sheet of paper I was working on; as my eyes tried to refocus I was reminded of what she said to me, to see a little of the sun. I walked over to the window, opened it up and looked down. The drop wasn't something that I was planning on doing any time soon. I walked into the kitchen, poured myself a glass of water had a sip. I went back to the windowsill I put my scraps of paper on the floor, and climbed through so I was half in and half out. I picked up the first piece of paper and jotted a title.

Kiev, Or Letters Spelt Out In Brickwork

I couldn't see the start of the piece from the words that I had, so I just started down the page; there was no point in fretting to myself over nothing. I'd pick up other pieces of paper just to see if I had missed anything, scanning pages quickly when I read a line out loud,

"Writing words on shards of glass, to be pressed against my head." I wrote it as the start, but I needed another line.

The words were spinning around in my head like a fairground ride, my mind reached out into the darkness and hoping for a fitting line,

"Hoping the meaning will find it's way in, if nothing happens I can always press harder." I looked down at the paper and said to myself, "That's it, I have a finished piece." I kept on working my way through the pages until every line was used. Some pieces got titles, others I couldn't think up titles. I heard her put the key into the lock, she came in looked at me hanging out of the window,

"Why am I hardly surprised?" she said, "Have you done anything today?" I moved myself back inside, picked up the sheets and handed them to her. She looked at them and then at me,

"I had a lot to say." I whispered.

"These are so… different, it's like an AK47 of poetry for the confused youth of our generation." I walked into the kitchen and poured myself another glass of water. She shouted out to me,

"What will you do with them?"

"I don't know, I expect I'll do little with it."

"NO!" she handed back the papers to me, "This is something that has to be seen." I laughed,

"No, you're fucking with me. I know that whole Clash thing that if you have something to say it will be heard. But this, I… I don't know, this is my demon's we're talking about here. If my dad were to find out that I was doing this, he would…"

"Fuck him, he's a self absorbed CUNT! Before you say anything, you are forgetting that I've met him; and that wanker thought because I'm Estonian that he'd have to talk slowly to me, he doesn't realise that there is no weapon sharper than the wit of my words. Condescending prick."

"Yeah that's the guy. You know what, you're right. I'll do this heart soft and headstrong." She smiled,

"You know it's the right thing to do." She looked around the kitchen, "We have nothing to eat today do we?" I looked around the room,

"No we don't, we'll eat out

tonight. But first…"

"We?"

"We take a bottle of wine, sit up by Sacré-Cœur and watch the lives that we don't have pass us by." She walked over to the rack and picked up a bottle, before opening the draw and pulling out the corkscrew. As she was failing at pulling the cork out she said,

"Are we going to take some glasses?" I had a look of surprise,

"*Are we going to take some glasses*? No, what a ridiculous thing to ask, of course not. We going to walk into a restaurant and be 'Oh Nevermind the glasses sir, we have our own."

"Well it's not like I've been sucking your cock in the last week is it."

"Touché." I closed it with, as she started to pull out the cork out. I saw it starting to break,

"N, n, n, n, no." I said to her, she looked up as she pulled the top half of the cork out,

"I thought that they were bigger than that." I took the cork screw from her

"I'll get the rest." I was just about able to get the rest of it out, I took a swig and I got the last of it. Which in turn made it's way to the sink, she nodded her head.

"Good, in future you can get the cork out." She had a shot of it and we made our way to the door.

"I got my key." I pulled it out just to give my own confirmation. We stepped through and I locked the door behind us. We walked down the stairs, as we got to the bottom of the stairs she handed me the bottle. Before exposing us to the streets. We walked up the street, passing the bottle between us, we walked up the back way to avoid the immigrants.

We sat on the steps outside the Sacré-Cœur, she said between taking a hit of the bottle,

"Back on your father, somebody said, and I'd be fucked if I were to know said it…" she handed me the bottle, "They said, The hardest thing to learn in life is which bridge to cross and which to burn."

I thought about California, she needed to see that corner of the world. The sentence she said was right, some people can't wait for life - and some need to be removed all together.

Day 21

I woke up, she was already awake. I didn't say anything, just gazed into the back of her head.

"Are you going to turn around?" I asked her, she spun around only to say,

"GO brush your teeth."

I got out of the bed, wiped the sleep from my eyes and walked towards the bathroom. The toothpaste was almost out, almost but we still had a few days life left in it if we were lucky. I brushed my teeth, and headed towards the kitchen. I picked up an apple and looked out the window as I took a bite.

"What do we have to do today?" I asked; I didn't hear any reply so I went to the bedroom door.

"We've not got to do anything today, why do you want to do something?"

"Nothing?" I asked.

"Nothing." She replied with.

"Nothing?!" I became quizzical.

"NOTHING! Not a thing, we have nothing to do." She put The Roots, on which lead for me to nod my head, I joined in with the lyrics during Thought @ Work and The Seed (2.0) before asking,

"Do you want to have a lazy day together?" she walked into the kitchen, I turned to face her seeing her naked in the kitchen really took me by surprise, she walked past me and picked up a banana

"No pun intended from this." I had to have a look, doesn't matter that I share a flat with her; when she doesn't think that you're looking its all the more reason to look. "Shall we have a lazy day then?" I asked, "We can watch some films, maybe…"

"Fucks sake!" I interrupted her, "As great a figure as you have please cover it up and leave something to the imagination."

She scoffed me and walked back towards the bedroom, just before she made it back into the room she shouted.

"Bring some food and I'll sort out some films for us to watch before we stop for lunch."

I grabbed anything I could find, and headed back to the bedroom. When I got back into the bedroom she was sorting out a DVD, "What have we got planned to watch today?" I asked.

"The Fabulous Destiny Of Amélie Poulain." I had to smile, she knew how to put me in a good mood; to me it didn't matter what else we were to watch I'd enjoy anything so long as I had Audrey Tautou on my mind I'd be fine.

"Well what are you waiting for?" I said, "Put it on." She put it on, and for the next 2 hours the troubles of both my life and the world didn't seem to matter. Everything that had gone on before with me. Anything and everything that I saw on the news, what had been going on with the riots in Kosovo, the start of Saddam Hussein's trial, Marlon Brando and Hurbert Selby Jr dying, Penance Soiree the beginning of the end for Jacques Chirac. It didn't matter that only a couple of years before he had been voted back in, his time was coming to an end, and the worst part for him was that he knew it. Me winning £330 on Greece winning the European championships, with a 66-1 odds bet. None of it fucking mattered as I was watching Amélie. When the film finished I asked her,

"When can we go to Café des 2 Moulins?"

"We'll go in a few days if you want to have a Crème brûlée." I nodded, "What do you want to watch next?"
I scanned my eyes through the DVD's that we owned and the ones that had been left here by the pervious occupants.

"Let's go with Almost Famous." She did nod her head to say with a grand overture in her tone, "Good choice." She sorted out the discs and as she was doing I asked, "Have you heard, the NHL is in talks to stop a lockout."

"I hadn't heard. How bad is it meant to be?"

"Really bad." She closed the DVD player; she clearly was more interested than me on the matter. We watched Almost Famous; we laughed, we cried, we once again fell back in love with 1970's blues rock music all over again.

We stopped for lunch, as we stood in the kitchen sorting out a salad together I asked her,

"What do you think death is like?"

"Do you ask because of the aeroplane scene?" she replied with. I did nod my head as it turned to face her

"It's something nobody wants to think about…"

"You've come pretty close a couple of times, but not close enough to be able to say what is going on, on the other side."

"But to answer your question, yes." I think she knew that I was thinking about it because of that particular scene.

"I don't know, and if anyone is to tell you otherwise they are clearly mistaken."

She was right. We finished the salad; I grabbed a French stick along with a couple of bowls as she got the cutlery.

"Seems a little unfair," I said as we sat down, "I get the joys of carrying everything."

We sat on the sofa facing each other, out of the silence she said, "Love's a bitch."

"What?"

"Do you want to watch Love's A Bitch?"

"Amores Perros?

She looked straight at me, she knew that I wasn't stupid; but couldn't work out why I would play stupid.

"You got things on your mind?" she asked me, I looked at the black TV screen; I sighed, "I never did say goodbye."

"It ain't easy to move on from love if you don't get the chance to say goodbye."

I rested my head on her shoulder, there was something missing - just one fragile part of me and it was something that I don't think anyone would ever be able to see.

"I wish time would take it back, take it all back."

"In a better world we would never feel hurt, but we are a part of this world and we do suffer. But what you are forgetting is that we know love." And with that I knew that at that exact period of time I knew that I was in the safest pair of hands in the world.

She got up and went to put a new DVD on, after changing and pressing play the film started. I knew that something wasn't right, they weren't speaking Spanish, this was an American film

"What have you put on?" I asked.

"10 Things I Hate About You." She said.

"It only works because they are not talking Shakespeare." She looked confused and sounded even more confused when she said, "What?"

"It's a take on Shakespeare's play taming the shrew. Didn't you know that?" She gave no indication, "huh, I thought everybody knew that." I finished off saying. We watched the rest of the film without a word being said, when the film finished I walked over to the window opened it up and looked outside.

"How does the world look today?" she asked.

"The world looks like it doesn't care about anyone's mistakes today, if we are what we seem - then we shall be fine." She gazed over towards me, there was no eye contact but I feel her eyes crawling over my body.

"Tell the world something from up here."

I looked down and there were a couple having an argument, I shouted out to them

"Hey, what is the point in fighting? You know you are not going to get any sex tonight if you carry on." He looked up only to say, "Does it really matter what we do?"

"When you do it on the streets yes," he went to interrupt me until I cut him off, "No point in trying to shut me up, you know I'm right." His girlfriend said something to him, and he walked up the street. She looked up and said, "You are too wise, too young."

"When he breaks it, don't forgive his worthless heart. If it means you have to do it in absentia do it, that guy is vermin."

I thought could see a tear starting to form in the corner of her eye, so I asked her.

"Do you want to come up for a drink?" she started to walk over to the door and we buzzed her in. she walked up and we were waiting by the door when she got to us. When she got to us, she asked, "What do you have to drink?"

"She is Estonian, so all we have is some vodka." She stepped in and the Estonian poured her a glass.

"Estonian?" she looked over, "But you're English, how did you 2 end up living together in Paris?"

"It's a long and complicated story," the Estonian said, "But the fact of the matter is that we need each other; and we don't want to live in our home countries right now."

"What is Tallinn like?"

"In the winter it's really beautiful, I saw it for the first time when I was 14."

She looked a little bewildered at both of us before asking, "is that the first time you met each other?"

we looked at each other to confirm from one another, "We met just over a week before that in London." We said simultaneously, the bewildered look she had turned to pure confusion. Before she had chance to say anything I closed it with, "We did say it was complicated." The Estonian then brought us back to why we invited her up.

"Do you still want that drink?" the French girl smiled, about 2 minutes later we each had a shot glass of Viru Valge.

"What is it the Russians say? Nostrovia? Is that right?" the Estonian shook her head,

"We get this all the time, it's Na Zdorovie."

The French girl clutched her glass a little looser, we all touched glasses and declared,

"Na Zdorovie!"

The French girl coughed quite badly after taking her shot,

"FUCK!! How can you both drink that?! That shit is horrible!" we started laughing hysterically at her

"Shit!"

"Fancy another I asked her." I asked her while trying to recapture my composure.

"No, no, nnnnnnnnnnnnnnnnnnnoooooooooooooooooooooooooo

I should head home in a second."

"How far is it to your house?"

"It is only a 3 minute walk from here, I live on Rue Milton."

"Does your boyfriend live there?"

"He is visiting from Lyon, when I get back I shall leave his things on the door step. He won't say anything the person in the apartment next to me is a doorman,"

"A doorman,"

"Yes, doorman; he is a doorman at a nightclub. I will be fine."

We said goodbye and as she was walking down the stairs she shouted out,

"That vodka has an interesting aftertaste."

"Take care." Was all I said back, I turned and walked back into the flat. As I started to sort things out she asked me, "What have we got planned tomorrow?"

"You got class and I'm going to sort out the flat, tidy it up a bit." She agreed with a nod. I put the washing up in the sink and filled it up with hot soapy water.

"I'm going to bed." I said. She was already having a shower; I had just heard the water running. I walked into the bathroom and brushed my teeth, as she got out of the shower I got in. Done in 2 minutes flat, I walked out of the bathroom, and got into bed.

"I'm going to finish this paper for class tomorrow."

"O.K," I said, "I'm going to muse

over the world." And before I knew it
I was gone for the night.

Day 34

I was leaning against the kitchen side, the heat was almost as unbearable as being. I opened the windows and drew the fly curtains, if I were to wait long enough I'm sure that I would watch them hit the fabric; but waiting is a long time. She was still asleep, I didn't want to wake her up. We both had the day to ourselves and I really wanted to take her to this quaint little Italian restaurant down in the 15th I had overheard someone mention it on the metro. I was eating an apple, trying to be quiet, failing in the process. There were a few glasses that needed to be washed up; I ran the hot tap, she could never get things cleaned properly.

I put the glasses in the sink, turned off the tap when my phone rang. It was in the bedroom next to her; I knew it she was to beat me to answering it then I'd receive hell. I raced in, reached out and grabbed the phone; it was only then that I realised she was still asleep. I looked at the number, +49 was that a German number?

"Hello?"

"Aha, you do still have the same number." It was Erin; I hadn't spoken to her in a while so it was nice to hear her husky voice.

"Aha? Have you been watching Alan Partridge?"

"Mmmhmmm, anyway - where on this beautiful planet are you living at the moment?"

"I'm in, sorry. We're living Paris at the moment. Why?"

Her mother was saying something in the background I couldn't fully hear what was being said.

"Put your mother on." I said, she put her hand over the phone, and around 30 seconds later I heard her mother say,

"Hello you,"

"Good morning," I said back, "She is as always quite excitable. So what is going on?"

"Erin wants to know if she can come and stay for a while in a couple of weeks."

"I don't see any reason why she couldn't, when did you have in mind?"

"We go away to Dublin for a week in a few hours. She wants to prove to us that she is mature enough to go away by herself. I asked her where she could go by herself other than to see her Grandmother in Salzburg."

"And she suggested me."

"Yeah, that is her great plan."

I thought about it for a minute, before I decided that I would let her stay.

"I'm in Paris these days, so it will be easier for her to just get the train from Köln to Gare Du Nord, and I shall collect her there."

Erin's mother put her hand over the phone and said something that I couldn't understand, there was a slight pause before I heard Erin scream with joy. Then I just about heard Erin say to me,

"I'm so excited!"

"I gathered that."

"I'll see you in 2 weeks! I'll phone you on my way here." She then just screamed down the phone.

"OK that was just loud." She screamed again before,

"Sorry." She started to calm down.

"Is there anything that you want to do while you're here?"

"Go to places from films, can we go to Les Deux Moulins, Pont De Bir-Hakeim. I want to look out from Sacré-Cœur, there are so many things that I want to do."

"Make a list and we shall work our way through it sweetheart."

"I will. TAKE CARE!"

"See you in a couple of weeks." She had to have the last scream,

"LOVE YOU!!"

"Love you aswell." I said back to her with my head about a foot away from the phone. I hung up, looked over at the Estonian whom I had woken up.

"Sorry." The look that she gave back to me was one that said my apology had not been accepted, I waited to see just what response I was going to get back.

"I was having a really wonderful dream,"

"Were you?" Her head did nod.

"Yes, I was a dolphin. I was swimming around in a phosphorous sea, eating mackerel. Then you came along answered the phone and shat in my blow hole." My sheer look of confusion was all that struck her.

"I don't think I did," I said before adding, "I would have remembered doing something like that."

"Well you did, and that is the end of this conversation. What are we doing together today?" I sat down at the foot of the bed with my back to her, reaching over to the pile of clothes that needed to be put away; I picked up a pair of socks. While putting them on and getting dressed I said,

"I was going to take you to that Italian restaurant that I heard about down in the 15th, beyond that I'm not sure if we have any plans." She reached past me and picked up a t-shirt, I think it was one of mine; before I had chance to add to what I had said she said,

"Can you pass me some underwear; I need something to go with what I'm wearing."

I thought about what she had just said before saying

"Don't you already have a pair on?"

"Yes, but they don't match with my clothes today." I turned to face her,

"The ONLY person who is going to see your choice of panties today is me; and I quite frankly couldn't care less as to what you are to wear." She reached past me and took a white pair, the pair that she was wearing quite ungracefully flew over my head and landed to the left side of our clothes pile. She got up and went over to the clothes pile, she started to hunt through the array; rooting her way right down to the bottom.

"What are you looking for?" I asked, her hands and eyes didn't stop looking.

"My white dress, it really shows off my features."

"You mean your ass?"

"Yeah, my best feature. Have you seen the girl who lives in the flat below?"

"I was the one who told you about her, I thought that black women had ghetto booties?"

"I don't think that her boyfriend grabs her ass when he fucks her. Then again, you don't do it to me."

"I don't fuck you, so I guess that I don't." she eventually found the dress, slipped it over her head and turned to face me,

"So how do I look?" she gave a twirl,

"Well; your hair is a mess, you

need to brush your teeth, I CAN see a slight tracing of hair out of the side of your panties and you have a huge clump of sleep in your right eye. Other than all that you look gorgeous." She saw the sentiment in my analysis, and went to the bathroom. I finished getting dressed, just as I put on my T-shirt she asked,

"Who was on the phone, am I taking it that we're having someone to stay? I hope it's nobody from your family."

"No, and do you think it's quite bad that nobody has phoned me while I've been out here?" She rinsed out her mouth, spat down the sink,

"Were you expecting your father to have called? He won't phone as it'll cost him more while you're here, tight man. Where is your shaver?"

"It's in there, you'll find it." I heard things get moved around, when it suddenly occurred to me as to what she was going to do with it. I raced to the bathroom, smashing myself into the door frame,

"SHIT! That hurt. Don't even think about it." I was too late and she was midway through doing it. She stopped, turned and said,

"Better."

"Are we good to go?" I asked, she looked at me and we started to walk towards the front door.

I locked the door behind us; just before we started to walk down the stairs we heard footsteps coming up from the bottom.

"Breakfast on who guesses wrong?" I asked, within an instant she said back,

"The old Asian lady who lives above us, we'll be out of here before she reaches our flat."

"It's the black lady who lives below us." We started to walk down, she went a few steps ahead of me crouched down, looked and was only able to shake her head and say,

"Shit." I caught up with her to watch the black lady unlocking the door to the flat below us,

"She has a horrible ass that just falls away from the rest of her."

We got to the bottom of the staircase and exited into the street, we walked across the road and into the bakery.

"Bonjour,"

"Bonjour, elle passera commande aujourd'hui et je te demanderais à propos du poste de boulanger."[27]

I turned to her and said, "Brioche and something else, do surprise me please." The look on her face was one of pure annoyance at being wrong.

"Désolé pour ça, elle a perdu un pari."[28] She smiled, "Le poste est-il

---

[27] Good morning, she will be ordering today and I'll be asking you about the baker's job.

[28] Sorry about that, she lost a bet.

toujours à pourvoir?"[29]

"Oui, ça l'est toujours. À propos, tu parles très bien français pour un anglais."[30]

"Merci. Je peux postuler?"[31]

"You are the only person to have applied for it, when can you start?"

"Is midnight OK for you?" she nodded her head, "The kitchen never actually shuts, if you want to take something simple that is fine. What would you rather do?"

"If I can just do my own thing that would be great. I normally just plug my iPod in and work by myself."

"Is there anything that you specialise in?" I turned to her and asked, "What is the French for biscuits?"

"Biscuits" I motioned back to the bakery owner before the Estonian had her input, "He's really good, you have to try his biscuits they are better than anything else you would have tried." She smiled at her, rotated her eyes back to me,

"I will see you at midnight, sorry you didn't say your name."

"You'll never forget me, so you'll never need to know my love."

She smiled at me, unknowing that I don't like to give out my name that

---

[29] Is the job still going?

[30] It is, by the way you speak very good French for an Englishman.

[31] Thank you, can I apply for it?

easy. Women's intuition. The Estonian was waiting outside; I got to the door and said,

"Thank you." her reply was concise.

"Your welcome." I don't think I had heard a French woman speak English willingly, I find it hard enough some days to get a word of French out of them. I walked out of the store, she handed me a brown bag,

"votre petit-déjeuner," I took the bag, "Are we going to walk down to the 15th?" I tilted her head upwards,

"Why would we walk to the 15th on a day as beautiful as today?" I knew she was annoyed by the comment that I gave her, she just didn't want to show it.

We started to walk down the street towards the church, she looked up at it all the way round until we had got to the other side of the church. When she had to pay attention to the road again she asked,

"Have I ever asked you what you think of God?" we crossed the road pretty quickly as the countdown said we only had 17 seconds.

"You've got a very different idea on God to me." We had made our way to the other side of the street as we meandered our way through the streets past Gare St-Lazare and towards the Arc De Triomphe and into the 16th.

"If God put us here to test us he very much is doing that?" we were waiting on the corner of Haussmann and Courceelles.

"I know what you're going to say." She said,

"That we see nothing but the bad in each other, man looks at man and if the other man has what he wants he tries to put him down to make himself feel better about his lack of existence in this world. I know that isn't saying why I don't believe there is a God, but what kind of God would allow man to divide and segregate into classes and then allow those who claim to be better to act like they are better? Just because they have more money? If people are equal, we don't have to respect our elders. Wisdom doesn't come from age; wisdom comes from… well I don't know what wisdom comes from. My point is, if there was a god he at no point designed us to experience life like this." By the time I had finished saying what I had said we were looking at the Arc De Triomphe.

"Your voice changed so much during that, it was hard to keep up with what you were saying."

"Sorry, this is pretty much the end of the world. Humans have become a parasite on the earth that won't survive beneath our feet long after we die."

"That had no relevance to anything did it?" she said, "You were just ranting for the sake of ranting weren't you?"

"Yeah. Come on, let's go walk across Bir-Hakeim. I'll feel better after that."

Life is short and I don't know it's point or purpose, I was never going to lie to her about that at least.

"God is whatever you want God to be to you. How you see God and how I see God are very different. Which is guess is why they say God made man in his own image."

"So how do you see God?" She asked,

"He's a twisted fuck." We walked around the Arc clockwise getting ready to enter the 16th via Avenue Kleber, "Worship me and I'll treat you like shit because I can."

"I think you're missing something in that."

"I expect that I am," I said, "But right now it's not really apart of my agenda." We looked at the Eiffel Tower from afar,

"You know we were never meant to look at it, it took 2 years to make and he only wanted it up for a single year."

"Bit ironic isn't it." We carried on walking down Kelber, breaking off just before the Palais De Chaillot. We stood on Avenue De New York looking at the Seine, I couldn't see Pont Bir-Hakeim, behind the other bridge. We walked along under the trees which were in full bloom, the tourists walked around us; it made me feel like a stranger in a strange land.

"Why do you like Pont Bir-Hakeim so much?" I shrugged,

"To be honest with you I'm not really sure, could be the things with films, but then again I do love the structure and the layout of it. Of all the bridges in the world that I've seen this is so much better than anything." I was finally able to see it, I climbed up onto the bank; looked down at her,

"Want a hand?" she reached out and I helped her up, she squinted her eyes as the sun was reflecting on the river,

"I'm no fucking Buddhist but the view is something close to enlightenment."

"I have to agree, it's seriously beautiful. I'm not sure if I even know the English word to say what I think of it."

"Do you know what it is in French?"

"transcender, I don't know if that is it. But it is close."

"Transcending. I guess I can see why you would use a word like that."

"If anything were to have changed, what would it be?" she asked,

"Nothing." We carried on walking along the wall, a series of groans came from her walking behind me, like she was a mechanic giving an M.O.T to a middle class woman's Jag, ready to rip her off for every broken pound that he could.

"Why would you change nothing? Most people say they would change this and change that, why not?" I got down I wasn't trying to manoeuvre my way around that random statue.

"It's that thing that by changing one little thing, if I were to bring her back. I don't know… things would be so different. We wouldn't be here, Erin most likely wouldn't be coming and I wouldn't have lost my innocence." She grabbed me on the shoulder,

"I could live until I'm 100 and I'll never meet another person in this world like you will I?" I grabbed her around the hip and we carried on walking.

"I very much doubt that I'm an original entity, but this is a world where nothing is original."

"Was you or was it someone else who told me the quote, It's not where you take things from - it's where you take them to."

We eventually came to Bir-Hakeim, standing directly in the middle of the bridge, looking down towards the 15th, I looked at her dodger blue eyes looking down the symmetrical structure with pure wonder.

"I see why you love this bridge so much, it's so beautiful." Was said in a long and drawn out way. We walked across the bridge, and down Boulevard De Grenelle right down to the roundabout when she grabbed my hand,

"Like shit we're going to walk around this, I'll show you a short cut to César Franck, and just so we're clear it's in the 7th."

"Huh?" we walked along some street of which I didn't read its name. turning down Avenue De Suffren we walked south and come the 3rd right we arrived at Rue César Franck, I looked up at the street sign.

"I fucking knew I was right." She looked a little confused, "7th my arse. What were we betting on this? Are you going to be spending more out on lunch for 2 as well?" quick as a snap she replied with,

"No, No. you insisted on bringing me down here, we shall dine and you shall pay." I couldn't argue the matter, it was annoying yet amusing the way we would flicker between who had the upper hand. It's a blasé thing but it was something that kept us going through our existence with one another.

"Are you sure this is the place?" she asked, "It doesn't look much like a restaurant does it." I opened the door and said,

"Shall we go inside?" she looked up at the sign on the glass,

"Da Stuzzi, this is either going to be quaint and cute or really awful. Either way you're paying." She walked in first and I closed the door as I followed behind her, we were greeted by a very fashionable Italian lady in her early 30's standing behind a deli counter, she smiled before saying,

"Welcome." I smiled and she said,

"Can we sit anywhere?" she motioned with her hand that we could sit anywhere, there was a couple sat in the window we looked closer to the door and sat at a long table, which in hindsight was a harsh thing to do, but we don't like to be seen as a couple.

"You're not French are you?" she asked,

"No, and from your accent you're Italian but you speak English better than most." She looked at me, "Do you want to share a bottle of wine?"

"We can drink the rest tomorrow night as I start the job at midnight."

"We'll have it before we go out tomorrow night." I looked at her and asked,

"Can we have a bottle of white wine?"

"Italian?" she asked; I smiled,

"Thank you very much." she walked off to get a bottle of wine and left us be.

Day 41

We were stood on the bridge looking up at Notre-Dame, she interlocked her arm with mine,

"I read somewhere, the Germans wanted to blow it up. The man they left with the detonator, he couldn't bring himself to destroy the building. He felt it was too beautiful for nobody to ever see it again. Then again, it sounds like a myth." I turned and started to walk away, she slowly caught up but her dodger blue eyes were enraptured by the architecture.

We walked into the 5th, while standing on Montebello she asked,

"Are we going to act like total tourists and go along the river bank? Or, can we weave in and out of the streets to wherever it is that we're walking to before we go home?"

"Do you want to lead the way?" I asked her, there was a smile on her face,

"There is nothing better than to see a city away from the tourist." She grabbed my hand, and started running across the road with traffic heading towards us on both sides. A Volvo almost clipped me on the heel, as I made it onto the pavement I gave him the finger; I'm certain he saw. We walked along turning off on

Boulevard St-Michel, as we walked down she pointed out a few buildings that I snapped with the expense of holding up traffic. I didn't care. I took a picture of a couple of women sat on their balcony, each drinking a glass of wine.

"Did you ever see Only Fools And Horses?" I asked her, a brazen smile crossed her face, she turned to a business man walking towards her,

"You plonker Rodney!" I had to laugh, as the man walked on by knowing that he was very much outside of the castle of knowing to what had just been said to him. "I love it, I only saw it for the first time a few years ago." We stopped in the midst of the asphalt as people walked around us like we were the centre of attention at a forensic scene. We each let our eyes get glazed over as we got lost in the features of the other. Her eyes looked past me towards Jardin Du Luxembourg,

"Can we go inside?" she asked, I looked over where a group of lads that clearly had just left school were walking in with a 4 pack of cheap French beers. "I'm sure that it will be tranquil."

"There is a wine store just round the corner."

"Is there?"

"We're in Paris, there has to be a wine store in the next few streets." She pulled up a fist, I knew exactly what she had in mind.

"1, 2, 3." We both revealed, she looked down confident with the same rock that she plays every time, unaware of the paper that I play each and every time she insists we play this repetitive game.

"You can't do the same move every single time we have to do this. Can you?" she walked over to a father with his daughter walking their Belgian Sheppard. I was watching as she asked and I felt that the dog was quite unfairly treated given that she still had all her hair, underneath all that fur she must have been sweating like there was no tomorrow. She walked back to me, grabbed my hand, hers were soft but starting to dry out.

"There's one, just down here." Pointing down a street that I had never walked down; so the name eluded me. "He said that we should be able to buy a bottle quite cheap and that they will take the cork out for us."

"So why are we stood here?" she looked at me, "You could have told me that while we were walking to the shop." We walked down, it could have only been 6 or 700 yards down the road when we came to it. We walked into a 12 foot high room, wine bottles stacked so closely together that it made my eyes blur. The tinges of the bottles reflected off the sun and burnt my eyes. I wasn't even thinking about mum, my sisters, I wasn't even thinking about lost love and how I knew the seconds, minutes, hours and days of my life would slip away from me from days before to the day of my death. When my mind came back to the room I watched her pay for a bottle of white, I didn't recall being consulted about the choice at any stitch in time. She walked back to me,

"What just happened?" I asked, her eyes rolled as she shook her head,

"Your eyes looked like you were in a different pixel of time and space, I tried to ask you but there was no chance you were coming out of it; not with me saying anything." We walked out of the shop after thanking the worker that helped her pick the bottle, on our walk back to Jardin Du Luxembourg she passed the comment, "I was tempted to slap you, don't know if it would have done anything; guess we'll never know now." We came to the entrance to the park, as we walked in a series of joggers nearly knocked us over I looked over as they continued on their pointless circuit, only to shout out,

"PRICKS!" A couple looked back, but nobody came to confront me. As we walked through we looked at all the families, I feared it was going to rattle her brain and she'd start mentioning kids, I could barely survive my own company for a day let alone the company of someone that was dependant on me for the next 18 years.

I did give thanks to whatever Gods the other tortured souls of this earth looked to for solace, as she never said a word. We continued our walk through the park, if anyone were to have come looking for me, they would never suspect me to be here. In a very famous park, a tourist spot to say the least. We sat down, keeping the bottle of wine hidden, you could never tell if there were plain clothed police in the terrain. An Asian family sat opposite us, they were all wearing anti-pollution masks. I don't know why but I was really offended by it, all 8 of them; spanning 3 generations from grandparents who must have been in their 80 to the children who couldn't have been any older than 7 or 8. She asked me,

"Why are they wearing anti-pollution masks? Paris isn't an industrial city to the extent that Beijing or Shanghai are, you can see the sun and the sky here. There's being safe, and there's being paranoid." I did wonder if she had an opinion on them, guess I didn't even need to ask. We passed the bottle of wine back and forth, comfortable enough that we didn't even complain about the saliva that the other would leave. The order of repetition of which we had created.

"What is it called when you see pictures in the clouds?" I asked her

"I'm not sure, but when you see clouds forming Munch's The Scream do let me know. I'd love to photograph it." Before she finished with, "When I say I'll photograph it, it will be taken with your camera." Shock, I thought to myself. We continued to watch the Asian family as they shared a bottle of water, barely making their lips visible from lifting the masks.

"There's something so tragic about them, they fly some 5,000 miles to make themselves feel the exact same as what they did back in China. It's just a case of the same shit, different surroundings." She took the bottle from me, and uttered after reaching the halfway point with the bottle.

"Some people are only happy when they are trapped inside their comfort zone." We'll never be like that, me and her are 2 undesired souls. I see her falling in love with someone else, getting married. This is just her preparation to realise that men are just as fucked up as women, and whoever she marries is no better or worse than me.

"In bed," I started, "When you turn away from me, your figure is like that of Scarlett Johansson." She spat out her wine over a flock of pigeons that were feasting a few feet away from us, as they scarpered away she looked at me only to ask,

"Do you look at my underwear?"

"Lost in Translation, the Gods made a masterpiece with her body." She stood up, handed me the wine and we carried on.

We stuck to the path, following it south, the joggers kept on going; they were enough to drive any man insane. We looked around, it was then that we saw the group of school kids from 10 minutes prior, they had downed a few of their tiny bottles of beer. As we continued through the park we looked at the different groups of people who had all chosen this park as their sanctuary for the day. I pointed at a group of 10 kids playing a game of football, one team were all wearing PSG shirts and the others had the Lyon away shirt,

"We used to do that." I said

"What? Have a perfect segregation of teams, I thought you said none of your friends supported the same team as you?"

"Not that, though that is a great idea. I can't believe that we never had 2 simple colours and did teams that way." Such an ingenious system these French kids had thought up, "No, we would use jumpers and bags as goal posts." We watched the game progress; the French had a youth game that would very easily match the

Brazilians and the Germans.

"I have a question for you." She said, I looked at her. "If they are just using their jumpers as goalposts, how do they know if the ball has gone over the crossbar or not?" I tried to think back to when I was 10 years old and what we would do, then it came to me.

"You would just use your own judgement, it more taught you to play the ball into corners." We stood watching the game, she was holding the bottle when the ball came towards us; I did a few tricks as one of the kids wearing a Lyon shirt came over,

"Mr, if we both took the ball out of play what do we do?"

"You have a drop ball, it is the fairest way."

"You are English, who is your team?" he asked, before I had chance to answer he started listing teams, "Chelsea, Manchester United, Liverpool…" before he had chance to say any more I interrupted him to tell him,

"Tottenham." He looked at me like I had just said the name of a non-league club. He called out to his friends,

"We start from a drop ball, does anyone know Tottenham?" He asked his friends, most of them remained quiet. There was 1, he was wearing a PSG top who gave an indication that he knew.

"My sister is a fan, she says they

are too unlucky." I gave a nod,

"At the moment they are not doing very well, but things will pick up. They play entertaining football at least."

They stood around me, I had become the referee by default.

"2 players, everyone else 5 yards." They all stepped back, "I'll bring you lads back into play and then I must go, as much as I'd love to be playing like Cruyff or Zidane with you all. We have things to do."

"Another time." One of them shouted out,

"One bounce then the play continues." I held the ball at my shoulder height and dropped the ball, as I did the kid who was by me wearing the Lyon shirt jumped. As the ball hit the grass and came up he used the outside of his left foot to play the ball back to his team mate, who on the half volley pelted the ball, causing it to curve with such intensity that it rendered the goalkeeper useless as the ball glided straight past him. As the keeper walked back to collect the ball defeated I saluted the goal scorer who in turn gave his thanks for the assist. I walked back to her, she stood there wine bottle in hand. I put my arm around her waist, looked back and as we gave a wave to the kids who waved before continuing with their game.

"They are some very talented kids."

"The keeper didn't do much did he?" she said, I had to correct her,

"He didn't stand a chance, the keeper can't always be given the blame. Sometimes the players produce sheer magic that leaves even the best keepers in the world as spectators."

We returned to the path, making our way to the west exit. We took a slight detour that made us go slightly north, there were less people which made me happy. Paris is a crowded city, so it's nice to find isolated spots every now and again to be in a point of solitude. There were a couple of women sat on the grass with 3 children, 2 girls and a boy. They were all only between 5 and 10, they boy was chasing after a football, when he arrived he would kick it in a random direction and chase after the ball. I kicked the ball to him and he kicked it back to me, I walked closer to his mother gently kicking the ball when we made it to his mother I said,

"Parlez-vous anglais?"

"Oui."

"You have an adorable son, can I show him how to kick the ball properly?" The Estonian sat down with the girls and started talking French with them, she passed the Wine to the mother who poured a little into the glass for herself. I asked the mother,

"Can you tell him to kick the ball with the side of his foot so it's more controlled." She had a smiled on her lips,

"You will have to show him, he learns things better that way." I sat down next to him, and showed him with my foot where he needed to be kicking. I watched him slowly get to grips with it, it was quite inspiring to watch a child learn to do something that I do as an automatic action. The child came back over and sat down next to his mother, she was having a conversation with the Estonian, when the mother asked,

"So, how long have you to been a couple?" we both started laughing,

"We look out for each other, we share a bed, but we're not together." She finished her glass of wine,

"Shame, you look so fitting." I wasn't sure if she were taking the piss or not. Guess it was something that I wasn't going to find out. "So why are you both in Paris?" we looked at one another, waiting for the other to give an answer. I started to laugh,

"She is studying, and I'm escaping the world. I'm loving the wine, time with her, more importantly just being a stranger in a strange land." She smiled, her attention was drawn back to her daughter. I looked at her, gave a look that we should leave. She gave a look that agreed with my look.

"We have to leave, he has to cook me dinner." The 2 daughters jumped up and hugged her,

"We'd love to spend some more time with you, if we give you our number you can always phone us." I added, the mother handed her phone to the Estonian, she added our digits, before we waved goodbye and the kids waved back. We shared a kiss with the mother and her sister before we left the park.

As we exited we walked around to Rue D'Assas, I began to wonder; which I exclaimed outloud,

"What is the easiest way to Bir Hakeim?"

"Garibaldi, was the street named after a biscuit or is a person named after the biscuit?" I had to roll my eyes, if I had been able to slam my head on a table I would have done.

"When you say things, sometimes… the word TWAT just barges its way to the front of my mind." She looked so offended as we crossed the street, "Was he named after a biscuit, do you not hear ***JUST*** how stupid that sounds?" sometimes she refuses to admit defeat, this was one of those times.

"It's not a stupid question."

"To name someone after a biscuit? they will be rinsed day and night for that. There are things that you say that are so blonde it makes me feel like the most intelligent person in our flat." We walked around to Garibaldi pretty much in silence, by the time we had made it to Bir Hakeim our silence had pretty much resolved us of whatever conflict was brewing.

"Do you want to walk the rest or would you rather catch the Metro?"

"We only planned to walk this far," before she added, "If we walked all the way home, it might be like we're cheating ourselves out of what our original plans were." She had a point, so we walked into the metro station.

Day 67

We stood inside Gare Du Nord, the 4 of us with one purpose. There were 8 minutes until the train left, I was holding Erin's things. I had my own things to carry as well though it didn't feel like I had the weight of half the world. I held both of our tickets, I had to take her home. I didn't like to leave the Estonian at home by herself; this was something that had to be done.

"Thank you for putting up with my esoteric ways." Erin made me laugh with the way she said things to the Estonian.

"Phone me when you get home, I won't be able to sleep until I know that you are safe." They hugged each other, when they let go I said to the Estonian,

"She is with me,"

"That is a problem, given the things that you have done for me in the past." The journalist put her hand out to Erin, there was that look in her eyes and I knew she wanted more. The apathy that the earth projected on the days that passed, wasn't noticed by us in that moment of time.

"Oh no, I've waited too long I'm not going to settle for less than what I want." Erin moved the journalist hand to the side stepped in and went to work. We both knew that she had wanted to do such an act from the moment that she first laid eyes on her, Erin wasn't alone in the desire to do such a thing; she however is the only person to undisclosed her thoughts about the journalist.

A good period of time passed in their kiss, I'm surprised that she didn't try to frig her off. When their lips divorced I said to them,

"We should walk to the train." As our 8 feet shuffled up towards platform 8, Erin and myself had come full circle. 19 days earlier I had collected her, we had created havoc on the continent. A lot of wine had been consumed, and the 3 of us had grown as people.

"So… you really did want to kiss me didn't you?" The journalist wasn't too bothered by the way Erin kissed her,

"What can I say? You're a night I'd like to have." I could tell that Erin was about to do something, I just wasn't sure what. She handed me the last of her bags,

"AU REVOIR PARIS!! Well sadly I didn't get to fuck any housewives, but that is why I will be back!!" Her voice was able to echo off all the walls, so while everyone was looking at her, she shared a final hug and kiss with both the Estonian and the journalist. As she got onto the train to find our seats, I kissed the Estonian,

"I'll try and get back tonight, if not it will be in the morning." The slight smile that came across her face was brief, she waited until I hugged the journalist before taking her hand.

"I'll phone you when we get there, if I'm not back look after each other." I stepped onto the train; just before the doors shut I kissed the Estonian.

"You always did." She said,

"I did." Was my reply as the doors closed, and the train departed.

I went and sat down next to Erin, her feet slotted across my lap. We didn't talk much on the train over to Köln, I was surprised by the lack of border control. I did wonder if this was how all the Turks got into Germany, what is the point in flying? When you can go through undetected by train.

Part of the way in, I think we were close to Liege, Erin asked me about The Bell Jar. We spoke for a bit about Plath, and suicide. I told her I had decided to quit drinking, I didn't see the point in being a part of a scene that so many people I once knew were slaves to. I hadn't seen my father sober since I was 13, I realised that the day before. That was the kind of thought that would crawl through my head, leaving my brain fried. Some 4 hours and 30 minutes later, when we arrived in Köln, we walked the 12 minutes to Erin's house. As I rang the bell and I could hear the sound off footsteps racing towards the door, her mother opened the door; she looked the exact same as when I first met her 4 years earlier.

"Come in, come in…" as we walked in, she continued to fire questions at us. "How was she? Did you go up the Eiffel Tower? Did you look after yourself Erin?"

"She was great fun, it was the time the Gods wished they had spent on earth." I reached into my bag, pulling out a box.

"I brought you a little something." She looked surprised, as she opened the box to reveal a snow globe. Her eyes lit up,

"You are too kind." She went and placed it on her shelf full of globes from across Europe, I looked at the cities that I had visited and places that were to be plans.

"How was she?" There was a look that I can only describe as anxious scrawled across her face, I knew that she was asking questions between the lines.

"I wouldn't want to have anyone else come and stay, am I able to stay tonight?"

"Of course, you'll be cooking

tonight however.” Erin had started to play Target by Fugazi, as I walked to the kitchen and opened the cupboards to see what I had to work with.

Day 38

I woke up and crawled out of bed, she was already up and packing her bag ready for class.

"Good morning, what have you got planned today?"

I shrugged, my mouth was dry and I needed a drink. I walked to the kitchen and picked up the first glass that came to my hand, it had remnants of wine from 3 days ago. I tipped the little bit it had left away, before rinsing the glass out and filling her up with water. I turned to face her again,

"Now I feel better, sorry what did you say?"

"What have you got planned today?" again I shrugged,

"Nothing, I might head up to Guy Môquet. I'm not going to be in the flat for long." She kept looking at me and I couldn't for the life of me work out why.

"What is it?"

She shook her head, looked down and then looked up again;

"I don't mind you walking around our flat in just your boxers, but please either walk like a crab to the bathroom or readjust it so I don't have to see it as prominently." I looked down to discover morning glory was at full mast. I pointed at her, changed my answer before I had even begun to say anything. "I'll get right on it." Was all I ended up saying, and with that I ended up walking to the bathroom.

I return to the bedroom and hunted around for some clothes that smelt clean, the constant action and reaction of picking pieces of clothing up sniffing them before tossing them to one side. After finding a semi clean pair of jeans, I eventually found a blue t-shirt with something faded on it, I threw that on as she walked into the room,

"Ma just praegu sain millestki aru."[32]

"Sorry I didn't get that, what did you say?"

"You've had the same pair of underwear on for like 3 days now?"

"The rest are in the wash, what am I suppose to do?"

"Every single pair?"

"Hate to break it to you, but yes."

She went over to her drawers and started to rummage through,

"What are you doing?" I was ignored. She turned back to face me holding a pair of black boy-shorts.

"No," I shook my head, "not a chance."

"They smell and you ARE wearing them. You're a writer not a homeless person." I huffed, "Fine."

[32] I've just realised something.

"You rip them because of your cock, you buy me a new pair. You wank in them, you will most definitely be buying me a new pair."

"Fine." I put them on, walked back to the kitchen and collected a few things to eat, stuffed them all into my bag and headed towards the front door.

"You coming with me?" I shouted out, she walked past and merely said, "Oui." Opening the door I slipped through, she closed it right before I locked up as she was waiting by the staircase. We descended together for the first flight in silence before she asked,

"When are you going to ask this journalist around?"

"I don't know, I'm not even too sure how old she is. She looks a lot younger than what I suspect she is. It's very deceiving."

"How old do you think she is?"

"She looks no more than 21, but from the way she asks questions and how she acts I'd say she was closer to if not 25."

We reached the bottom of the staircase, as we walked to the front door she asked, "Would you fuck her?"

"Sorry?"

"Would you fuck her?"

"I don't know, I think at the moment I wouldn't want to fuck anyone. Why would you be jealous?" She just looked at the door.

"Guess I'll never know unless you were to."

"Come on," I said, "Lets go and carpe diem baby."

"Either a worthwhile usage of Latin or a random dropping of Metallica."

We walked up Rue Des Martyrs; the kids were outside the school smoking, I looked at her and held her hand, as we walked through a voice shouted out towards us.

"Tu peux me passer une cigarette?"[33]

"Sorry, no."

We carried on walking on by, the kid shouted out at us.

"Connard, sais-tu combien c'est dure d'être étudiant?"[34] I let go of her walked up to him, grabbed him by the throat lifting him up against the wall and said through my gritting teeth,

"I said no, then you choose to be rude. If you see us again, you say nothing. Clear?" He nodded his head

"Think it's hard to be a student? Try being a writer." I walked back up to her, grabbed her hand and we continued to walk up the street.

"You didn't need to do that."

"Yes I did, people shouldn't be rude to strangers for no reason. He asked, I said no. That's it you say

---

[33] Can you spare a cigarette?

[34] You prick, do you know how hard it is to be a student?

no more.

She knew that she couldn't argue the matter, so she said nothing. When we arrived at Pigalle metro station I asked, "Do you have enough money to last you the day?"

"I should be ok, if I need anything I'll just head back to the flat. Where are you going to go today?" I looked around scrunched my face and said, "I'll start at Sacré-Cœur and see how I feel, I got some food. Keep your phone on you and if I stop at your lunch break we can meet up." We kissed and she went down the steps to the metro, I walked along the Boulevard De Rochechouart before heading up some street what's name I can't remember, the Indians and Arabs were opening up their shops to get money from the tourists on over-priced crap. It was early enough to miss the immigrants scamming the dim witted tourists, if you were to sit at a café and watch each of them work for a day they could easily earn a couple of hundred euros selling shit that will either break or be pick pocketed. I walked up the steps and looked over the view of the city; the sky was a certain shade of green. There were a few people there taking photos of the cathedral, I put my head phones in scrolled through the iPod before deciding on Head Like A Hole. Just as I was about to press play I received a tapped on the shoulder, I turned to face a woman in her late thirties, "Excusez-moi, parlez-vous anglais?" I had to laugh at her accent; I had never heard an Australian speak French before.

"I do, and try not to enunciate everything; it really does show that you're not confident with your words."

She looked a little surprised, "Can you guess which part?"

"I've not been, so I wouldn't know a Darwin accent from somebody who lives in Adelaide. So anyway, how can I help you?"

"Do you live here or are you just a tourist?"

"You didn't stop me to ask me if I am a tourist."

"You're right," she looked around, "I'm here for a few days and I really want to try some delights from a French bakery. Do you know of any good ones?" I had to nod my head, I pointed back the way I came.

"Follow me," and I started walking; she was just stood there. "Are you coming?" she started to catch up,

"thank you," she said, "Is this not out of your way?"

"I'm not sure, today I have no plans. I think I will go Metro hopping today." She looked a bit bewildered by my day's plans but she followed me nonetheless. I walked back down Rue Des Martyrs, this time there were no school kids outside. I asked, "How long are you in Europe for?"

"About 18 months, I've just got Spain, Portugal and Britain left. Then it will be onto the states and Canada, then down to Belize."

"Why so long in Europe? Come to think of it, why Belize of all places?"

"There are a lot of places in Europe, so many countries and such beauty in the churches and the natural environment. Belize, I know some people who own a sugar plantation, so they make their own rum. Got to try some of that." It was a fair point; she just expressed it like a drunken woman suffering from a midlife crisis.

"Right," I said before adding, "Did you stop off in Estonia?"

"Estonia, Latvia and Lithuania. I loved each of the Baltic States for very different reasons." She said as we approached the patisserie.

"This is the place, Where I work. I wouldn't say it's the best in the city, but it is in the top 1." We walked into the shop as an old man was walking out, I let him pass as he did he raised his hat. On stepping in I added, "I owe a Latvian woman my life, and I'm living with an Estonian." The lady on the counter greeted us,

"Salut."

"Good morning and how are you?"

"I am excited, today after work I am going to the cinema."

"What are you planning on watching?"

"The film on Ché…"

"The Motorcycle Diaries."

"Yes, it is showing in Opéra. So I am going with a girl friend."

"We have no plans this evening, maybe we could join you?"

"That would be nice. Right, what are you after?" I looked at the Australian, "What are you thinking looks good?"

"I have no idea as to what was said, but I really want something French." I turned my attention back to the girl on the counter, "3 brioche rolls, 2 brownies, a pain au chocolat and," I turned to the Australian, "you just have to try these." Before adding, "3 Paris Brest."

"Three?"

"I'm meeting her for lunch so I shall take her one. That is all."

"€11.40 all together."

"How much do I owe you?" the Australian asked,

"€4.20. But you have to savour the taste and texture of the Paris Brest." She gave me a €10 note and wouldn't accept the change that I was trying to give.

"I will see you tonight lapochka."

"8.00 we shall wait for you in the foyer to the cinema."

"Lovely, see you then. Bye."

"Have a good day."

We walked out of the shop; I looked around for the nearest Metro station.

"I was distracted by the pastries. What on earth did you two talk about?" she asked,

"We arranged to meet up tonight to watch The Motorcycle Diaries together." I located the nearest Metro station at the bottom of the street, just behind the church. "I have to go, so it was lovely to meet you; enjoy your stay in Europe and stay safe."

She put out her hand,

"Thank you very much for your help, and I hope you have a lovely evening with her." We shook hands and with that, we set off in our separate directions. She walked back up the way we came; I put the headphones back into my ears and pressed play and head down the street towards Norte-Dame-De Lorette Metro station. Down the steps all the while reaching into my pocket, placing the pass on the sensor just as the chorus kicked in. I head to the southbound platform; the next train was only 2 minutes away, though it did feel like longer. I got on looked around and decided not to sit down, as I could be more spontaneous with both getting on and off the trains. The 12 line south, I watched the stations go - Trinité – d'Estienne d'Orves, Saint-

Lazare, Madeleine, Concorde went passed and I decided to change at the next junction onto another line. I played the waiting game for another 4 stops until I came to Sèvres – Babylone. At which point I jumped off; and headed west on 10 line to Duroc. The sad thing about the Metro is that nobody talks to each other; people can be together all day and the second they get onto the Metro they become different people.

From Duroc, I headed north to Invalides where I made my way up to the gates to phone her.

"Hey," she said upon picking up.

"What is the nearest Metro station to you?"

"I'm by Gare Du Nord, Shall we do lunch at Notre-Dame?"

A picnic by the cathedral, what a pleasant way to spend the afternoon, sat down by Notre-Dame cathedral with her.

"I'll get a bottle of wine." I added,

"That'll be good, I'll be waiting you'll see me."

She hung up and with that I ran back down the stairs and got on the rapid train to St-Michel Notre-Dame.

When I came up back onto the streets, the sunlight blinded me having only experienced artificial lights for the last couple of hours; I went down Rue De Jacques where I knew there was a good, but relatively cheap wine shop. I walked in, there was a couple looking at champagne and expensive bottles of wine, and I found them to be quite pretentious asking to try the bottles to see what they like. I picked up a bottle of white, and headed toward the till smiling at the lady helping with the other couple; she came over and said, "Just this?"

"Yes," was my response before adding "Is there any chance you can open the bottle for me?"

"€4.50 and yes that is fine. Do you want to buy some glasses?" I had to laugh at the comment saying, "We're teenagers who can barely afford our rent let alone glasses." It got the attention of the couple who seemed quite annoyed I had taken their sommelier away from them. She smiled as she opened the bottle.

"You're not French are you?"

"I'm English, but I do live here."

"It's a nice bottle, so enjoy it; and enjoy your date."

I had to correct her, "It's not a date. She looks after me."

"Well, have a nice time."

"I shall. Merci, au revoir."

"Au revoir."

I walked out the store and back towards Notre-Dame where I saw her walking out of the Metro station.

"AHA." I shouted out to her, she turned and waited for me to walk up to her, upon arriving we carried on up to Notre-Dame.

We sat down on the grass, I handed her the bottle of wine as I opened my bag. I pulled out an apple and a peach, weighing up in my mind which was for each of us as she tried to pull the cork out of the bottle.

"Give it here," I said, handing her the peach. "I really don't want to watch you struggle anymore." She looked at the peach in the most quizzical way,

"Why do you always eat apples?"

"An apple a day, keeps the dentist away."

"The dentist, you mean the doctor right?"

"I'm not scared of the doctor, besides apples are full of vitamin C which is good for your gums."

"Hence why I get the peach?"

"I'm sure that a peach contains something good for you." She laughed and started eating it; I took a hit from the bottle before I started on the apple. A few people walked past us, but to them we must have just looked like a couple of students in love. We ate the food that I had inside my bag; the wine slowly went down, hit by hit. We had been silent for about 7 or 8 minutes and at which point I asked her,

"How was class and what were you doing up at Gare Du Nord?"

"I got a little bored with the class today; we had a different teacher who just wasn't able to keep my attention at all. What are we doing tonight?"

"Sorry to hear that," I said as she handed me the quarter full bottle, "But tonight we're going to the cinema."

"What, where, when and who with?" was then asked at lightning fast speed.

"The Motorcycle Diaries, Opéra, we are to be there at 8 and we're watching it with the girl from the bakery."

She smiled, took the bottle back and had a hit;

"That'll be nice, she is a really lovely person."

I returned the bottle to her, returned the cork before putting the bottle in my bag, so I had her full attention.

"I want to know, is this going to get easier? Or am I going to be trying to put on a front to people and have only you seeing me as the fragile person that I am?" She didn't say anything, I didn't give her a chance to say let alone think an answer; I just shouted, "FUCK!!"

"I don't know, I can't answer any questions like that. All I'm going to say to you is, that every day you will just have to rebuild the world; eventually you will learn to fly and learn to love the world again." With saying that she took a hit of the wine, which turned into her finishing it off. I don't think that she even realised that she had done so. I knew she didn't have any of that planned, she couldn't have; I don't think that anybody could be prepared for anything like that.

"Do you have to go back to class?" she nodded, and started to put bits back in her bag. I handed her a few bits that I had taken off her, I stood up first and then helped her up. "Where do you need to head to?"

"I've got to go to République, what are you going to be doing?"

"Back to Metro hopping for me, I think I will join you to there and then see where I want to go."

We started walking back towards the station; she clutched her copy of Ulysses by James Joyce, she said whether to break the silence or not I will never know.

"Do you know what you should do?"

"No, do tell."

"You should throw a stranger an unexpected smile, help an old person, photograph a lonely woman telling her that she is loved and send a tourist in the wrong direction. You know, really make yourself smile."

"Alright, and if I'm able to do all tasks then you are to pay for all 4 cinema tickets."

"Seems like a fair trade." She closed the conversation with as we validated our tickets.

She was walking towards the rapid train, when I grabbed her hand and dragged her in the direction of the 4 line,

"That train is quicker…"

"And in the time we spend waiting for it, we could have got to République." She saw my logic and didn't argue. We got down to the platform, stood facing each other with about 9 inches separating our noses.

"We haven't yet shaken on it." She said, I thought about it before realizing that we hadn't.

"Spit or kiss?" I asked, she moved her head in and we shared an Eskimo kiss.

"Challenge starts now." She said. A backpacker walked up to us and asked in a thick Irish accent,

"Do you know the way to get the train to Amsterdam?" he was looking at her but I had to rise to the challenge and answer for the bet.

"Yeah, you need to get the express Metro C line to Gare d'Austerlitz. They had a big shift and change up of all the train stations, didn't tell anyone caused loads of problems. Almost fully sorted now." He looked like he knew I was lying, but he picked up his bags and said,

"Thank you, I'm heading to Amsterdam to find me some good weed." And with that, he was leaving.

"Why him?" she asked,

"I hate Irish travellers; they just want to get drunk and move from one bar to the next." The train pulled up and we got on, 2 stops and then we were to change to the 11 line. On the walk around to the 11 line, we passed so many people content with just getting to where they needed to be that they missed so much of the world that was around them. I spun my bag round to the front keeping it on my left pulled out my Nikon FE2 before zipping my bag back up.

"Just have to be ready." I said, she hadn't noticed what I had done, looked and then we just carried on to the eastbound platform. There were a few minutes between us arriving at the station and our train arriving, in which time I had circulated my head to see who was getting onto the train. She looked at me only to say, "Which one do you have planned next?" The only reply that I gave was,

"You'll see."

The train rolled in and as everybody got off, we look at each other forgetting it was the end of the line, so as we stood there thinking thoughts like what could these people possibly need to do here? What is so interesting about Châtelet that we have never noticed? We got on to this crowded to the max Metro train, it was hot, sweaty, summer and overfilled. But in we went, like sardines into a fucking tin. Those 4 stops saw very few people get off, and nobody really able to get on. If I were them I would have walked, but I'm not them I'm me; and today I was Metro hopping. We left Art Et Métiers, as we were looking at each other I said,

"Ready for the second?"

"Which one will you try your luck at?" she asked. I could taste her words; there were mere inches between our noses. I could feel that we were almost at République so we moved to the left hand side of the train as we did I said in a raised voice,

"May I have your attention," as people raised there eyes to see what I was going to say I carried on with, "We are just about to leave the train, so you shall all get a little bit more room in which to breathe." The train rolled into the station, "I hope that every single one of you has a divine day, and who knows we might meet each other again one day. Until that day, I shall depart here and leave you with something along with a bon voyage." The doors opened and we stepped out as the train doors closed and departed I pulled an apocalyptic smile. She looked quite shell-shocked by what I had done, all that she could say was,

"2 down, 2 to go."

"Well then make it more of a challenge for me."

"Fine," she snapped, "The lonely

woman has to be at Stalingrad station, and helping an old person can't be inside a station and also no helping people cross the street; that is 1. Too cliché; and 2. Too easy. The last 2 challenges are now set."

"No problem, I can do that." She set off back to class, I couldn't think of where you'd have a class in République. I wasn't going so it wasn't my concern.

I walked around to get the 5 line, as I walked onto the platform the train was leaving;

"Fucking typical." I said to myself. The next train came straight along, it was fairly crowded but I was still able to find myself a seat in and amongst the luggage. Nobody got off at Jacques Bonsergent, a few left at Gare de L'est, but it was at Gare du Nord that I was left by myself in an empty carriage. The next stop was Stalingrad, where my challenge was to take place. I didn't know how to go about it, the minutes flickered away and I wasn't seeing anyone worth photographing or looking lonely. I looked at my clock only to discover that 80 minutes had ticked away, and I was still no closer to finding a lonely woman.

The minutes were wasting away and it varied on who I was to see, between old couples, students and housewives with far too much money on their hands. It was before I knew it,

I was close to encroaching 2 hours and there she sat. How did I let her pass me by? It doesn't matter how; the fact is she is there. I reached into my bag and pulled out my camera, took focus and - SNAP - as I took the picture she looked up, it didn't come out too bad.

"Pourquoi est-ce que vous prenez des moi photos?"[35] she asked, my response was simple,

"You needed to be photographed, you are quite magnificent. I don't know what it is but…" I was cut off with her half shouting,

"I don't like to speak English! Tell me in French or I will smash your camera!" I leaned into her and said, "You are beautiful, you are loved, and this world asked me to tell you so." She wiped the tears away from her eyes, stood up and brushed the dirt off herself.

"Thank you, you are a kind stranger. Whenever I feel down I shall think of you."

"May you remain beautiful until the day this world ends." She put her hand out, I shook her hand and she said,

"This is my train," she reached into her pocket, "This is my card, phone me some when and let me buy you a drink." I put the card into my pocket and closed our encounter with,

---

[35] Why are you taking my picture?

"I'm sure I will do soon enough." She got on her train which was heading towards Riquet; I walked around to get the 2 line west.

I rode the train until I arrived at Nation, where I switched onto the one line up to Gare de Lyon. Quick switch to the 14 line down to Bercy; then the 6 line west to Place d'Italie, before the 5 to the Bastile. Where I ran with the 8 line across the city to Opéra; where the 3 came in very handy up to Villiers, before I was back on the 2 line across and back home to Pigalle.

I walked out of the station, and on my walk back to the flat I saw an old man with a bag of empty bottles walking painfully slow towards a bottle bank. I walked up to him as he was walking and crouched down beside him,

"Puis-je vous aider à recycler les bouteilles? Je ne pense pas que vous avez assez haut pour mettre les bouteilles dans." He looked up at me and smiled,

"Merci, j'allais avoir du mal avant de décider de les laisser pour le ramasseur de poubelles. Mais maintenant je peux rentrer chez moi."[36]

"I feel better for helping you," I

[36] Thank you; I was going to struggle before deciding on leaving them for the bin men. But now I can get home quicker.

said, he gave a warm smile. I then added, "Now the girl that I live with has to buy the tickets at the cinema."

"Aha a woman, I hope you treat her well." I nodded. "And what film are you taking her to?"

"The Motorcycle Diaries, it is about Ché Guevara."

He stood up straight and looked me square in the eye; I just knew he was going to say something important.

"I read that book when I was a bit older than you are, it is so influential. Read it, and become the man you want to be."

"I shall." We shared a handshake, I took his picture and with that, we departed. I walked back down Rue Des Martyrs, as I walked down I pulled my keys out of my bag in perfect time to arriving at my door. I let myself in and walked up the stairs, she was already inside as I entered.

"well?" she asked.

"4 tickets for The Motorcycle Diaries tonight, on… YOU." With a click of my fingers I put my bag on the floor and walked into the bedroom. I found a semi clean shirt; changed to it walked back to the living room only to be confronted with,

"Are they still in one piece?"

"Are what?" She picked up a clean pair of boxers and threw them at me, I subsequently realised what she was going on about.

"Yes they are, and you can have them back…" I walked past her grabbing her hand, "When we return from the cinema." We headed straight out and onto the metro where from Pigalle, we changed at Saint-Lazare and then went straight to Opéra. When we got there, the girl from the bakery was already there. She walked across the road rather excited to join us,

"You made it. Oh, I can't wait to watch the film. My friend shall be here any minute." We got to her and she gave each of us a kiss, before I said,

"She lost a bet, so the tickets are on her tonight." It started to lightly rain, it wasn't going to last long but we stepped into the foyer. The Estonian asked her,

"Your friend does know we are joining you?" she smiled as the door opened and her eyes were directed towards that.

Day 60

I was waiting backstage, the Estonian had a bottle of Grey Goose in her hand. I don't know if she had brought it in, or if someone had left it for me.

"Hand me that would you? Please." Pointing at the bottle, she passed it over to me. I took a shot, Erin was somewhere around; I knew she wouldn't be feeling as nervous as me.

"Do you have your order sorted?" she asked, I took another hit straight from the bottle. I looked at the papers as I clutched them in my hand, I stood no chance in finding an order in which they could be read and work together as 1. I handed her the papers, walking elsewhere I said,

"I need to go for a shit, think I might be sick." I had a serious case of stage fright; I didn't like to perform anything. In my eyes there was no need for art to be performed, you appreciate things in there finished form; the mistakes that are made in live performances are there to ruin a person view and perspective of someone else's art. I had grown to hate painting from seeing them with my own eyes.

I walked back to the Estonian, she was standing there with the papers rearranged; the journalist was sat by a table while Erin was sat on it.

"This is your order, don't create disorder or you'll fall flat on your face and we'll never be able to save you." She handed me the papers, the string, Blu-Tack and just about anything else I could use to keep it together.

"Kiev as the piece to start with?" They each nodded their heads, "Right, well do I at least get to see the rest of the order?" They each looked at others, I wasn't really sure what was going on with the 3 of them.

"No, keep the surprise and we'll see how your improvising skills are." A woman came up to us, tapped me on the shoulder and said,

"It's time."

"How many people are out there?" I asked, hoping to heard that there wasn't too many.

"It's pretty packed out there, I think we counted 287 people pay for tickets. Guess they are all here to listen to you." That was fucking terrifying news to be given, I didn't even know 287 people. I didn't even know 28 people in Paris. I took one final hit of the vodka, I looked at the 3 of them, I felt just as nervous as when I had to walk back home from the graveyard; that seemed like a lifetime ago.

I had to do it, I grabbed the 3 of them; unaware of who I was going to hug first. I just embraced the group.

The 4 of us, nobody knew - but this was our moment of time.

"Just wait for me at the side." I asked, they each smiled or gave a nod. I looked down at the papers, hoping to the Gods which I highly doubted cared for the stones which had replaced my heart - that I would survive this. The journalist grabbed my hand pulled me towards her and kissed me, there was such passion in her lips I couldn't bring myself to release mine from hers. I walked onto the stage, thinking to myself if I were to just look at the paper and the corners of the room I would be free to some extent of the other entities which were all staring at me.

"Good evening, thank you for all coming out." The applause died down, "I'm going to start with a poem called Kiev, Or Letters Spelt Out In Brickwork." I turned my head to the scraps of paper being held in my left hand, I took breath. Unhappy with the distance between myself and the microphone, knowing that my voice won't carry I grabbed the microphone and pulled it closer. Taking a new breath, I closed my eyes in the blackness behind my eyelids I couldn't make out the words; I knew I was going to have to read with my eyes open.

"Writing words on shards of glass, to my pressed against my head; hoping the meaning will make their way in. if nothing happens, I can always press harder. This internal paranoia will try to seep its way out, and I won't say a word. My list made sure, it was sure to multiply; cosmonaut missing the awful weather, the muscle is racing. West Nile slipped through a net, into the scores just like the catacombs. Lost in and without, the love that we all pissed away. I split my confessions between those wrapped in barbwire, and 4 deafening bells; nobody could hear a thing. And my trail of thought was wasted trying to say, somebody please tell me what I really need to say."

I fear that what would happen next would be like that episode of the Simpsons when Lisa goes to the poetry reading, and the art students just click their fingers to show their approval. What I got was an out of synch applause from the people in front of me.

"Thank you," I whispered into the microphone, I still couldn't bring myself to look around at the people sitting, standing transfixed on my words. I turned the page to see what the Estonian had left next for me, I turned to look at Erin stood at the side of the stage.

"I need a drink." I mouthed to her, she stood there looking confused by what I was trying to indicate. I tried mouthing it to her a few times, the blank look on her face had aggravated me that I walked over and and decided to take the bottle from her.

"Still nervous?" she asked,

"Fucking." I declared back, there was no doubt in my mind that I really shouldn't have been up there; but anything to impress a woman.

I walked back on stage holding the bottle, after taking the top off I said,

"Sorry, nobody provides me with a glass." I was just about to take a hit when a girl in the front row said,

"Excuse me," I looked down at her, blocking everyone else from my mind. "Would you like to use mine?"

"Thank you." I said, as I knelt down to collect it from her. She had prominent red hair, eyes wide fluctuating with colours that I couldn't work out. I poured myself half a glass, felt like I was tasting moonshine in a public place. After taking a sip, I knew in my head that it didn't feel right. The writers of my bookshelf wouldn't have been happy; Bukowski and Hemmingway would have most likely knocked me the fuck out. Emily Dickinson, I can see her wondering why I had left the house. Plath and Crane sitting there patiently for me to pause before asking me why there was no mention of suicide or the heart yearning for something that wasn't going to be. The Russian, all of them questioning me, as to why I would either get to the point so quickly; or not have any moral to what I was writing. This was something I'd never win, no matter how hard I was trying. I gave her the glass back,

"Thank you, but it doesn't feel right." I stood back up, returning to the microphone.

"I don't know the order of these that I'm reading, but this is for the adorable girl who offered me her glass." I turned the page, looking down at what I had next. Trying to find the microphone without having to look at the audience in front of me.

"Ok, so this is called Love Lights And Flash Fights In A Citadel." There were murmurs around the audience, I'm guessing it was over the ridiculous names of the poems. I started to read, ignoring the inaudible words of the crowd. As the words rolled off my tongue, I could hear the silence as the chatter faded away and the ears, the hearts were all listening to me. I scared myself when the thought crossed my mind about 6 poems in that my voice was being heard and would be remembered by these people that had paid to see me, this isn't something that I'd want to do on a regular basis - but in this moment the only place I would rather be is at home with the girls watching some films.

There are things that I can't change, finding them as things I am unable to do anything about is part of life I guess. My past I realise now, in this very moment standing in front of the crowd as they watch me and the words that are projected from my mouth, has to be left to die where it lies. I stopped as they all stood facing me on their feet; I'm not a rock star, I'm no prophet. I don't know what will begin or end with this world, I have little understanding of myself; but here, the men are searching for that one line of mine they can steal and use on their women to have their brains fucked out. The women sit looking at me connecting with the tragedies that my heart possesses, and yearning to be able to say that they were the muse of the next love poem that gets read. I turned the page, I felt more confident in what I was doing. I looked up and glanced my eyes across the room, I couldn't believe that such a small space could hold so many people. And for the first time in front of a crowd of strangers I could look at them and interact.

"Thank you all for coming out, first of all I'm sorry for the length of the titles of the poems. Inside jokes and all things like that. Anyway, this is a poem that I barely know given the fact that I can't remember the title." I looked down to recall what I should have already known, "Ok, so this is a poem that was inspired by something that the girl over there brought into our flat." I pointed at the Estonian, and everyone looked at her. "This is called 7 story Russian Doll." I picked up the bottle of vodka and had a little before offering some to the redhead who only took a little.

"Time would forgive the Gods, but we weren't supposed to know. It was time to applaud the right things, but the seasons had lost their control. Nobody dimmed the lights out so when I looked at everybody's souls, I didn't realise there wasn't one I could call my own. I had become suck a wreck, feeling like an unfinished Russian doll; nobody noticed the cracks in my bones. Was I the only one that heard it raining stones? My wallet was short to pay the boatman his toll, he looked at me like a tattered card deck. They never told us to be ourselves, so we just became fragments of once broken entities. We left our home towns, drinking bereft words when not a soul forgot the order, hold the motion." The pause that then came as some of the audience were waiting for the next stanza was hopeless, hopeless like a waiter that couldn't read out tickets or take plates to the right table. I stepped back and picked up the bottle again, I was so far beyond apprehensive that I was almost perspiring confidence. As the handclaps started, I drew breath to relief myself of the situation. I moved the papers from my left to right hand, putting my head in my left hand certain that I had fucked up. I looked over at the journalist who was sat on the floor, tears in her eyes pointing out towards the audience. I look round to see them women that make up my spectators, with tears in their eyes; those who had tissues were using them. The men looked on jealous, as unaware as I am as to the connection that had been made with the women in the room.

"Thank you, I wasn't expecting any reaction." I looked at the journalist, as she was drying her eyes I quickly walked over to her,

"I got dressed up for you and you bring me to tears, what goes on in your head?" I stood there unable to answer her question, "You have to give them more, you've given them your heart. You have this room in the palm of your hand, capture them." I walked back once again to the microphone, this time I took the chord out of the stand. The Estonian walked over to me,

"What are you doing?" I handed her the papers, knelt down and picked up the Grey Goose. My eyes never left hers.

"Improvising, there is a voice in

my head right now that won't be still."

"Sylvia Plath," I nodded my head, "Own this room." We shared a kiss, and I watched her as she walked back to Erin.

"OK, so this is a poem that could be considered to be in my head. You can call it, Do Piano Wires Get A Place To Retire?" The last of the girls were drying their eyes, and in this moment eyes from all directions were focusing on me. My time to show the mind I had was now or never.

"I stand barely a man, from a land I don't recall. This is a place, little friends; smaller home." I pointed at the Estonian, "She is a girl, tending to me like I were a lamb. I realise now, I don't have a wish I want to own. No father ever wanted me as a son, that's as far as I say of the motherland. Feeling of nothing, it's not like I were a baseball card. Round and around, all my thoughts still go. Feelings of death, and of pain. I thought I was clever, but now I'm back to being alone." I looked at the crowd, they were wanting more; I felt so faint. Not enough to eat, and too much vodka to calm my nerves. "Can't distinguish my name, or lies. I didn't do anything to this world, then why am I here?" I looked over at Erin, she was waiting to see what was going to be said next. "But from the start, I was alone like a rock on the beach next to the unforgiving ocean; that was the place I longed to be. Born, I should have been a florist, removing the thorns to show just how unique roses really are." I fell to the floor with exhaustion, looking at the audience I said with my last ounce of thought,

"All I could wonder was how long? I didn't know if I ever was going to be saying, your love was strong enough." The audience stood up clapping, as I led there the thought came through my head reminding me that I still had more to read.

Day 43

I woke up, it was like waking up from nothing. She wasn't in the bedroom, I didn't even bother looking at the clock; I walked straight to the bathroom, I took my time to brush my teeth. I couldn't have spent any longer than 3 and half minutes to brush my teeth, it just seemed like quarter of an hour longer.

"Where are you?" I called out, there was no reply. I became slightly annoyed by it; my voice had become a silent cry. I walked into the living room, she was sat by the coffee table hunched over a pile of papers reading with the intensity of a power surge in New York. I looked closer, she was reading my scraps of paper. Some were finished, some were just lines I didn't want to forget. I was hoping that she hadn't taken them out of the order that I had them in.

"You've not rearranged my order of disarray have you?" she said not a word, when she finished reading the page that she was on she placed it facing down on the 2nd pile and looked up at me.

"Why won't you show people what it is you're doing here?" I didn't want to share my sorrow, but I had a different thought come over me.

"How are you able to read my

handwriting?" That had annoyed me to a high extent, I had taken my time to really create a font that I felt was pretty much encrypted to all entities but myself. I guess I was wrong. The morning sun made its way through, I couldn't see out of my left eye; but that wasn't too much of an issue.

"I spend so much time with you, we always leave each other notes. After a while you just get so use to what is being written it becomes so easy to read."

"So what are you thinking of it?" I sounded less nervous than what I was feeling, she was spending more time reading the pages than what I had spent writing them. I started to fear that they would mean more to her than they ever could me, I looked at the piles, she must have taken everything.

"Do you have every scrap?" I asked, she gave a slight indication that she did before she hunched back over the papers. Hemmingway would write in the same way, the only difference being that he would have downed 2 bottles of rum before contemplating suicide or to write a word.

It was making me feel torturous, waiting for her to finish; her telling me what was right, what was wrong; and what she really thought I should do with them. I went back into the bedroom, I got dressed. I knew that I had to leave the flat. I got dressed so quickly, I just threw on anything that I picked up. I walked back to her, she was still hunched over the papers; I was surprised that she wasn't taking notes.

"I'm going for a walk; this silence is going to kill me slowly." She looked up and didn't say a word, as I went to leave the room she said,

"Wait!" I stepped back into the room, hoping that she would tell me to stay with her. I was that sure in my head that in went to sit down, she focused on me out of the corner of her eye; only for her to say,

"Your top is inside out." The smirk on her face was enough for me to know that I didn't even need to look. I took my top off and put it on properly,

"Do you want anything?" I asked,

"This piece doesn't have a title, did you not plan on using it?" we looked at one another, "I think that it's lost without a title."

"Then call it, Lost Designation. Now, do you want anything?" she shook her head,

"You shouldn't share that just yet, it's ahead of everything. It's like 21st century poetry zenith." She went to hand it to me, I refused to take it,

"You'll know when the right time to hand it back to me is, you look after it. Words are forgettable and meaningless bits of ink on pieces of paper, how you're reading my work is how I have to read magazine articles; otherwise nothing sinks in." she put the piece next to her, knowing that for the rest of time it shall have a name. "Text me when you're done." I called out to air, she wasn't going to reply, if it wasn't for the fact that it was so early we would have both had a something to eat. I closed the door and started down the stairs.

When I made it outside the blistering heat was instantly unbearable, another summer's day in Paris. I didn't know where I was going to walk to - but then again it wasn't too important, I just needed to be out of the flat. The second I walked outside I knew it was a bad decision to wear jeans, but I wasn't prepared to go back to the flat. I walked up to the corner of Clichy, it was then that I realised it wasn't the same as the day before, an unexplained reason she wanted me to publicise my life away. Instead of walking along Boulevard De Clichy, I chose to head along Rochechouart. It was a market day, and the way of avoiding the hustle and pickpockets was too walk to the far right side, behind the market stalls, sometimes if you were lucky they'd have a few apples and bananas by them that they wouldn't notice you take 1; today was a day like that. Most days I would turn and walk down towards Gare Du

Nord, today I felt the urge to go along and to see the 19th as I don't think I had ever seen it beyond a Metro station. I kept walking along, a few cars would pass by me, but I was making peace with the solitude. I eventually came to Stalingrad Metro station, and I didn't know… I wasn't sure where I should go, or what I should do. The lack of peace I had found in myself from not knowing where I was going, what was really happening in my life or what the future had in store for me. I looked over and had something of an anxiety attack, the building that was in front of me, I don't know what it houses or the relevance it has towards Stalingrad. I reached into my bag pulled out my camera, after setting it to black and white I took the picture that I wanted to take. I put my camera away and said to myself,

"Makes all my poems look false." I walked past it on the left hand side, and up the lake that ran up to the reverse of the building I stood by the bank, a couple walked across the bridge by the church, I started to think of the one I lost. I could hear her voice telling me to write her a song; I never want to pick up a guitar again. And I wrote my songs for her, yet my fingers never even cared. I wanted to just sing a song I wrote to her in the street, right there with everybody around, if I didn't think that they were there, would they be? I looked down the lake; I was surprised that there were no ducks situated there. I guess that I'm unaware that ducks like the scenic parts of Paris. Fussy things, all they do is swim, eat and go quack. I stood there, wanting to sing to the air, knowing that I would be regarded as somebody totally mental if I did. I looked down at the water, when a tap on my shoulder startled me; I turned around to see to my surprise the journalist.

"Hi,"

"What are you doing here?" she asked, she sounded quite surprised.

"Ummm, how do I say it without sounding mental. She has banished me from the house until I get the call that I can return because she has finished." The journalist looked at me in such a strange way, her eyes shut for a moment when she opened them she said,

"Guess I'm not dreaming. So as she has kicked you out, do you need somewhere to stay?" I pointed to the church,

"Can we go up to the church and I will tell you what is going on?" she linked arms with me, she looked at my face side on,

"Have you been crying?" she asked, there was an almost worried tone to her voice.

“I was thinking about someone that I used to love. It made me a quite sad, but I’m ok.” She squeezed tighter with her arm, her attempt at comforting me was a little outdated but I take my hat off to her heart for caring.

“So why aren’t you allowed in your apartment?” she asked as we came to the first bridge, I spontaneously dragged her across.

“Because she is reading my work, I think that she is trying to see just what I’ve been up to, and to work out what all the flower references are all towards. And, maybe she just wants to see if there are any poems about her.” As I finished my sentence the journalist rested her head on my shoulder,

“And are there?”

“Maybe like a line here and there, but nothing too solid.”

“Have you ever written any for me?” she asked, I stopped and leaned against the railings, she let go and looked at me,

“I can’t,” my eyes couldn’t be taken away from those dark almost black eyes of hers, “The Gods, the stars and the sun would all be jealous if I had to remind them that you are more beautiful than they are.” There was an old lady walking her dog coming towards us, as both shuffled their feet and my anticipation of what was going to happen after they had past, I couldn't believe just how slowly just this old woman was moving; snails had moved faster than her. The journalist leaned over grabbed the back of my hair and kissed me, letting go just before the old lady got to us.

"You caught me off guard." I said after it returned to being just the 2 of us.

"If you ever feel the world here is too much you can always stay at mine." It suddenly occurred to me that I had to meet with her the following day.

"If I didn't know better I'd think that you were trying to lure me into bed." She gave a smile that if the lost one had given would have made me hers within an instant, "And that is something I really can't have right now, I'm lost. This won't help me." She took my hand again, as we walked up towards the church she asked,

"If the circumstances were different, I probably would have." We took about 6 steps in silence before I asked,

"Where am I meeting you tomorrow?" she gave no reply, I looked up at the church, my phone started to ring.

"Hello?" I answered, I didn't bother to look to see it was her; although I knew it was.

"I got 75, you need to come home." I hung up and turned to the journalist,

"You have to go," she said, I pointed back towards the flat. "Will you at least think about spending more time with me?" I gave her a kiss and said,

"You live up this road, and it's now time for me to get going home." She readjusted my t-shirt, gave me a final kiss and left me.

Day 46

I looked at the clock, quarter to 5. Made me feel thankful that it was only a 2 minute walk to work. I knew that she wouldn't wake up, I still couldn't bring myself to turn on the light. I brushed my teeth, and made my way down the stairs. I could see inside the shop, the baker that was taking over from was by the door talking to someone, I opened the door and slipped in undetected. I looked at the rota to see what I was on, Paris Brest and biscuits, easy morning. Shame I was working until 2pm. There were 2 others working with me, after I got changed and had walked into the kitchen. One of them asked,

"Have you spoken to your mother?" I couldn't distinguish which one asked the question while I was over at the flour bins, collecting what I needed to use for the task at hand.

"I spoke to her yesterday, she saw an old friend of hers; I used to play with her son when I was like 6 or 7. She was shopping in London and she went to give a homeless person some money, and it was her son."

"Sad, did he go home with her?"

"I don't know, I doubt it. He would just run away, he is a fool."

"It must have broken her heart."

The other said. I didn't want to think of it, he was a fool never wanting anyone's help. Everybody needs someone sometime.

"Did you do anything with your days off?" I asked, they were silent; I wasn't too worried if they weren't to say what they had been up to. The room was slowly filling up with each of the things that we had been making, I still wasn't fully used to the early starts but I knew that Erin would be in the city in a couple of days.

Time inside the kitchen always flew by and this was no exception, as the other people started work and the shop opened I started to clean up before getting brownies and sweet pastry ready for the following day.

As the time ticked away and I heard the girls out front talking to customers, I ended up by myself for an hour. As I looked up at the clock and saw it was 1:50 I said to myself,

"Almost time to do nothing." I was trying to think of what I could do with the rest of my day, I thought about phoning the journalist to see if she wanted to go for a walk. The Estonian had suggested a picnic the day before, I was thinking about seeing with her if that was an option, when one of the girls; I don't know her name, poked her head in and said,

"Tu parles anglais non?" I gave a

nod and she followed it up with,

"Peux tu parler à cette fille? Je ne comprends pas ce qu'elle dit."[37] I threw my cloth to one side, dusted off the excess flour that was on me and walked into the shop.

Standing there was an American girl, she was about 5'10" there was very little of her. The blonde hair was starting to show their roots, with eyes that had the ability to enrapture God; I stared at her knowing I wasn't the first and wouldn't be the last person to fall for her in those black plimsolls, barely visible denim shorts and plain white t-shirt. I wasn't ever going to complain and not seeing a great deal of her denim shorts, her legs were second to none.

"Which part of the states are you from?" I asked, she looked quite surprised that I knew before she had said a word that she was American.

"New York, I don't recognise your accent." I laughed, I had to.

"I hear that a lot, my accent is very hybrid. How can I help you?"

"Can I have a baguette, and one of these," she pointed at a Paris-Brest, I bagged it up for her, I feared that I was going to drop something and make a fool of myself. "What is it?" she asked,

---

[37] Can you talk to this girl? I don't understand what she is saying.

"Paris-Brest, its choux pastry filled with a praline and cream mixed together." She was salivating the flavour, as she scanned the counters to see what else she wanted.

"Can you recommend me something?" she said as she smiled, I moved over to and pointed at the marble brownies.

"You would have never tried anything like this before." She seemed patronised by what I said, so I cut a little off one and gave it to her, as she ate it everyone in the shop could she how she found the taste to be so delectable, her eyes grew and were almost falling out of their sockets.

"You found a goldmine, my mother would love this. Can you give me the…" I shook my head,

"I'm sorry my chickadee, but nobody but me knows this recipe. I plan on keeping it that way for as long as I can." She respected that, as she reached into her bag for her purse she asked,

"I'll take 2 of them and how much do I owe?"

"I'll let the girls deal with the money; I regard it as an ugly commodity. That and I've now finished work, so it was my pleasure to help you."

"One thing before you go," I looked to pay more attention that what I was, "Can you tell me where the nearest Metro station is?"

"If you hold on a minute, I'll walk you there." She smiled, "I'll be right back." I returned to the back, filled in my hours and very quickly got changed, throwing my whites down on the pile, before heading back to the shop. I did fear she would be gone from my life in just as quick a fashion as she emerged.

When I returned she was looking out of the shop door up at the apartments, I tapped her on the shoulder,

"You ready?" I asked, she pointed up,

"Those apartments are so picturesque; I'm envious of people who live in them."

"I live up there, it's not that great." She looked at me with a level of jealousy that I could only describe as ridiculously high. "Come on, I'll take you to where you want to go."

"I have to get to Gare Du Nord, I'm meeting a group of friends there in an hour. They are arriving from Brussels. You're not really a baker are you?"

"As in do I do anything else beyond my job? I'm writing a lot of poetry at the moment." We started to walk up Rue Des Martyrs, when she then asked,

"Can you show me your apartment?"

"Why do you want to see the flat?"

"I want to see the view, and if

you'd let me read your poetry…" if anyone else had asked me I would have instantly said no, but she was the muse that every great artist would want to have.

"OK, but only on the grounds that you're the 3rd." she got all giddy before asking,

"Third what?" I laughed to myself, we crossed the road and I unlocked the door to let us in. as we walked up the stairs she asked again,

"What do you mean by third?" We made it to the door, as I put the key in the lock I told her.

"The 3rd perfect 10." She wasn't picking up on what I meant, I thought to myself that nobody could be this naïve. I shook my head, "First there was Juliette Binoche, then there was Cate Blanchett. Now, now there is you. A perfect 10 is just a means of never being able to find a fault with a woman."

"But I have plenty of faults." I laughed slightly at her,

"I don't see them." She was walking around the flat, picking up random objects as she went. She came to the pile of poems, lying on the table as scraps of paper. She picked them up,

"Did you write these?" I looked over at her and gave a nod,

"Why do you write?" she asked the hardest question anyone could ever ask, most of the time I'd try and shun the question. The other day I did find the perfect quote for such an occasion.

"I write because a voice inside my head refuses to remain quiet." She smiled before glancing at the paper,

"What is it that you're writing about?" I just pointed to the page, she looked down,

"It's just relevant I guess, I don't think it has to mean anything."

"My short time was feeling like centuries, snow falls here and nothing does grow. I know Paris is my summer, later life - before the beginning; doors fall off their hinges, they don't need mending. I heard what the pastor said, Sing - Sing. And I crumbled down when I discovered that she was more infinite than me, so like a fly I was caught, guess that made her my Venus flytrap. Like everyone before, I was so alone." She looked up at me, "This is fucking heavy shit, and whatever you were in this is some sort of self-therapy. But, does it help?"

"It's just poetry," I looked at her differently, "Can I photograph you for a poster as I'm doing a poetry reading in 2 weeks' time." She put the papers down I positioned her how I wanted her, and started to create snapshots, but something wasn't right. I reached over and grabbed a marker pen, walked up to her and started writing on her shirt. She looked down after I had taken my hand out from her shirt to keep my writing steady.

"The Atmosfear Of The Blank Door."

"It's what I call the collection." I returned to photographing her as she got back into position.

"Will this be a book cover?" she asked,

"No idea, if it becomes the case I'll give you the book." I took a few more pictures, "Let's get you to Gare Du Nord."

"And my t-shirt?" was looked like she was going to fret over nothing.

"Never wash it, it belongs to the Gods of time now. If anyone asks you were doing a photo shoot. You don't need to say anything else." She smiled and wrote down her address,

"If it gets printed as a book I want a copy." I smiled, picked up my bag, put the camera on top of the poems and as we walked towards the door I went into the kitchen and got a couple of apples, giving her one I asked,

"Do you have everything?" she looked down at the t-shirt, knowing I had made it more complete she said nothing.

Day 7

I thought I was in love, but actually it was a dream I hadn't released that I was in. She was still there; I could see the different colours in her eyes, her left was green and her right an obscure shade of gold. The tattered Abbey Road t-shirt that she had, it had an ever growing hole under the arm, exposing her skin to me and only me. She was sitting on the side of my bed, fixing her hair so it was up. I could smell the shampoo, and the faint aroma of her perfume. I looked at her delicate figure, I knew everything there was to know about her. As I gazed at the hour glass that she had been blessed with, she concentrated on my poetry books. As I sat next to her I led backwards, so unable to take my eyes off her. I found myself lost for words, I'm not even sure if there was a reason for it.

"Why do you only collect books of dead poets?" she asked, I felt awful because I couldn't see her lips move. She led backwards and looked at me,

"Does this mean that I will be the only person who cares about you while you're alive?"

"I don't know, but I could muse off you until we both end up in the graveyard."

I woke up, scared, I couldn't tell if I was in a dream within a dream. I was breathing so heavily I couldn't hear myself think, if this was reality then I must have woken someone up. I looked at the clock it was 8.45 I turned my head to the other side, she was barely asleep. I don't know if she was pretending or if she was actually asleep. I walked to the bathroom and brushed my teeth, my bedhead was some kind of crazy. I washed my hair, it felt really bad as I hadn't washed it in a few days. There was a knock on the door,

"Just a minute." I shouted,

"OK," Shouted back my sister. I couldn't work out which sister, but I was fairly sure that it was my older sister. I finished and opened the door, there wasn't anybody outside. I walked back to my bedroom, there wasn't anyone around. I opened my bedroom door and she was sat up talking to my mum, who in turn said to me,

"So when were you going to say that you were moving to Paris together?"

"Well when I thought you were up, you don't start work until 10 today."

"So what has brought this on?" she snapped, "You can't just run away from your problems."

"And you also can't stay with your problems, ignore them and stagnate pretending nothing has happened can you?"

"You looking to get away from how bad Spurs did as well." She played her Ace cards,

"They will bounce back, don't you worry about them." I said, "But mum, I have to get out of this place for some time. I got my lecturers number, so if I need to start later I can phone him and let him know."

"I don't think it's right, I mean how long will it be before you're to phone me and your dad asking for money? A week tops I'm guessing." I was really offended, I wasn't letting that snide comment going under my radar.

"I've never asked you or dad for money, I'm able to not waste my money on shit like people that I went to school with." My mum turned to her and asked,

"You will take care of him?"

"Don't worry; it would take an act of the Gods to keep us apart." She said, "I'm going to be studying, so I'm going to be in all the time working on my French papers. We'll be just writing together asking for notes."

"Will you at least take him to a church, he's missing that."

"I've not been to church since I was 12."

"Your grandfather is a reverend!" I did nod my head,

"Yes he is, but you know better

than anyone that that is out of convenience and so people think more of him than if they were to know him and realise that he is nothing more than a rude old man, who has nothing to say." I put on my shoes, "We'll discuss Paris some more tonight. But now I need to go and see someone, let her know that I'm safe and heading out on the road." She left the room and got her things for work. I said to her,

"What are you going to do today?"

"I'm going to have a look down the North Laines at the clothes stores and the small independent stores, see if there is anything that I can get for Paris." I smiled, "Who do you have to see that is so important?"

"Just a girl that I was really kind who works in Boots, she told me to keep in touch with her." She got out of my bed, and walked across to her pile of clothes. As she got dressed, I felt indecisive. I opened my wardrobe and pulled out a plaid shirt and went with the jeans I was already wearing, they had become so faded that it was almost time for them to be thrown, but for today they were mine to wear. I turned around and she was doing up her bra,

"Do you have a t-shirt that I could wear?" I opened up one side of the wardrobe and pulled out a Led Zeppelin 1977 t-shirt, as she took it I said,

"Don't even think about modifying it in any way," she had a slight grin on her face, "That is a genuine 77' t-shirt, if that doesn't come back to me like that you will feel my wrath." Her face acknowledged that I wasn't joking around. She put it on all the same. She picked up a few things, put them in her bag, and faced me.

"I'm ready, how much more do you have to do?"

"You need to brush your teeth, and I need to put a couple of things in my bag; then we will be good." She went off and brushed her teeth, I picked up my copy of Complete Poems by Anne Sexton. I had it for something to read, in case I was to get a little bit of time to myself today. She came back in the room,

"Ready?" she asked, I gave a nod. She picked up her bag, and we walked to the front door.

We stood outside mine, she watched me lock the door; as I turned to face her she asked,

"Who lives in the flat below you?" I looked at the flat to see if anyone was there anyone there.

"Rachael and Alan."

"Are they a couple?" she asked,

"No, it's complicated." We came to the bottom of the road and turned right to walk towards the train station.

"How complicated can it be? Either they are a couple or they are friends."

"No, they were together before I knew them and then they broke up. But they still live together."

"*What?*" the look of confusion on her face as we stepped up onto the pavement was priceless.

"I told you it was complicated." We carried on walking down toward the train station. When we arrived at the train station, I pointed down Guildford Road,

"That's your direction," I said, "Do you mind if we don't meet up for lunch? Just after being stuck in a room with you for the past few days have driven me to a day to want to be by myself." She smiled,

"You've saved me a job; I was going to say I'll see you back at yours at like 5pm?"

"That's good with me." She went to start walking down when I stopped her,

"Go into a shop called Resident, it's a small independent record store. That always have something good playing, you can waste so much time in there."

"I will do, ma armastan sind."[38] She said,

"Love you to." I replied with. She walked down and I started to walk down Queen's Road, there was more traffic than normal. The row of taxis

---

[38] I love you.

looked untouched, but who would want to be in the back of a taxi on a day that is so beautiful? I slipped between buses and made my way onto the left hand side of the street looking down towards the sea. I walked down; I wasn't in a rush to get anywhere so I took my time. I walked around the corner of Boots and went in the entrance on North Street. I walked around, when I was stopped by someone who worked in the store,

"Can I help you sir?" I looked around,

"I'm looking for someone who works here, she's like 6 feet 1, has kind of faded blonde hair. She has a slig…" out of the corner of my eye I spotted her.

"Not to worry." I said, as I walked over to her. She stopped what she was doing as she saw me coming.

"Good morning," she said as I got closer. I looked at her, the ceiling and then back at her,

"Hi." I said as I stopped.

"Is your hand any better?" I showed her my hand,

"It's a little better, but I've had a crazy few days. I was going to ask you, what time do you finish work today?"

"I finish at 1, if you wait for me on the North Street entrance we can go get a coffee and catch up." I smiled, trying my best to not concentrate too hard on her lazy eye.

But I did think her lazy eye is what made her more attractive than what she was.

"That sounds good, I'll meet you at the corner." She smiled and returned to her work. I walked back out of the shop. The lights were on amber so I made a run for it, barely making it across in time; but making it across nonetheless. I decided that to go to the beach and read Annie Sexton wouldn't make me feel better, but I'd at least feel something. Even if it were someone else's pain. I carried on down Queen's road, when I got to the beach, the wind was so cold that I said out loud,

"*No.*" I thought for a second, walked along to the pier, looked up at the pavilion and decided that I was going to sit there and waste away a few hours reading.

When I arrived at the pavilions there were people everywhere, I at least knew that I'd have some solitude in the pages of the book. I put my headphones in and just let the songs come as they may. The pages didn't always make sense to me, but I do guess that is the joys of poetry. I'd read the book quite a few times, and I'd always find a gem that I'd never read before hidden away, I'd always think I'd never read it but I guess things shine in different lights. I kept reading this one poem called

The Interrogation Of The Man Of Many Hearts

I wondered to myself, how would I answer the question, and who would be the one asking them to me? I rarely looked up to see what else was happening around me, to see usual things for this building at this time of day. Locals walking through, tourists stopping them to take their pictures, Mums pushing their prams through as the kids look at the world with open eyes and pure amazement, and of course - nobody that I knew. I looked at the clock and it said 12:49. I stood up and brushed myself off, put the book back into my bag and started to walk to North Street. As I was walking up, hoping not to be late for meeting her, I had a hand grab me on the shoulder, I turned around to see a copper.

"What seems to be the officer problem?" I asked,

"Would you mind coming with me?" he said. I pointed up the street,

"Actually I do mind, I'm going to meet a friend."

"That wasn't a request."

"It certainly sounded like a request." He paused for a few seconds,

"Yesterday we had a child matching your description escape from hospital, so I'd like to take you in for questioning."

"Well I'm 18 so society deems me to

be an adult, and surely if they were in hospital they would have had a name."

"It was a john Doe." Quick as a flash I replied with,

"Well that is simple, my name isn't John." He shook his head,

"No, a John Doe is…" He thought of me as being stupid.

"I'm aware as to what a John Doe is. Can I go now?"

"If you go I will have to arrest you." In the most theatrical manner that I could conjure up I shouted,

"*ON WHAT GROUNDS?!*"

"Wasting police time."

"You're the one who stopped me!" There was no chance I was going with him, "I'll ask you again, what seems to be the officer, problem?" he still didn't say anything, I looked at the time on my iPod, I was late. I rolled my eyes,

"And now I'm late, have a good day." I continued to walk up the street and I was able to see her stood where I told her that I would meet her,

"I'm sorry I'm late." I said, as I got closer, she smiled.

"It's OK, I saw you talking to the policeman, I feared the worse but thought it best to keep my distance." I didn't need to add anything to what she said,

"Shall we go get a coffee?" we walked up and across to Western Road, the coffee shops separated the rows of shops into more manageable distances for people who couldn't go more than half an hour before needing to sit down and have a drink. We walked into Starbucks; the queue was pretty much non-existent and the clerk at the counter said to us,

"Hi, what can I get for you?" I looked at the woman I was with; she was still making up her mind. Guess it up to me to get the ball rolling,

"Hi, can I get a medium hot chocolate, and she will say what she wants in just a second."

"What size did you say?" he asked me,

"Medium." I gave as my reply.

"We do 3 sizes sir, Tall, Grande and Venti."

"So is tall the largest size?" I was just beyond confused,

"No sir, Tall is the smallest size we do." I put my hands up and closed my eyes.

"Tall as a rules doesn't mean something small?" He stood there with a blank stare, so far beyond its own repair. "Why on earth would you call the smallest thing Tall?"

"I'm not really involved in the naming process, I'm just someone who works here."

"Right, glad we got that sorted. So can I please have a medium hot chocolate please." He started up again, I turned to the woman I was with,

"Shall we go?" she nodded before saying,

"There's another coffee shop a few shops down." We just walked out.

"He could have just done it and called it a medium, but you almost had me in stitches with refusing to call it what he wanted it to be called." I smiled, "You did kind of tear him apart on the naming of sizes."

"I did, I really did." As we walked along to the next coffee shop I said, "I only got out of hospital yesterday, I look pretty bad. All I want is, urgh. I don't even know what I want…" we walked into the next coffee shop.

"I know what you want." She said, the woman working in the Costa we had just walked into said,

"Hi, what can I get for you?"

"Can I have, a medium hot chocolate with marshmallows and cream and anything to make him feel like a princess; and I'll have a cappuccino thank you." I had to laugh to myself. She was mocking me, and I didn't want to do anything about it.

"If you want to find yourself a seat, I'll bring the drinks over in just a minute." We walked over, I watched her sit down at a table big designed for 4.

"Here looks fine to me." I sat down opposite her, "Your hand looks better, can I see it?" I showed her my hand, it tickled but she looked at it so intuitively that I wouldn't have felt safe with anyone else.

"It'll feel sore for a while, but it will heal up just fine." As I brought my hand back to myself the waitress placed the drinks down in front of us.

"… Thank you." I said looking up at her, in that moment I felt as insignificant as an ant before a boot steps on it. She smiled and returned to the counter.

"So what is it that I want?" I asked her, she giggled to herself a little,

"I wasn't thinking like that. All you want right now is a friend who will listen to your problems." She was right and I wasn't even sure if this was the right place to tell her.

"How do you know know…" she cut me off, it was more often that not the other way round.

"I'm a psychology major, I don't want to be one of those people but sometimes, people are so obvious."

"One of those people who think that because they're at uni they know everything?"

"Exactly, so what has happened since I first met you?" I looked around me; there were about 20 people in the café.

"Here?" she gave a simple nod,

"If you don't talk about your

issues to a crowd, they will never get resolved." In that moment I could have said 'Fuck it.' Got up and walked out, instead I thought 'Fuck it, I'll tell her.'

"Well after I left you I went to my old Art teachers house, cooked dinner for her. Ended up falling asleep at her house, I woke up the next morning, she said as a joke we had fucked. I couldn't live with myself so I took all the packets of paracetamol she had in her house, went home asked my neighbour if she had a bottle of wine. I told her I couldn't write, and I wanted to feel like Bukowski." I knew she was seeing where I was going, but I continued to tell her anyway.

"I wasn't thinking about what I was doing, I did it anyway. I think the doctor said I took 14 packets worth. Such a selfish thing to do." I took a sip of my hot chocolate, I looked at her, she had tears in the shape of every country she had ever been to. "Do you want me to stop?" she wiped tears away from her eyes, in an instant I saw Cyprus, Mongolia, France, that month she spent in Cuba. They were all gone in that moment.

"No, you're ok. I just need to regain my composure, please continue." I was quite reluctant to continue but I did all the same,

"I walked to the hospital." I had to catch my own breath, "I asked the doctor if he would call the Estonian for me, she came. The doctor then told me that he would be giving me up to the police, because a suicide attempt is attempted murder." I had to stop, I wasn't sure if I could carry on.

"…Fucking, hell." she mused, "When I have, a bad day. I think to myself, 'there's always someone worse off than me.' What do you think to yourself when you have a bad day?"

"I normally read books by… dead poets, they understand my pain." we sat staring at each other, in that time she saw my life, and I saw the countries that she would head to in the pupils of her eyes.

Day 8

We had just collected our tickets, there was a queue leading up to the ticket inspection and my *MOST* favourite people in the world; Custom Officers. We were facing each other; in Waterloo my mind does seem to wonder. I loved to listen to the little things that people say when they walk past you.

"I don't get it," she broke our silence, "You love to fly?" I acknowledged what she said, "Then, *why* are we getting the train to Paris?"

"Simple, it's so much cheaper." I said, "Besides, you hear people say much funnier things in train stations than in airports." I looked around, "I want to go get a drink. Do you want anything?" her look of annoyance was crystal clear to anyone who would have passed a gaze at her.

"Really? There's like 7 people ahead of us. Can't it just wait?"

"There's only a newsagents in there, *and* I expect by the time I get back the queue will only be down to like 3 people; and that is me being quite generous." She picked up my bag and handed it to me,

"Mocha,"

"Pretentious." Was my rapid-fire response.

"And as you said that, I'll also have something sweet. Thank you." I moved the backpacking bag which had enough clothes to last me a week, but was designed for an indefinite period of time to my back, my rucksack I moved to be on just one shoulder. I normally put it on my left, but I felt like a change. I walked over and up the escalator, the floor was clattered with people looking at train times, on their way to different platforms. I was walking across the floor towards Caffè Nero, there was a man walking towards me holding a newspaper,

"Excuse me," I said as he got closer, "Have you finished with the paper?" he handed it to me,

"What trash you want to read." I took a look at what he was handing me, The Socialist Worker. The tone of his voice would lead anyone to believe that his public school education would teach him to not want proletariats to understand the way of the working world. After all we're nothing special to this world, if we die there will always be another person to take our job.

"Thank you very much. My kind of paper." I said with a smile. He looked disgusted by the approval that I had for the paper in his hand. "Beats reading The Guardian doesn't it." Ah the rage etched on his face was a delight to a true Marxist.

Sadly that wasn't me.

"Have a good day sir, and thank you for the paper." I continued across the floor to Caffè Nero, I would step aside of people as they were walking towards me. Most people would think that they'd step around me, as I was the one with the luggage. But, people are people; why should I be an inconvenience to their day?

As I got closer to the shop my eye was focusing on one person. Someone who I thought was an old school friend, I didn't want to say anything and make myself look like a moron who shouts out random things to strangers. I was trying to make up my mind as to whether it was him or not; when he said,

"It is you!" I walked up to him, put my bag down which led to a convoluted handshake.

"How you been mate?" I asked him,

"Good, I'm just waiting on a train down to Southampton. Have to go down for my brother's wedding." His brother was like 8 years older, I think I had met him once or twice. "What about you?" he asked.

"I've been ok. I'm just getting a coffee before we get on our train to Paris."

"Who you going there with?"

"My friend from Estonia."

"The same…"

"Yeah."

"As when you were…"

"YES!" he seemed satisfied with the answer that I gave, he cleared his throat and then asked,

"Do you remember a girl from when we were at school?" there was a look of bewilderment on me,

"There were a lot of girls when we were at school, narrow it down a little."

"*The rumour.*" I started to chuckle to myself, I knew exactly who he was talking about. The rumour was that she went to the funfair and had sex with a gypsy who worked there.

"What about her?" I asked, he pointed into Caffè Nero.

"She's inside." My eyes lit up, it was my last chance to do a childish prank. "Just sat there, reading her paper having a coffee."

"Well I have to buy some drinks, we have to go inside." We walked inside, I went up to the counter and he waited by a table,

"Hi,"

"G'd morning, can I have a hot chocolate and a mocha, please." As she went off to do the drinks my friend started up with the fanfare. The rage was becoming so blatantly etched across her face, like she had left high school moved to a new city where nobody knew anything about her. Only for that tune to be playing in an innocent, but malevolent manner. Like a dripping tap, it means no harm but, very quickly becomes the source of so much frustration. The girl put the drinks in front of me; using a marker pen she labelled the drinks for me. Just as she was about to tell me the price, I heard the scraping of a chair on the tiles. I looked at him, looked at her, and then out came the words for all of SE1 to hear.

"I DIDN'T SHAG HIM!!!!!! I ONLY WANKED HIM OFF!!!!!!!" We both burst out laughing; he fell on the floor, I ended up on the counter. The poor girl was looking at us perceptive that she was very much outside of the castle of knowing on the turn of events that had just taken place inside where she works.

"I think I'm going to piss myself." My mate said between bouts of hysterics and him gasping for air. I was just about able to compose myself.

"Can I also have," I looked down at my friend, only to discover that he had pissed himself which got me laughing again. She walked past him only to get him laughing again.

"Sir, I have a queue of people waiting. Is there anything else that you'd like?"

"Can I also have 2 lemon muffins please?" She put them into a paper bag and then said,

"That's £7.35 then." I placed a £10 note in her hand saying,

"For such an amusing trip to buy coffee, I thank you and leave you with the change." I moved the items from the counter to the table before I helped my friend up.

"I got to go mate, you take care of yourself." We shared another convoluted handshake.

"Let me know when you get back in the country, we'll go for a drink." I gave an approving gesture with my head. I picked up my bags, sorted out the drinks and left the store.

I walked back across to the escalators, as I was standing still when I was going down I was certain I could hear her kicking off over something that I couldn't quite work out; but as always with her, I feared the worst. I ran over to her, gave her the mocha and hot chocolate,

"And the problem is?" The glance that she gave me was one of total aggravation,

"Which one of us has the passports?" I felt my back pocket, there they were. 2 passports, I pulled them out and just handed one to her. She hit me on the head with the one that I had handed her,

"Helps if you give me the right 1." I switched them over, and she gave me the train ticket. We handed them to the customs officer, he looked at both passports.

"Are you travelling together?" she smiled, I stayed deadly still.

"We are, yes." He handed back her passport, turned to me and asked,

"Have we met each other before?" I let out a long exhale, looked and her contemplated asked her. I turned my attention back to the customs officer,

"I don't think so, I'm not particularly good at remembering faces." He handed it back to me,

"My mistake, have a nice trip."

"Enjoy your day." I said back. We walked through, she handed my hot chocolate to me,

"So why did you take so long in getting the drinks?" I chuckled to myself.

"I saw an old school friend, got distracted by singing the fanfare; found out that someone we went to school with wanked off a man who worked there. You know the usual things that happen when going to buy a drink." The baffled look that she had on her face led me to say,

"What?"

"I don't see why that would cause you to take so long."

"We took our time falling about laughing." We sat in silence, she started to eat her muffin and I looked at mine. I wasn't feeling like eating at all. I looked at what she was wearing what looked very much to be like MY Led Zeppelin t-shirt, a vintage pair of jeans and a pair of plimsolls that looked ready to be taken off and thrown in the bin.

"Why are you wearing that?" I

pondered to myself, I hadn't realised that I had said it out loud when I then heard.

"Why am I wearing what?" I pointed around and at the t-shirt.

"Unless you found one in a shop in Brighton, THAT looks very much resembles MY t-shirt." She smiled like a Cheshire cat,

"You never asked for it back last night, and…" I cut her off,

"You were wearing it, and we had to pack. Do you really think that me getting you to take my top off was high up on my agenda?"

"Normally I'd say yes, but with you in your current state of mind, I'd say it's more like the 7th or 8th thing on your mind." She knew me too well, I'd give her that.

My mind wondered, I started to think about who would notice that I had left. Would my sisters be too bothered at me leaving? Who would take my place where I work? Would there be one less person in the crowd at rock shows? I started thinking about the month before, we went to see The Red Hot Chili Peppers in Hyde Park. I was wearing the t-shirt that I bought that day, they played this new song. I'd never be able to describe it. Part of me wanted to hear it again, and something inside me said,

'That was a moment you spent with her, it's gone. The words of the song will fade given time, memory is something that was designed to be forgotten. To remember everything will just leave us so sad.'

All of a sudden I heard an announcement from the Tanoy system,

"The 14.01. Train to Paris Gare Du Nord is now ready for boarding. All passengers are asked to promptly make their way to their coaches. Thank you." I looked at her,

"Ready?" I asked, she stood up and started to pick up the bags.

"What were you thinking about?" she questioned me, I picked up the bags and we started to walk towards the platform. She nudged me when we had our first glance of the train. I shifted my eyes over to her.

"You never answered my question." And then it hit me.

"Sorry I was miles away." I started to open my mouth forgot what the words in my mind were and said nothing.

"You've forgotten the question haven't you?" I let out a long breath of air,

"Sorry, my mind really is miles away. Yes, I did forget what you were saying." She could see that my mind wasn't really with it, but she still asked again.

"What were you thinking about?" I could have lied to her, said that I was thinking about us, about the future. I could have even said I was thinking about things I do think about when my mind strays - whether it be football or Ché Guevara, I thought to myself - No, I should tell her the truth.

"I was thinking about her, we went to see The Red Hot Chili Peppers last month. There was this one song that they played, it was…" she cut me off,

"Otherside?" she pondered.

"They played that, but it was a new song. It was kind of futuristic and something that I'd love to here again. But then again, I wouldn't." I sourced the words in my mind. "Shame, it'll fade. Shade, shade… shade. The leverage of… the leverage of space."

"When it tilts, and becomes something new. The contours of the understanding that we have for the world… will become something new."

I took the bags from her, watched her get onto the train, before getting on myself. We walked through the carriage and found our seats, she sat next to the window while I put our bags above us. I sat down and looked around, the carriage was very quickly starting to fill up. What when we got on was a sea of empty chairs, had become a barrage of heads. I looked at her and through gritting teeth said,

"I Want To Swap Seats." She looked at me,

"Well out you go." She said. I wasn't doing that. I lifted up the armrest, grabbed her right leg and the panty line on her left side and lifted her up. I slid under her, as I did a middle-aged couple that clearly had a stagnated marriage, sat down opposite us looking at her sat on my lap, with me gripping onto her underwear. I slid her across to the aisle seat, before saying to them,

"I only did it to show I have the biggest dick at this table." I didn't get the reaction out of them that I had hoped for. I was hoping for shock, I got disgust. She looked out the window as we pulled away,

"How do you feel?" I kept my eyes of the train tracks that surrounded the outside.

"If I had a voice, it would be a cataclysm."

"Sorry?" she pulled back to say. I grabbed her by the side of her head and pulled her back to me,

"It's ok. I'm with you, I'll be fine and we'll be here for each other until we're ghosts." She rested her head on her hand, which in turn was resting on my shoulder, in that moment I looked at myself in the window; I smiled, I knew nothing, and I wanted nothing. The only thing that I did know was that I was free.

Day 53

Erin was putting things away that we weren't going to be using right away, I was consolidating everything that we were going to use to a single chopping board.

"I said it earlier, I am not chopping onions." There was little authority to Erin's voice when she spoke, but she tried.

"That is fine, we're only going to need 1." She most likely scorned me behind my back, as we put the last of the things away I looked at the iPod and put on Temple Of The Dog, as the chords started to play Erin skipped it onto the next song,

"Reach Down, it's a 10 minutes long song, but it just doesn't feel that way." I let it play I didn't mind, Chris Cornell had a voice where you could feel his pain and anguish at the death of his friend. Erin picked out a bottle of white wine for us to start off by cooking with, and then the 3 of us will drink the rest of it.

I chopped the onion, as I was getting ready to prepare everything else my phone rang.

"Can you get that?" I asked Erin, she shook her head;

"No, it's bad luck to answer somebody else's phone. You get your own phone." As it sat there ringing, I looked to see it was the journalist, 'better Erin had not answered it.' I thought to myself, I answered the call,

"Hey,"

"Whatcha' doing?" The journalist asked me, I moved into the living room,

"I'm not free to come and see you."

"You'll never guess what I'm wearing while I'm sat on my bed."

"That isn't going to free up my time, I've got Erin here; and we are in the mist of cooking dinner."

"Oh," she sounded like I was the one, who had cancelled on her. I was preparing myself for the hang up when I asked,

"Do you want to come and join us for dinner?" I could hear her brain ticking away, as to if she was willing to share me with 2 other women.

"So it'll be the 3 of us?"

"4, the girl I live with is eating with us."

"OK, I'll bring a bottle."

"Great, I do have one request." There was a sigh, she tried to cover it up but everyone and their brother would have been able to have heard it.

"Don't come here dressed like you had planned to give me a lap dance, Erin is a lot younger than you, and I don't want her to be led astray."

"OK."

"Ring me when you get here." I said

"I shall." Was her reply, she then hung up. I walked back in to see that Erin had finished preparing everything,

"Sorry about that. We have another person to cook for."

"Who?" she seemed to not like the idea of cooking for a fourth.

"Friend; she is a journalist, she's quirky in her own sort of way."

"Does she write about you?" I gave a nod as I started to sweat off the onions, she picked up the bag of risotto rice and poured the lot in. I added some white that Erin had clearly opened and helped herself to a glass of while I was out of the room.

"Do I not get a glass?" I asked, she smiled and started to laugh nervously.

"Oh but it was my every intention to pour you a glass, I just couldn't find any."

"*Oh shut up you tart.* Thinking I wouldn't notice, how does it taste?" After having a little bit, she started to mull over the flavours in her mouth before concluding,

"Better for cooking in my opinion."

"But as you've not paid for it, you shall drink it without complaining." She laughed as I added some water, and then started to look around. Opening cupboards, Erin kept the pan moving. I eventually found it, grabbed 2 cubes and returned crumbling one into the pan.

"What's that?" Erin asked, I looked at her, unknowing why she was asking such a ridiculous question,

"An OXO cube." I said, she still didn't look like what I had said had sunk in.

"You mean a stock cube. Du bist so ein Spießer. Deine Sprache ist wirklich lächerlich, warum erfindest du irgendwelche Wörter?"[39] I had to laugh, she knew I didn't know what she was saying.

She eventually poured me a glass of wine, I knew how to cook and drink. I had worked with worse chefs than me doing it on a regular basis from as early as 8:30 besides, I knew what I was doing. We must have been about 14 minutes in when the door opened, she walked in and we instantly heard,

"Who's cooking?"

"Why?" I asked, as I changed the song on the iPod to Cropduster.

"You share too much with Eddie Vedder, and I'm only asking because it smells good." I tried to work out what she meant, I guess we are both fools. The world made us think that we thought and created the world how we wanted it to be, what fools we are; the world finds us, chews us up

[39] Your language is seriously ridiculous, why are you making up words?

and spits us over to the wolves. Erin was constantly stirring the pot like she knew to do.

"We're both cooking, so remember compliments don't buy drinks." She poured herself a glass, finishing off the bottle. As she looked over again she past the comment,

"That's quite a lot for 3 isn't it?"

"Well now we're cooking for 4, so it should be fine." The doorbell went, I knew it was the journalist so I buzzed her up. I waited in the doorway as she ascended the stairs. I should have realised that she was going to try and do something to titillate me. When I first saw her she looked no different, but then it struck me that she was wearing a dress. Her legs seemed to go on longer than time would ever last, I contemplated life and the relevance of the earth beneath my feet. The blue and yellow plaid print ended a good 8 inches before her knees, I had never seen her in a dress, and frankly didn't know why she wasn't in them more often. The thin straps pressing against her skin gave the effect of making guitar strings look like piano keys. It became obvious in my mind that all she had been wearing at her apartment was the black French knickers that I noticed hiding under the thin fabric. Even though she was lacking a bra she still radiated elegance, composure and the confidence of a spider that had made a web that could never be avoided. A better man wouldn't notice, but she was enough to get a priest hard wearing that dress. She took the last step to the landing, with a bottle of white wine in her hand. That much I could notice, but my eyes just went back to the figure that was standing, hand on the rail, looking at me. Most days I would rate her a 9.4 but at that moment, she was enough to make the Gods jealous and declare war on us.

"You look like a modern effigy of some Greek goddess," she for some reason gave a curtsy, twirled. "You're not playing fair. We did talk about this." She knew, and it didn't bother her; we were at some point going to end up in bed together, and then she'd get what she wanted. She knew she had me - hook, line and sinker. She smiled walked up to me and kissed me on my cheeks, for some reason she did it 3 times.

"So how many of us are there going to be?" I put up my thumb and 3 of my fingers,

"You, me, Erin and the girl I live with." She smiled as I stepped to one side to let her in. I walked her into the kitchen, where Erin was listening to Eric's Trip. Amongst singing the words, she had taken dinner off the stove. She looked up and the journalist asked,

"Erin?" to which Erin pointed at her,

"You must be the journalist," her eyes gazed briefly towards me, "You are far more beautiful than what he makes you out to be. Are you single?" I couldn't fucking believe her.

"There's a guy I like, he's just got out of a relationship, so I'm waiting for him to be comfortable with himself." Fuck, fuck, fuck. I thought to myself, Erin would put 2 and 2 together and get 4.

"Are you going to dish up?" Erin asked me, I walked round and started to dish up. "I cooked." Erin announced to the journalist, sometimes she would say things to try and annoy me.

"And as I'm dishing up, I take ALL the credit." The journalist handed Erin the bottle of wine, Erin grabbed another glass and let the journalist pour herself a glass.

"When I went to California," The Estonian came back into the room, and I had the 3 of them looking at me. "We went to a vineyard, it's as boring as shit. But they take you round, let you eat the grapes so you can act like a tosser and say you can taste other flavours. Then right at the end of the tour they finally let you try the wine, by which point we were seriously bored. Everybody says something pretentious like 'It's cheeky, but arrogant. It's subtle, but striking.' I had to go 'it's shit but free.' We left very shortly after that." The Estonian had heard the story before, she still gave a smile as the other laughed.

"So what are we eating?" the journalist asked, Erin was laying the table.

"Asparagus and Parma ham risotto, his recipe my cooking. So… if you like it you can take me home with you." The journalist started to laugh, she didn't realise that Erin was after a scissor sisters session. We all sat down and started to eat.

"What do you all do after you've eaten?" The journalist asked, looking at each of us.

"We normally sit out the window and enjoy the view of Sacré-Cœur. We're basically an old couple, when we go out it is really sporadic and normally ends up with us going to really seedy places." We carried on eating, there was a few minutes of silence before the journalist then asked,

"Will you let me take you all out to dinner for you cooking?"

"I would love that." Said Erin, I had to roll my eyes; she couldn't make it any more obvious.

There was very little conversation for the remainder of the time that we were eating, when we finished the Estonian cleared the plates, as the journalist finished her glass of wine she return the glass to the table before musing,

"Can we sit out of the window and you read your poetry to me." I looked at Erin,

"As long as you don't tell my mum I've been drinking I'll help clean up before joining you." We all stood up and as Erin went to join the Estonian, I picked up my papers they were nothing more than scraps being held together with string. I handed them to her as I opened the window, she handed them back and opened another bottle of wine. As she climbed through the window frame I caught a glimpse of what she was wearing under that dress, I knew my days of resisting her were diminishing with very little I could do about it.

Day 63

The sky looked older than grey, there were hints of blue; though I think without Erin being there it would have been totally grey.

We were on a beach, it was definitely England. The way the sand looked reminded me of my childhood, trips away with my mother. Erin gazed out facing the sea. A pensive expression that was strung across her face as her clothes weren't too suited for being at a beach. Her eyes were cast out towards the unforgiving ocean; I must have been around 15 feet away from her when I crouched down to photograph her. As her lips started to move, I had premonitions of the words that would flow from between them,

"You looked at the lights then turned your head," I tried to interrupt her by asking,

"How do you know that?" Nothing could stop her, she had started so she had to see the poem through to the end.

"What you saw inside of your mind will haunt you every time you sleep. I twisted 13 words from the books on the wall, looking into the mirror on the floor all I could do was scream; 'Where does the beach become the water?' Looking backwards as sweet as she is lying on my floor, knowing that she won't wake up: Caught between two dreams; and my one remaining thought." Those 79 words had rendered me more useless than halogen light bulbs during a power cut.

I looked at her; she was now holding a heart. I had little idea as to what was going on.

"Where does the beach become the water?" She repeated herself to me, until the words blended into a sound.

A pinch of salt should be taken with dreams, before reality crashes down on us.

Where does the beach become the water?

I was brushing my teeth, I could hear them talking but couldn't locate where they were in the flat. I was in need of a shave, I had started to feel quite grown-in. I went out to find them, only to discover they were in the kitchen. I remained leaning in the doorway, as they made sandwiches. The Estonian couldn't spread butter to save her life, she would always tear the bread; and she wouldn't swallow her pride and ask Erin to do it for her.

"You know, Erin can butter bread without tearing it. Maybe in future you should let her make the sandwiches rather than you wasting what I bring home from work."

"It's nothing to do with me," she uttered, "The recipe is wrong." Erin first looked at me, then her; bewildered by what was just said to us, Erin felt compelled to see what was really meant by the previous announcement.

"How is the recipe wrong?" We both glanced at Erin, waiting to hear what she was going to say next. "It's a 1,000 year old recipe, it's far from wrong. You can't butter bread, as he has said, I feel that I can vindicate it." There was nothing left for us to say, Erin had the last word in the matter.

Life was a tree of blurred lines and poetic pictures, that all fitted together like an unorganised jigsaw puzzle. The journalist, Erin and the Estonian were all hosting their own lines and branches; with pictures I had taken of each of them no matter how sparsely dress they each were, I saw each photograph as a leaf that had either fallen to the ground for others or was still on the tree, an audience of me. Everything tells their stories.

I observed them as they bagged up the newly made sandwiches that Erin had made, before collecting some other items from around the kitchen.

"So where are you both going today?" They put the last of their bits into Erin's bag,

"We're having a girl's day out and tonight we're going to…" I knew what the Estonian was going to say and we had already talked about it.

"No, no it doesn't matter how you dress it up or how many times you ask the answer will always be no." The child in the apartment below us started her piano lessons, I heard each key tap. Even the notes that she missed, the notes that got lost between more dominating sounds, and the crescendos that she hadn't quite mastered.

"What was it Wilde said?" she asked, I could see Erin had the cogs in her head searching for the quote that really did ring true with whatever it was that she was trying to prove to me.

"Always forgive your enemies; nothing annoys them more." The shaking of her head was our only indication.

"No, it's too obvious a quote. It's more likely going to be 'To live is the rarest thing in the world. Most people exist, that is all.' I see nothing changing with you, so I'm thinking I'm right." The Estonian smiled, I got it first time - just like every time. Her body language would often make little twitches, I have over the years been able to pick up on them. Her constantly going on about this for the past few days had started to begin to annoy me, I didn't want her going and I certainly didn't want Erin going.

"But we're having a girls day out, so sorry but you're not able to join us." I had no choice but to respect what had been said to me, it would be nice to have a little time to myself without being at work. I opened the door to let them out, they left and after locking the door behind them I found myself going back to the kitchen to clean up the little mess that they had made. As I was wiping down the sides, I threw the cloth into the laundry basket. As I straighten up the kitchen to how it needed to be, I could hear my phone ringing. Running back to the bedroom where I had left it charging, I hit the answer button and lifted the phone to my ear.

"Yeah?" I hadn't looked to see who was phoning,

"That's no way to start a conversation." The journalist replied with, in a tone which I think sounded like I had hurt her.

"Sorry, never had time to look. What gives me the pleasure of your phone call?"

"Are you doing anything today?" I had to remember what time I had work.

"For the next few hours I'm free, I have work later on. Why do you ask?"

"Do you want to come round and spend some time together?" I knew in my head that she would get me to have a few drinks with her, which would subsequently make it easier for her to lure me into bed.

"I'll tell you what, I will come round. But, you have to meet me at Gare Du Nord."

"Why?" There was a certain level of innocence to her question, she knew that I was wary of her seductive ways.

"Because I don't want the first image that I see to be, you in some lacy underwear that you know I'm going to find hard to resist."

"How long?"

"How long, what?"

"How long until we meet at Gare Du

Nord?"

"Shall we say like 15 minutes?"

"OK." She hung up before I had chance to say anything else to her, guess she was going to surprise me with what she would be wearing. I finished getting dressed, grabbed my keys and made it to the door. As I locked the door and headed down the stairs, my mind started to race with thoughts of what she would be wearing. I had never had thoughts about the journalist, none that weren't to do with interviews; I feared that whatever power I had was soon to be lost to her. The streets didn't have any part of my attention, a car nearly ran me over; I apologised without kicking up any kind of a fuss. When I came to Gare Du Nord, the journalist was waiting in the entrance by the taxi ranks.

"Long coat, little cliché wouldn't you agree?"

"I would," her eyes fluttered, and I was falling, falling, falling. "But I wanted to show that people still did it."

"So how little have you got on underneath? I can see that you are wearing stockings, but how much more hides itself from my eyes?" She looked around, her hand reached out and took mine. As she dragged me inside the station I asked, "Where are we going?"

"Photo booth." Was all she gave as

a reply, when we came to a photo booth, I pulled back the curtain to reveal 3 people inside doing a series of comedic pictures.

"Excusez-moi," I said to them as I drew back the curtain, the wait for the next minute was more awkward than missing your spot at a deli counter and being accused of queue jumping. As they came out, and we entered I very quickly drew the curtain behind me, holding it in the corner so nobody would ever be able to enjoy the view that I was to be blessed with.

"Well are you going to show me?" I whispered, she unbuttoned her jacket separating the lapels. She stood in front of me as a Goddess, nothing more than a tightly strapped corset and the stocking that I had already observed.

"We'll be leaving shortly." She whispered, I could hear my breathing getting heavy; I was hoping that she couldn't.

"Yes we will." I waited for her to button up her jacket before I pulled back the curtain, and she led the way.

Day 64

And like 2 generals that had lost all their men, unable to admit defeat they picked up whatever guns they could find to really fight to the very last man. The Estonian should have known that I was going in all guns blazing to our Mexican standoff, with no shortage of bullets.

"How many favours have I asked you for in my life?" her fingers weren't doing anything in the way of counting, but the mind was ticking trying to calculate the answer.

"Including that, I make it 6."

"And do you have any idea how many favours *YOU* have asked me for in the time we have known each other?"

"In the 4 years that we have known each other I've asked you for 7 favours." She makes it difficult sometimes not to laugh at her, she knew that it was a blatantly a lie; though it still would have never have stopped her from saying it.

"You have asked me for 54 favours in the 4 years we have known each other, do you want me to list them?" She started to shake her head, fully aware that I could list them all.

"No, there's no need. I'm sure that you've added a few; but I'll let them slide." As we stood apart leaning against different parts of the kitchen, staring daggers at each other. Erin walked into the deafly, awkward silence that we stood in.

"Feels like a mortuary in here." Her words were just suspended in the air between us, the words holding their own before falling to the ground. I didn't say anything, I hadn't even acknowledged that Erin had entered the room.

My need for the Estonian to know that she was in the wrong was bigger than my love for her. Erin cast those eyes of hers back and forth between the 2 of us, I thought that Erin was looking a little lethargic.

"Have I done something?" The innocence possessed in Erin's questions, made it virtually a necessity to give her an answer. The Estonian must have a heart made of razor wires, as her eyes stalked Erin before reverting back to me.

"Did you fuck the journalist as well?"

"What do you mean as well?" She threw her arms up into the air, much in the same way that a football manager would do when his side is 2-1 down in the 78th minute when his centre-back passes the ball backwards to his keeper; only for the keeper to not predict the play - and as the ball rolls into the back of the net. The manager is the first to know that his team is fucked, while the player makes peace in his mind that next week his will be dropped from the starting 11.

"You know full well what the question is implying, I already know that you've fucked me, you fucked Erin last night…"

"No I didn't," I really didn't know where her mind picked up information from. "I am very much unaware of fucking Erin last night and I'm me." I was trying my best to keep my composure.

"And that's why when I got back and walked into the bedroom, you were inside of her." I looked at Erin in shock, it was at that moment that I knew the Estonian wasn't making stuff up for shock value and she was in fact telling the truth. Whatever gibberish I was about to start up with, Erin shot me silent by saying,

"Look it was there, and I wanted to lose my virginity to someone special."

"That doesn't mean, fucking me while I'm asleep." Erin put the glass that she was drinking from on the side, after wiping any excess water from her lips; she asked,

"Why not?" I didn't think the question was serious, I looked at the Estonian. That proved to be a mistake, as she only returned to shouting.

"So did you fuck her?" My expression was blank, perspiration had started. My eyes were beginning to lose their colour, as everything that I knew and loved was in little over 2 months dying in front of me.

"Well as I have just found out, I guess I have to say yes I did."

"I already knew about that, did you fuck the journalist?" she screamed. I looked at her, if I were to lie she would know in an instant. If I tell the truth, I'm well and truly fucked.

"What if I were to say that I had?" I felt that was the only safe thing I could say as a reply, my eyes cast the room. I had the feeling that there were 10,000 eyes looking at me, with the intensity of more cities than I have ever been to.

"Well I'll have little choice but to ask if you have had anyone else."

"Then yes, and no I haven't slept with anyone else." Fortunately for me, the answer caught her off guard enough that she didn't swing for me.

"You lucky fucker," Erin sounded beyond surprised, "How was it?" If there was ever a wrong person, to say the wrong thing, at the wrong time, it was Erin. Here I am trying to bring as little attention to myself as is humanly possible, when admitting to one girl that I have slept with another girl; while Erin is there in a state of envy. In layman's terms, I am truly fucked.

"So why did you have sex with her?" The Estonian was close to tears, Erin looked like she was riddled with guilt; unable to say that she was sorry to her. The 3 of us had been reduced down to being animals, I didn't know what the right thing to say was. Erin turned and walked out of the room, my blank expression went from the door to the Estonian. It was 30 seconds later that the front door went, I focused on the Estonian like a macro lenses;

"We have to go, she needs us."

"She needs you, we don't know each other well enough." I left the room to put on my shoes, as I slipped my feet in I called out,

"You can't leave me to find her by myself, we are supposed to be a team. I know I fucked up by sleeping with the journalist, a world without mistakes is not a world that contains us. This world does contain us, now get off your arse and help me find her." I walked towards the door, it wasn't the way that I wanted to be going to save Erin - by myself. I shut the door and ran down the stairs, when I made it to the street I didn't know which way to go. I was affixed to the spot, unsure if I should head up or down the street.

"You go up to Sacré-Cœur, I'll start heading towards Bir Hakeim. She will at one of them." The Estonian had a heart. I started my way up to Sacré-Cœur, there were an increasing number of tourists; this is why I had been avoiding the cathedral for the past few days.

As I looked through the crowds for her, unable to see her I headed off to Bir Hakeim. I found myself running through the streets, streets which I hadn't been aware existed. I was running along Rue La Boetie, when I ran into the Estonian.

"You're only here? If we run, we'll get there in no time." She grabbed my hand, dragging me towards the nearest metro station. As we went into Miromesnil, the Estonian turned to face me, as we came to the barricades, she pulled me close and kissed me; placing our Metro pass down allowing the both of us to slip through.

"C'est sympa de voir le jeune amour à Paris."[40] An old lady said as we came across the other side, synchronised as an embrace. As I took my hand from her hip, I replied with;

"We are a forgotten generation that do try." The race to the metro tracks didn't seem as far as it normally was, then again - this wasn't a station that I frequented very often. As the train went the 5 stops to Trocadéro, as we ran from the 9 line to the 6 to commute a single stop; with the hoping that Erin would be where we were to look.

As we departed the metro, heading down the stairs 2 at a time. As the

---

[40] It's nice to see young love in Paris.

metro train continued overhead, on towards Nation, via the south side of the city. I was able to see Erin, lost and all alone. It was a mirror of my life in Brighton, was it little more than a reflection of myself?

"What are you doing?" I asked her, the sullen look of her eyes reminded me that never was as long as you could stand it to be.

"I needed to get out, that argument was too much of a burden in my hands." I held her hair, holding her close to me I told her,

"You haven't fucked up, you've picked up on how I was feeling back home. The 3 of us are here to stand for each other. We need each other sometimes." The Estonian arrived as I let go of Erin, the look in her eyes was one that showed she really wanted to apologise. As the Estonian gave every indication that it wasn't needed, Erin still said,

"I'm so sorry."

"Don't be," was the initial reply given, "What we don't realise is simple. The second we're no longer rooted we act like roses, we look beautiful for a while, then we die." They both cast their eyes over to me, wanting a source of inspiration to be given to them.

"All this is right now. We're actors doing an adlib scene, waiting for the director to say cut."

www.ingramcontent.com/pod-product-compliance
Lightning Source LLC
Chambersburg PA
CBHW030548020726
47494CB00005B/1522
* 9 7 8 1 9 0 9 8 7 8 7 3 0 *

The Atmosfear of the Blank Door

By Him

Published by New Generation Publishing in 2013

First Edition

www.newgeneration-publishing.com

New Generation Publishing

85 Unless You See It Snowing

Snails say, quick face.
Lights heart with mouth heat
Shimmering
Pacing myself not to fall out.
Chess pieces, falling from the board
To the floor.
Step aside for the bride,
Just step aside; this isn't the day
In her mind.
Pacing myself like how the trees
Will go black as they act like
tourniquets
Before it's their time to die.

Suffering, but I know this can't be
Just what I mean.
I was just enraptured by
The changing of numbers,
Did a tear look like my new number?
Or was I hopeful of it snowing?
Life fast forwards in my mind,
And I've found my heart still
Without a father.
The voices in my heart
Say nothing, say nothing more,
Nothing more than,
Walkaway.
It's your heart etched so cold,
This must be
Like Nerine, the only showing.

Love Lights And Flash Fights In A Citadel

Not a word in the whispers,
Though anything said
Could be ignored.
Peony act like they
Light up the night,
We already know
About illuminations.

I do care what I can do,
The tongue sticks out
But we all see stitches
Across the mouth.
Final toleration;
Frankness to resist,
But who was the one that
Ignored time and space?
Tragic,
Everything was caught
Head in a heart lock.

Kiev Or Letters Spelt Out In Brickwork

Writing words on shards of glass
To be pressed against my head,
Hoping the meaning will sink.
If nothing happens, I can always
press harder.
This internal paranoia
Will seep its way out,
And I won't say a word.
My list made sure it was sure
To multiply,
Cosmonaut missing the awful weather.
The muscle is raging.
West Nile slipped through a net,
Into the scores just like the
catacombs.
Lost in and without
The love that we pissed away,
I spilt my confessions
Between those wrapped in barbwire,
And 4 deafening bells.
Nobody could hear
A thing,
And my trail of thought was
Wasted, trying to say
Somebody please tell me what I
Ranunculus need
To buy.

View From A Place Where Time Is Flat

I had a face, it wasn't my own;
The night makes it look so black.
Eyes capture what
The camera forgot to photograph,
Another day
I never sat in the front seat of a car.
Step into a florist,
Freesia to the left;
With some on the right,
More appear when the day hits dawn.
The only thing I knew about death
Was my body would be
21 grams lighter,
Than the instant before.
Nobody told me the secret
To see your halo,
Everything is everywhere;
Nothing might not exist.

7 Story Russian Doll

Time would forgive the Gods,
But we weren't supposed to know.
It was time to applaud the
Right things, but the seasons
Had lost their control.
Nobody dimmed the lights out
So when I looked at everybody's souls
I didn't realise
There wasn't 1 I could call my own.
I had become suck a wreck,
Feeling like an unfinished Russian
doll;
Nobody noticed the cracks in my
bones.
Was I the only 1 that heard it
raining stones?
My wallet was short to pay the
boatman his toll,
He looked at me like a tattered card
deck.
They never told us to be ourselves,
So we just became fragments
Of once broken Waxflowers.
We left our home towns,
Drinking bereft words when
Not a soul forgot the order,
Hold the motion.

Topical discussion

Sit still for just a minute,
Nobody wants you to break a sweat
Then again,
I just want you to be REAL.
Why can't we watch the sun set
From your roof top?
I need a hand to rest
With mine.
History isn't a case of
His story, her story, your story,
And certainly not my story.
Tremors of Caspia,
And earthquakes are cries.
You're my one and only
Friend,
Same as when I was 14.

Any time is a time,
So long as a clock is near me.
Everything will ruin
Our lives.

Angry Swedish Kids Create Masterpieces, Americans For The Next 20 Years Will Try To Replicate This

Nobody was ever to know
I couldn't keep myself afloat,
Things are happening
Nothing that I knew at the start;
With nothing I know now.
Regret for the things I didn't do,
Cracks riddle the ground.
Let us gather round to see what
happens,
Empty vessels making unbearable
sounds.
Light flash bright,
Just to stay in your eyes.
Radio and airwaves become visible,
Reach out and grab them.
Shame nothing is like tulips.
Cynics say new romantics,
Critics utter hopeless antics.
Whisper Lumex revolutions,
Nothing happens without casualties
Or bad solutions.

Throw Me To The Spiders, I'm Not Scared But Throw Me

When they said anything
I heard everything,
My name wasn't spoken as a word.
Did someone say
I reflected off the chrome,
Inside my heart
Is a silence that
Shows me the way.
Maybe I was born to haunt myself,
Something like Ivy.
The rivers separated thoughts
Why does sand always make the same
patterns,
When the water has left to expose
remnants?
I wanted to feel the worth
Of my ordinary words,
Then there was nothing left
Just holes inside.
Let this world feel the wealth
Of these ordinary words.

The Universe That Consists Of Me And Angels

Nobody told me
The angel of desire
Had become depressed like me,
A puzzle piece
Lost its way;
Entities wonder who
Placed it on the floor.
The angel of lust
Was inside me,
Confused between women;
Name me 1,
Name me 4.
The angel of serenity
Had ignored everything,
Explained her plans to everyone.
The Dahlia I bought
Were futile.
The angel of the day
Spoke for me,
In strange tongues
I didn't understand,
This tiny universe
Stays within my grasp.

Bright Lights And Requests Denied

I dreamt of New York,
Right before I realised
That
I had woken up in Paris.
No lights as bright,
Though the smell of cigarettes
Did drag me across
To the wonder.
Queen Anne’s Lace coffee,
And the lights were
Once in the sky;
Before my pyre
I’ll watch them
Change colour to
Illuminate like fire.

Miserable Feelings Feeling Different

Nothing will appear
Never ending,
And I'm glad of that.
Imprints of the moon
Held together with a
Victorian spinning wheel,
Who knew what the
Following design was to be.
Lost in such space,
All I wanted was to sit
On a rooftop
Watch the colours change
The lights in a Telstar.
While the children smoke,
Rain be quiet so the
Questions can be asked.
Nothing is here to be
Thought about in the
Wrong context.

Guerrilla Ideas Or Castro Firearms

Dying star and when you become
A new light in the sky,
We could all be blinded.
But until we find another earth,
This might be the best option.

The black Cosmos petals we could only
Compromise with, a grand idea
Multiplied by my rage.
As nothing made sense
Not even a paradoxical version
Of myself,
I do not believe
I know I'm something less.

What Is The Point To Guitars If You Won't Play Them Loud?

Ice shards freeze in front of my face
Reducing my lifelines,
Pendulums slow down
Everything but the pace.

The view from the bottom
Was the only one that I could recall,
The warnings started to be reduced
To nothing, not even Safari Sunsets.

Keep breathing she said,
I was starting to get the hang of it.
2 pictures before and after,
Tragic everything became
Incandescent.

My body mass has reduced
To almost nothing,
Such a shame my mind
Was heading in the same
Direction.
Eyes blurring over when I read
A billboard saying,
Come on remember who you are!

Unlucky Lottery Tickets

Scratch away
And the night becomes
Day,
Medicate like a passing
Of light.
There is nothing wasting away,
I won't let my words
Be forgotten by intrusions of others.
Shake a broken hand,
And it crumbles down to dust.
Nothing would
Nothing can tear it
To tear it all away,
Field of Pincushion and it collapses
down
Like the time we've lost.

To be Dressed In Blue

I left snow and sky
And for what?
Grey rain, summers that
Left me feeling cold.
Don't account me as a part of this,
Even when I stand on my toes and
their tips;
I can't see over the mist.
Double crossed eyes,
No intention to focus on your nose.
Go ahead
Break a tip
It can be broken,
Break it up
When it says
It'll never be broken.
Close your eyes,
Fingers to hold Safflowers.
Seduction with
Those eyes, even
When she keeps them
Closed.

Order Yourself About

Ask yourself why.

Why you want the power
Disordering you.

God make a sign if your
Eyes are blue,
Even if you do it is only
To show you have power.
I did however say
If you have all the order,
Then I disorder you
To order yourself around;
Walk left,
Sit down.
Breathe in a Monte Cassino.
As we exhale disgust,
From thinking you were a God.
Fooled once,
Ready to be
Caught in a fight
If you think twice isn't enough
And you wanted 3.
Order yourself into that disorder,
Shift right;
Move left;
Spin round.

Broke Down, But Not Like A Car

I'm in a safe
Locked away from myself,
Nothing in spite of
The words I have.
Haze this mirror,
That way nobody can pout.
I could taste the world,
It's lights running down;
They ran out.
Children shine lights
Into the eyes of a car,
Have, you for 1
Can have my feet;
Walk away.
Let all the colours in my Hydrangea
grow,
Trap the melancholy;
When people think their
In a demotion,
From the beauty
Of these emotions.

The Universe Reflects Onto Nothing

The people I knew were conceited,
To the point when I had to
Reject the essence of
Their Monkshood.
Everything is beyond,
The words are gone;
Somebody struck piano chords.
Hell didn't see me as restless,
But what does hell know about fury?
Well you can have
Please just have my
Face, my name
Listen to every heart murmur.
As I wonder what happened
To my heart,
Even if it did ever exist?

Does a heart have a shadow?

Action Faked

How I follow
You know I follow, baby
Knowing I shouldn't.
Sea submerges me,
Lungs breathing it all;
Hands being all I feel,
Hands not my own.
Never to be fully sure
Who I am,
And because I feel it all
I knew that I couldn't
Be with you.
And because I feel everything,
It was you who didn't love;
You just latched.
Sleep in fields of Larkspur,
While the rest
Of us work around
99 and a half.

Hello Here, I'm A Lie. You Didn't notice Did You?

I had once been resisted
Now to leave a faux salvation,
We're becoming lines of people
Heading to our only destination.
Being on the road seems
Like a long way off from the post
office,
The mountains,
And Los Angeles;
Snow in summer.
Is chaos, but to me
Chaos is better described
As a child's free thoughts
And imagination.
Nothing in this world
Riles up thoughts,
Like uprising of Ornithogalum
And the defecation
On a wasted tragic nation.

Metalist Marksman

I was once hopeful for me,
Nobody else shared my view.
And so I asked the pastors of time,
My words had become
A flat line.
No-one hears,
No-one cares,
My God didn't care.
Show him my name
My face, my Arum.
He told me all didn't
Belong in this place.

Most people in the room
Don't suspect
Their life's the same,
From birth to death.

The Lowly Poverty Of This Earth

Should have taken a
Photograph, no brick wall
Will answer you back;
While I've learnt from enough
Mistakes.
Tell me my father's dead,
Smile regains the upside.
I hammer the pieces of a heart
Some say is mine, I hear word you're
still alive
Things fall apart, and I find my
action doesn't end.

Son of a bitch,
I'm not even sure I'm an entity.
My memory doesn't
Serve me,
So why would it you?
Let the Vanda tell me,
I'm a million miles away
Why won't you die,
At the moment
I want you to?

21st Century Hungry Entities

I don’t mind
Stealing from the order,
But I won’t be the one
Who fires shots
When the streets fall
Zapata black and red.
Scars exposed like Sedum,
New days that didn’t look
Set to arrive.
Natural light not here
To provide warmth,
Guiding light.
First hospital day,
To conclusive hospital stay.
Nurse asked me,
And I told her
My life was to stay
Curious,
Stay wild,
Stay hungry.

Paris, What Are Those Words Spoken By You

They decorated your heart
To hide who you really want
To be,
Sad Trachelium weren't here;
Had you gone?
Where had my heart gone?
Heart replaced by question mark,
Why aren't all maps
In Russian?
Save me the temptation
Of walking outside blind,
Could have asked yet
Your eyes always looked
So far away.
Colours glazed with green and yellow,
Moss on you designed
To stay.

Clipped And Left As Remnants

Myself isn't really
Something I want to face,
Lights start to break.
Frequency of quirks
With the distortion,
Nobody ever expected
The dot to dot.
Only created an unblemished
Flower - a Begonia.
Something that I didn't know,
Musk and pollen
Left on my fingertips;
Never mind.
Landscapes came
Flashed,
Never to be seen
The same;
Sky was fading.

As we saw
Flowers dying where others had
Words raging true,
Recalling words
The general always
Said, we were fashioned
To die in war.

Economic Central List Coffee Stained

Such a shame none of us
Whistle during our own pyre.
Central not near here,
We've got lives
Captured decisions not set.
When once
I chose to die,
But it wasn't really
People I did miss,
Just the surroundings.
Nobody said words like
The Gods,
While ringing in my ears
Had been created
To keep me awake.
And the height of Sunflowers,
Were where feathers
Stopped being fake.
Fear and our own
Melancholia,
Swallowing the
Earth beneath my feet.
Now I'm a man with
My last breath
Unlike braille
I can see my lines.
I can read my lines.
I can feel my lines.

Tinged A Sacrifice Green And My Shoes Brown

My short time was feeling
Like centuries,
Snow falls here
And nothing does grow.
I know Paris is my summer
Later life - before the beginning,
Doors fell off the hinges
They don't need mending.
I heard what the pastor said,
Sing - sing
And I crumbled down
When I discovered
That she was more infinite
Than me.
So like a fly
I was caught,
Guess that made her my Venus Flytrap,
Like everyone before I was so alone.

And when my voice became
Electric,
I knew how insignificant
I was outside
The sacred heart.

First And Last Names Shouldn't Begin And End With The Same Letter

Nostalgia looked like daisies,
And the city lights
Reminded me of times
I had not been around to
Ever witness.
The dreams I started
To have were looking at me,
With intricate eyes.
There started to be
Little words used,
In and out of context.

The Lines Separated Themselves From The Square

Tiny Bee,
What New England Asters did
You pollinate today?
I'm not sure what
Any of us have to say,
How come nobody visits these days?
I hear the still words
Of a girl that refuses to visit,
Why haven't I gone to her?
When will I go to her next?
No love has been lost
For she had no love to give,
Brackets didn't surround anything.
While I had a realisation
That if needed
I can still tell lies,
Nothing should ever
Say goodbye.

Messages Restored Inside

I heard this was order,
I didn't believe them.
Not a soul was regretting
Such order,
Fame was nothing but a word;
Steering ground.
The skylines raise themselves
Like sunflowers to the sun,
Everywhere but Manhattan
Appears to blend into 1.
Faked like that
Glass eye on the floor,
Shine towards
Murmur a name black and blue
In the Crocosmia.
What's a difference
If nobody knows my name,
Guess it doesn't really
Matter.
A soft focus was when
The macro of the world,
Had begun to
Look like the hell
Below.

Kangaroo Courtroom Drama

I was once an existence
Unable to hear
Trapped as an 8 year old
Stuck in these nightmares,
Disabled to separate like lots
Of horseflies.
Nothing was what it seemed to be,
Time pictured itself out
Look at Dracaena on methadone.
Bending past 1,
Go ahead and call it 2;
The world was small at the
Top.
Words of everything were
Everywhere,
Keeping my passion
I'm now the director,
So now few want to give
Credit to me.

The Time Spent Waiting

And I won’t take the name
Of my father,
Who else is waiting
For time to be done?
Complete past complete,
He’d refuse to admit
That he is the
Vainer one.
All my sisters stood by me,
Shame I still lacked
Any real figures.
No Kniphofia reflected into
My name,
While not a single Lilly will be
Left on his grave.
I wasn’t yet ready to
Enter mine.

2 pennies kept to pay the boatman.

Rebooting Atoms To Unstable Levels

All colourless words
Are etched in stone,
Seen for time;
Unless black rain
Thins the levels
So they are the same.
This blood that I gave away
I wasn't ever able to feel inside,
The cells were no longer mine.
1 then 1, 1 following 1.
I leave for reasons of my own,
Wasn't to be forgiven
Etch Lisianthus on with
Graphite pencils.

I heard them ring the alarm bell,
Joyous tune;
Today is the only time
That hasn't ever happened,
So what's the point in being scared?

Always Wasn't A Promise

I held her,
She wasn't even
A woman.
It was just something
In that voice,
Tones of good
Words that
Time didn't
Want to have.
I never loved
Somebody,
I never, never,
Never, never,
Never, never
Saw a Forsythia cry
Until the day
I left you.
Time was flat
From that point,
And we couldn't
Hide in the pages of songs.
And I could
Never, never, never,
Never, never, never
Grasp 15
The way that I held you.

All Sound Just Fell Away

Gloriosa had died in the kitchen,
While all I wanted to be was
Starting from the bottom;
No intentions to move
Too far.
Had to say the view of the stars
Let man reinvent constellations,
To pictures more relevant to now
So as the sky pixelated,
All colours went crimson;
Rot set in oblique to the core
It’s forcing me apart.
I’ll never find me
As the one in love,
There was no reason
To love you.

Parcels Returned To Sender

Woman's weep
Reformed cigarette burns
On the floor,
I feel I'm going
Close to going
Gone, sleep tight we're gone.
Reflections are promises,
But what did they say
Under the sound of that gun?

Plans making sense,
While the lights
Bolt backwards to forwards.
Unknown a mirror does
Scream,
The bass guitar growls
Fuzz.
And the Zinnia open up,
Rescinding words of
Love.

These Lies Illuminate Under UV Lights

Lines burnt metalist
Under blue eye
Ridges,
So houses are inert.
Flash wand synched better than
Muscari,
Hunting like a bounty
Of things
Savage - like scanning
For your own noose.
The wrong tracks
So the timeline
Consists of things,
Things that became oblivious
To human existence.
Relax - I hope you fade away
Nobody knows his name,
Society has a level of caring
The needle reads much the same.

Ursa Minor Rotating The Wrong Way

God created the waves,
Boys ride the waves.
Krishna invent a phase,
Girls be the phase.
Ride on.
Right on.
Heart keep your fight strong,
Voice may you be heard long.
Flowers keep your beauty
Like when you were young,
I heard the tolerance
Was at an all time low.
Scan the world
And see where cancer
Should hit home,
Oceans tell us
Your real names.
The world's dead eyes
Watch this tidal fade.

40 Blank Stares

I found a trace
Of a person I once thought
I knew.
Fade day to day,
You had my fate.
My eyes couldn't
Focus - life started
To look like a blur,
I can taste myself
Vanishing.
All my eyes
Could distinguish
Were Phlox.
My windowsill
Is missing
Like parts of me,
My time won't be wasted
I'll find myself in the end.

The Almost Eternal Sojourn

So while we burst
Ourselves your big mouth
Says too much,
Letting repercussions take
Their place.
Snapdragons get to have
15 minutes in the sun,
Tick the clock so
The riots had ended.
Our city sat in rubble,
Now she can sleep
Fumigating the people.
Recreate me
As the same,
Somebody give me
The name that
Is their only
Link to sustain.

Half Way To Something

Challenger complacence,
Eyes of a nations.
Hellebore for forgiveness,
Really deceit.
Challenger complacence,
Eyes of a nations.
Hellebore for forgiveness,
Really deceit.
Fracture little lines,
Tearing the break nines;
Same time zones.
Would anyone even know
If we lost character,
Before we found ourselves?
Nameless, unable to hold any flowers,
Wastelands known as
Siberia.

It Wasn't The Fault Of The Devil As To Why I Lost A Friend

We haven't spoken to each other,
Do you even know how long?
I believe it was a culmination
Of many things,
Though I don't know what
Was dropped
And what did smash.
Little bits of us fell away,
Stand, slip, trip, honest,
Stay clear.
Nobody new will dance,
You can't fix us,
Lost friends.
That lady poured a
New bottle,
From the oldest glass.
Who let the devil
Stand like a friend?
Nobody wanted to
Take the blame,
So we all bought Carnations.

Secondary Colour Landscapes

Contended is
A pay telling mountain,
Under lights with
Nothing that we’ve
Been searching for.
I was still trying to
Find the roses
To leave on a wasted
Grave,
There are days
When I feel like
A parallax;
Caught up serene,
My heart was cut ready to
Break.
Know it is good to end
What others do start.

Sanity Is A Cold Vein

All my troubles disappeared
When I made you my fix,
Putting your lips right to my
Veins, was just like Narcissus.
Complicated like ever.

I Am An Assumption Like How White Are The Teeth Of The Dead

You can’t become
A brief moment to a loved
City,
I once held those
All on the surface
Of a box.
1980’s
My lifestyle was 2 words,
Eastern bloc.
The curtains opened
Right when I realised
There was only 1 way down,
My reflection looked
Distorted, I couldn’t tell I was
Looking at me.
Helenium flashed as a motion
The vodka felt mature like
A lifeline,
Hairdresser made her new look
Sublime.
Far from wrong to fail.
Nails held every man still,
Thoughts about nothing but tail.

Rock, Paper, Chainsaw

Such a shame there are less muscles
Used in swearing than to break a
Smile,
The answer could be that I'm
Alright.
Guess I just need a Sunday message,
And to drink with Shakespeare
characters.
Nod your head
And give it all away,
Suffocate yourself - but
Keep those hands holding onto
The prize.

Swallow your hollow heart,
Bleed in and bleed fast.
I have no need for the name
Of you,
Saffron Tuberose with a
Mouse's whisper.
Eat your ham on rye
And disburse.

The Modern Ironic Scene That Is Rebellion

You thought what you
Were doing was revolution,
The conformity in what you were
Doing was starting to
Stink the air out.
Using dialect so
Scene, it couldn’t even be
Scented to resemble Bouvardia.
Everything broken was
Hers, in ironic context.

National Pride Outside Of North America Is So Fake

I became intoxicated from
The colours the world projected,
Lacking the love was all
She ever said; she never
Read the signs in my eyes.
Some days my intention was
To shoot the vain,
Others I wanted to shoot inside
Older women.
My streets are filled with
Rats and fascists,
But that was just
The weather forecast.
The hoping to having
Alstroemeria, was a great
Distance away.

Do Piano Wires Get A Place To Retire?

I stand barely a man,
From a land I don't recall.
This is a place, little friends;
Smaller home.
She is a girl,
Tending to me like I were a lamb.
I realise now,
I don't have a wish I want to own.
No father ever wanted me as a son,
That's as far as I say of the
motherland.
Feeling of nothing,
It's not like I were a baseball card.
Round and around,
All my thoughts still go.
Feelings of death, and of pain.
I thought I was clever,
But now I'm back to being alone.
Can't distinguish my name,
Or lies.
I didn't do anything to this world,
Then why am I here?
But from the start,
I was alone like a rock on the beach
Next to the unforgiving ocean;
That was the place I longed to be.
Born, I should have been a florist,
Removing the thorns to show
Just how unique roses really are.

All I could wonder was how long?
I didn't know if I ever was going to
be saying,
Your love was strong enough.

The Trees That Were Cut Down So I Could Write And You Could Read

Fallen from disrepute and
Overdosing on caffeine,
The moon rolls
While people look up at the
Polluted sky to try to watch;
The sky fall from there
To nowhere.

Music passes through us all,
But the future will stay
Close to my Chrysanthemum.

Muse Over Words That Are Painted Black

My blood was the only
Thing I truly did own,
Nobody could take it away.
Only I said who had
Any right to take
My purest property.
I couldn't believe
The vanity,
Then again it was something
Like money proclaiming
False dreams were for
Everyone.
Guess my Zantedescia knew better.

Thin Threads Holding Thrads Together

So far the lights
Hit all equinox,
Witches push the buttons
So the laws of freedom
Are restricted.
Such a shame there
Are always
Ways and means around
Problems,
Everybody punch your fist
When asked why. Simply say,
We were bored,
We were bored,
You left us fucking bored.
Room of static space truckers,
Pointless sounds of a 4/4
Every dulcet note,
And every Oncidium
Had a destination - unknown.

Singed Paper But It Wasn't For Estella

I collect hearts,
Much outdated cigarettes;
Displayed like potpourri.
We held no story,
Even though it's something
I would never forget.
The room looks like a closet,
While it feels much the same as a
tomb.
In madness they said,
Friends become;
Lovers so long as when
We're done they revert
Back to being pretend.
She was done smoking menthols,
Words etched in wood
Within a mausoleum.
See everybody hates me,
Then they love me;
Before they hate me again.
I'm starting to realise my generation
Is fucked up, and full
Of imaginary friends.

Odessa And The Prussian Blue Sea

I didn't want to die in
A hospital ward,
The lack of flowers
Would have left me
Worse than before.
Did I have any alarm,
Or know how long
We'd be lost at sea.
I miss a few people
And 75 tulips;
Yes all I needed to know,
Try as I might
So I did try as
If it were my life.
Now stand up and fight,
Days fade into pain
My words right or wrong;
Didn't matter
My lust in life
Had all but gone.

Who Else Left Me This Way?

New levels of disbelief,
Fantasies were there
While the room listened
To your lies.
Friction locked up
Reminded me
Of a broken heaven,
Orchids had nowhere
To grow;
Plans given a new
Director.
Welcome to my world.

The Disintegrated Through Your Words

Nobody was on good terms,
As I only knew 6 people
People point their fingers;
Saying they know more
Than what I sold.
Brick shit talking house
Of glass or cards,
Don't light a match
Or you will burn
It all down.
Even the bulbs I planted
Did nothing,
Not a seldom Strelitza
To take solace in.

Oh, leave me here forever.

C10H16

Tourniquet, while a black
Concept doesn't show
Anyone what it is we
Really fucking mean.
There lies the bride,
There lies the bride,
A casket drowning
The cadaver with
Black turpentine.
Listen to these tongues,
World was once here
Now it's only snowing.
Revive our hearts,
Etched to dissolve.
This turpentine isn't
The seed to Iris I once held
While the wind is blowing.

I Guess This Is Goodnight

Clock ticks backwards
While my heart is all but
Tearing everything apart,
This wasn't an episode
When the lights
Were to burn to ashes.
Shame my poems know
Who you think about
When you masturbate,
I'm closer to nothing
Than what I care
To believe,
Sky revealed as blue
I find myself
Unable to stay happy
As it isn't
Dodger, or Tottenham.
This wasn't simple,
Like the colour of Eucharis
Like the storm
In the eye
Of Jupiter.

Everything Is Ignorance Until You Consider The World From Her Point Of View

Well I gave it away
At the blood bank,
Waiting as time did tick away.
My little sister wouldn't
Join me,
Saying it was the one thing
Nobody could take from her,.
Listen now to someone's guitar
Future's caught in a sunset,
While the Scabious didn't sit
Right in the sky.
And all the high notes have nowhere
To go but up,
Chase the night
Chase it just without me.
Register the room for coats and
hooks,
Return to the game.
Pawn takes a rook,
So the board becomes lighter.
Pages keep getting turned
Indecisive people glider
And a new machinegun.
Calories from ham on rye.

Not Even Bright Lights Could Show Me Something

I was born to listen
Shame there weren't
Voices to begin
A girl,
As a florist
Who sets botany
Higher.
Resolve the lights
Of photosynthesis.
Clap your hands,
Dive
And start to swim.
Nobody planned to wait
For me on the other side,
I fear that now
I'm 1 not 2;
Nobody will remember me
Like they do you.

Summer Rain Over Faulty Microphones

Sinking in the ocean
As I try sing your song,
My lungs fill up;
I'm starting to
Worry my money
Is tainted with blood,
So the boatman
Gives request denied.
Electric sparks like a
Tesla coil,
The rain on Paphiopedilum
Is more than I do know.
Flicker my radio,
Become seduced
By a voice
I no longer know.

A Period Of Time Before Simple

Counting off different ideas,
Would anything become
Of them;
It wasn't for me to say.

Past, present, future
Couldn't even sort
Any of it out.
Do I know exactly
What has happened
With what the Agapanthus,
Say they are expecting.

Money Recalled Then Rapport

Words written like
Inaudible sounds
Chincherinchee holding all
Attention,
Am I alone in understanding?
Just let me go,
Staying out
Please leave me
At home.
Now I try to listen
To sounds cutting through
The tree.

New Torrent, Old Space

Taste from the plate
Expect a lightning strike,
Clock ticks love to hate;
Nobody says they love me
Then again,
Nobody said they did
Before.
There isn't a word I can
Describe like tantric,
Dying Verbascum
In the graves of
Our new born waves.

Goodbye To My World

I didn’t have time
Reminder - reminder
Anticipating nothing,
Ruin.
I don’t recall dreams,
But they tear this world apart.
Do only I remember
That I was faulty,
But then that was
All aged 14.
Time passed And I was unsure
That anything had changed,
Who is even able to love?
Fields of Oleander,
Then I was 18
And I had lost
My world.

Railway Lines Lead Home

I’ll thumb a car down,
Unaware of either
Destination.
Young and ruined,
Hearts were the end
Of strings all pulled.
The Saint Bernard’s Lily has
Had the plug pulled,
We no longer have
The face or the
Fragile smile to be
Drunk;
Our hearts are
As read as flowers.
Still what is the
Real value of yesterday?

Bridesmaid Blues

In the list were
Hours wasted, because
The heather given by
Gypsies was
Destine to die.
As shallow graves
Remind us of
The fire inside,
Bad time.
While what should
Have been,
Really should have been.

Planets Light Upon Me

Tasting
What this life
Gave as a sacrifice,
Were these dreams
Preparing themselves to die.
What's 120 seconds,
To a wasted life?
The colours of Lantana
That were only
Described,
Never by a name.

Her, Then Me, With Lies - Lies

Did you miss them?
They stood around
Shared a cigarette
Minds connect,
She'll join me once she
Grabs some Spanish Oysters.
I left the house
With a gun,
While the wind hits
Our eyes.
Another heart picked,
Another dies.

Luck Is Something Not All Of Us Have

They spelt my name
Incorrectly on
My birth certificate,
Didn't change my love;
Or my heart.
Was I defining my name
By people,
Shakespearian tragic people.
They hold Mallow over graves,
Their friends were
Alcohol and shame.
Why would the dead want flowers?

Sleep Whispers

I heard these moments
Were broken,
So just this element
Is different.
I didn't know
What the thoughts were
By my peers,
My mind contained
Old songs
Each holding
Bindweed; I have never
Seen before.

And then I heard
That song,
My body knew what
To do.

Short Frantic Seconds

I burnt castles
Which were up in the air,
A portrait of
Tortured Blue Gem
And 1,000 desires.
With what I held,
But I had more grip
Than a picture frame.

Another Contract Expires

Then again I am me,
And for her
I'll wait forever.
She didn't say
Now was never,
She held Foxtail
At the start;
But this is the end.
Did we even switch
The lights off,
When the whispers
Haunted the air?
The love has died,
Why the hurry to move on?
Let us move forward together.

Back Before Days

It was hurting
A stranger,
Something I didn’t
Even know happened.
Archaefructus left in
The garbage,
But I am yet able
To face myself,
Life seems a long
Long time ago.
I lost before I loved,
Nothing sounded good.

No Memories Of Melodies While I Was Dead

Pictures of sunflowers,
Nothing had the urge
Or desire to purge.
The heart I had was on loan,
Then again, it wasn't
Really a problem;
As nobody could hear
The beats.

Roots heading
Into the ground,
The poppies
Taking colours and shapes
To flags.
The national anthem
Sings in the eyes
Of a beautiful stranger.

79 !